I0733906

CINDY M. AMOS

REKINDLED FROM ASHES

By Cindy M. Amos

Horizons of Hidden Promise Book 1

Dedicated To:
The resilient ranchers of Clark County, Kansas

*Here is the message from the Lord—Do not be
consumed by your fears,
for I am calling you out by name as my own people.
I will be your safety when you pass through deep
waters.
Should you walk through flaming fields, you will not
be burned up.
I have paid a high ransom for you. See how precious
you are to me.
Isaiah 43:1-4a*

Chapter 1

An irreverent wind rifled through the shortgrass prairie of western Kansas. The first week of March seldom reached eighty degrees, so Burk Crosby determined to make the most of his work day. He studied the sagging top wire that enclosed his largest pasture and opted to tighten the fence with a splice, a quick fix that would keep the herd contained.

When the wind gusted, he nearly lost his hat, an irksome hindrance. He grabbed a length of barbed wire and slid fence pliers into his back pocket. Having already taken the head count on the cattle, he gave the ailing fence his unbroken attention.

The south wind rushed past again, sending his hat rolling down the fence line. He quick-stepped in retrieval mode with a grumble locked under his lips. A faint hint of smoke rubbed against his devotion to the fencing task, but he ignored it to set the wire splice in place.

A glimpse of the southern horizon made venom rise in his throat at the cantankerous bluster determined to mar the warm day. Under clear skies, he could see a good ten miles into Oklahoma from where his ranch sat southeast of Ashland. Today, a dark bush seemed to overgrow the horizon, making any distant outlook impossible. He blinked to better discern the blurred hindrance.

Unsettled, he dropped the wire splice and walked along a steady rise on the landscape. Further west of town, such a slope plunged into red dirt canyons that eventually framed the Big Basin. Cut by a creek, this pasture offered a more gradual transition, but he was grateful for the elevation nonetheless. As his boots kicked dust at the top of the rise, he paused and assessed the southern horizon.

First to the east, and then to the west—as far as his gaze roamed—the dark bush vented skyward. Plumes of smoke began to snake from the bush, licking the air. "Lord God above, not a grassfire..." By the looks of things, half of Oklahoma might be on fire. With the boisterous wind hailing from due south, his ranch sat in the direct line of advance.

He turned to locate the cattle. Surrounded by knee-deep grass—winter-bleached and crackle-dry—the terrain lay volatile as all get-out. Sweat tightened his hatband. He broke into a choppy run off the knoll, needing a survival plan and needing one fast.

~

Swamped with hollow satisfaction, Lyndie Leigh Sessoms accepted payment from the rodeo coordinator and handed the check over to her manager. "Here you go, Ernie. Thanks for coming over from Tulsa to catch the Oklahoma City show."

The coordinator tipped his hat and disappeared inside the arena.

Ernie Matthews kicked at some wood chips lining the chute area as he folded the plump check into his wallet. "You could still get on the playbill down in Enid the fifteenth of March—if you wanted to."

She held out an open palm to stop him. Goodness knows that man could draw out a two-word prayer, given the opportunity. "Look Ernie, we've already been over this. I need a break—some time off to think about my future. This rodeo circuit has grown wearisome lately."

"But folks adore you, Lyndie Leigh." He leaned in to give her a show biz wink while he tucked the wallet away. "You're a modern-day Dale Evans. The world needs a star like that."

She sniffed and squared her feet. "Maybe what the world really needs is a Roy Rogers figure—a hero on a palomino to ride in and save the day."

"Speaking of horses, would it be all right for me to loan out Tracer for sire duty during your sabbatical? We could cut the fee fifty-fifty."

Her gaze shifted to the horse trailer already hitched to Ernie's truck. The buckskin's muzzle appeared through the window. "Do whatever you think is best. At the end of three months, we'll reconsider where we stand."

He tapped the heels of his boots together. "That's a mighty long time off, Lyndie. You'll have to come back strong. Where you headed, anyway?"

"Someplace that needs me." She offered her hand in a parting gesture. "I'll be in touch."

"Don't forget your Friday night radio spot. That's still a go for Western Star duty."

"String around my finger to remember." She pretended to tie one on. "Hope you'll listen in, so you won't worry about me too much."

He shook his head and stepped back. "Try to find what you're lookin' for, little lady. Life ain't about foot-dragging, after all."

"Be well, Ernie. Time for me to head north."

"Watch that Kansas state line. I heard there's a wildfire out of control up that way."

She saluted and walked toward her rig. Maybe she needed direct exposure to fire. The camper trailer didn't necessarily appear flameproof—but she sure felt that way.

~

Ironic that he'd come out to *mend* fences, Burk now

clamped down on the pliers and snipped through the fourth strand. With a little cooperation, he could move the entire herd onto his winter wheat to buffer them from the intensity of the blaze. Over the last half hour, the dark line had crept considerably closer. If only the wind would lay back some, then the pressure might ease off a bit. Still, he couldn't trust what amounted to a lame wish.

He jumped into his four-wheeled ATV and threw it into reverse. Ill at ease from the smell of smoke, the cattle stood packed together along the far fence. He planned to herd them through the new break, optimistic that the lure of greening wheat would be too much to resist. For the second time that week, he flat-out needed a herding dog.

Once in position, he made some noise by tapping the vehicle's horn a couple of times. Those honks scattered the herd like an angry bust on racked billiard balls. None went straightway into the corner pocket of the fence cut—not one. He spat and checked the grassfire's progression over his shoulder. For the first time, he spotted orange flames where the sky met the land.

"Come on—cooperate for once." He swept an arc to the east around a majority of the cattle and drove them back toward the opening. A solitary steer wandered into the wheat field and began grazing. Like a roadside advertisement, the suggestion spread. Within minutes, three-fourths of the herd stood on fire-resistant ground cover.

Regret for not having a gate handy pinched his side. Another twenty-five head still stood in harm's way. He glanced south and saw that the fire had already engulfed the adjoining McMinimy spread. Sickened at the sight, he swiped a hand over his lips and headed north, determined to round up the remnant.

As a last resort, he could cut the northernmost fence and leave the cattle to fend for themselves up on the Guards' property. A double-sized pond up there would make the perfect refuge. Of course, the cattle would have to reason that out and wade into the water. Something sat on the broad edge of ain't-gonna-happen with that scenario.

Burk breathed in smoke and coughed. He shifted the bandana up over his nose and wiped watery eyes on his sleeve. The wildfire advanced on the devil's frictionless sled. Where he stood at the base of the knoll, he was about to get run over.

A square plot lined in spring green opened to the west. He'd completely forgotten about the old settlers' cemetery. Mowed last October, it held practically no fuel for the fire. Racing to the longer edge, he frantically worked the hinges loose from one wrought iron panel and rotated it open. Slowed by dread that accompanied the last-ditch effort, he trotted up behind the southernmost steer and began to wave his arms. "Hey-yah," he called, closing the distance.

The pried-open railing acted like a funnel to guide the animals inside. Once half the animals had passed through the portal, the vise-clamp on his chest eased off some. He walked the last of the steers into the cemetery compound and took the panel in his hand to close the pen.

For no apparent reason, the herd spooked from the rear. Fighting the smoke, Burk hastened to secure the closure and trap them inside. When he looked up, five hundred pounds of attitude bore down on the opening. He saw a white blaze that marked two flaring nostrils. A split-second decision, he spanned the gap with his body to thwart the skittish escape attempt. The panicked steer remained unfazed. A direct collision stole his breath. Reeling, he crumpled to a helpless embrace of the ground where his rescue turned motionless black.

~

Lyndie chided herself for thinking it would be easy to ride the coattails of the wildfire. Halted, a herd of cattle now claimed the highway as its domain. The last information sign she'd passed stated Sitka was two miles ahead. A gravel road to the west represented her only option, so she pulled the steering wheel in a full rotation to avoid the wide-eyed cattle.

Knowing country roads intersected every mile, she'd head north again at her first opportunity. The fire had already raked through this section. Wooden fence posts smoldered like abandoned cigarette butts down both sides of the road. All points in between could be described, in no uncertain terms, as lifeless black. The prairie had gone from landscape to lunarscape.

An improved road soon bisected this east-west road, so she slowed for a right turn. The gusty crosswind buffeted the camper one last time and surrendered to become a beneficial tailwind. With north her preferred direction, her chosen destination of Ashland must remain somewhere up ahead.

The truck geared down to achieve the climb up a steady rise. The damage along the way left a searing impression. In the corner of a pasture, a lifeless lump turned out to be a trapped steer. The somber sight dug at her nurturing instincts, but nothing could be done at this point.

Once the truck leveled out, an ornate arch appeared up ahead. Intrigued, she eased off the gas to take a better look. It marked a cemetery. There in the ashes, a cowboy knelt outside a wrought iron fence. Braking to a stop, she watched him topple over onto the blackened ground.

After throwing the gearshift into park, she killed the ignition. *Right place at the right time.* Slinking between barbed wire strands, she made her way to the downed man. Twenty-odd steers continued to graze inside the cemetery, extremely lucky to be alive.

Lyndie dropped to her knees at the man's side. With his shirt torn in several places, dried blood caked several of the holes. She touched his neck. It felt clammy cool. "Hey there, cowboy. Great job saving the herd. Looks like you outsmarted the wildfire." When he tried to roll onto his back, she assisted him.

"No…no smart to it," he replied in a scratchy voice. His chin wore a black-and-blue scuff. Hazel eyes the color of cedars in winter glanced away.

When she leaned closer to shade his face, his pupils failed to respond to the light change. "Okay, cowboy. I'm taking you into town for medical treatment. Think you can walk to my rig?"

"Point to my feet, will you?" The corner of his mouth twitched up as his entrancing eyes fluttered closed.

She tapped the toe of his closest boot, willing to play the comeback game. Her frank assessment began to pay a bonus dividend as the hazel-eyed rancher had been chiseled from a solid rock. When she locked her arms around his shoulders to help him stand, the rock analogy played out into a six foot-two muscle-clad man only a little the worse for wear.

His arm soon slid around her waist. "You lead."

She took a series of burdened steps. Glancing ahead, she spotted the barbed wire fence. "Hey, are you up to straddling the roadside fence?"

He rested a heavy head on her shoulder. "No—too in and out of it. Roll me under."

"Okay. Sure wish the steer back there with the white blaze could have had that option. I'm afraid you lost that one." She paused at the fence and lowered him for the roll underneath.

The man tucked a thumb into a tear in his shirt. "The two of us locked heads earlier, but I couldn't persuade him to stay in the cemetery."

"Sometimes winning seems like losing in the moment. It's best to make your final choice when you can stand up straight in your own boots." With that nugget of wisdom, she shoved him into a rolling motion and cleared her last apparent obstacle. *Goodness, what a find.* Those cedar-shaded eyes were another matter.

Chapter 2

The feminine apparition at the wheel seemed none too real. Burk focused as they crossed the bridge into Ashland. Loose blond hair framed a pair of high cheekbones. When he swallowed, two dayflower blue eyes gazed in his direction.

"There's a complication up ahead—a police barricade." She slowed and rolled down her window.

"Better let me do the talking." The road ahead appeared truncated by parked vehicles. "This looks none too promising."

She pulled the vehicle to a stop short of the barricade.

He spotted the deputy on duty, an old schoolmate several years his junior. "What's up, Levi? We can't come into town?"

"No, Burk. We're evacuating Ashland. Protection, too. Head for Coldwater High School. The gym's being prepared for overnight accommodations. Is your place still standing?"

A cold trickle ran down his achy chest. "I don't rightly know."

"Best get going up the road. Take care." Levi tipped his hat at the driver and backed away with a dismissive gesture.

"I'm turning around then?" She checked her mirrors and then gave him a quizzical look.

"Yeah, back along the highway. We'll turn north to Buckland, since Protection's likely sealed off, too. The hand of God will have to protect Ashland in the meantime."

The vehicle began its maneuver and completed a wide turn to head back east. Its driver seemed calm. "The Bible says his chariot rides the wings of the wind, so I think God will make it in plenty of time, given the wind speed today."

"Riding the express then." Movement north of town caught his attention. In seconds, he recognized the aged man on the tractor. "Lord above. That's Gene Shawboro."

"What in the world is he doing out there?"

"It looks like he's disking the perimeter of town for a last-minute firebreak. Way to go, Gene. See you at Coldwater, buddy." His voice broke with the sentiment.

The driver reached for him, but halted. "I'm Lyndie Leigh Sessoms. When I heard about the border fire, I drove up from Oklahoma City to lend some help."

He glanced at her to seal the name with the face. "You travel with a camper?"

"Yes, a majority of the time. Rodeo circuit mostly."

He clamped his eyes closed to keep his thoughts from ricocheting. The rodeo had trapped his free time once or twice. Her name seemed familiar though his head throbbed. When the Western Star show popped to mind, he had her pegged. "Well now, it's not every day a man gets rescued by the Sweetheart of the Rodeo."

She bristled at the mention. "Today, I'm just Lyndie, plain and simple. I left the circuit after the OKC rodeo. I'm on sabbatical—searching for some higher purpose beyond the life of an entertainer."

He mulled that over a quiet minute. If she hadn't gone maverick on her soul-searching quest, he'd be sucking cactus pads by now. "Lyndie, I'm Burkett Crosby, a third generation Clark County rancher. Right now, I'm about as grateful as a man can be. Hardly anybody comes out my way. Even the mailman complains."

She snickered and braked at the intersection. A barricade of empty cars forced the turn to the north. "Just for the record, I tried to come up the highway through Sitka, but a standing-room-only herd of cattle suggested a detour." She turned the vehicle north.

"Saints in my favor…and now the wind at my back." He shifted to kick off his boots and massaged his right calf.

"Maybe Coldwater has public showers. You could probably use a therapeutic washdown." Her shapely brow rose with the suggestion.

"Don't expect much more than a cot and a sandwich." He unbuttoned his torn shirt to check the damage. When he looked back up, a sanitary wipe dangled from her fingers.

"In case you're right, go ahead and start the cleanup process. I have some ointment in the camper."

"What? Do I look like I could use some improvement?" He pulled down the visor and readily saw why his jaw ached.

"Let's just say you give rugged good looks a dirty name." Her cheeks seemed to color in a blush, which turned her eyes a deeper shade of blue.

He wiped his face, letting her compliment work more improvement than the ointment likely would achieve. His thoughts shifted to Coldwater, and unease pitched a tent. "The townsfolk will be on edge at the shelter, not knowing if their homes are being spared. You might be able to chase off a few worries, given your celebrity status."

"Well, I could certainly hold a few hands and pray for people."

In retreat and beaten to a pulp, the emotional exchange caught him off-guard. He sat silently staring out of the windshield, trying to swallow. "That'd be real special, Lyndie. Thank you for being here." For the life of him, he couldn't manage to add anything more.

~

Lyndie's usual breeze-through-life sentimentality had not adequately prepared her for the tense scene inside the gym. The emergency shelter swarmed with distraught people. Some held blank stares, others appeared agitated. God help them—many of the children were crying.

Burk split off with a hobble as soon as they'd entered the building. A group of tight-faced men stood in the far corner of the gym. Their circle opened to allow him entrance. A few well-timed hand gestures no doubt meant he rendered a report on his narrow escape. A man beside him clamped a hand on his shoulder afterwards.

She blew out a breath and began walking to the back. Portable tables clicked into place by women wearing aprons. Maybe food would be served, after all. When she passed a family with two young children, a teary-eyed little girl halted her in her tracks. She knelt and made eye contact. "Hey, sweetie. You're really helping Mommy out by being such a good girl."

The child sniffed and leaned against her mother's leg. "We had to leave my doggie behind."

She exchanged glances with the mother. With a baby on her shoulder, she didn't seem to need yet one more responsibility heaped on her. "Do you know that animals have good instincts? Your doggie will smell the smoke long before the fire arrives and run far, far away."

"You think so?" She sniffed again, but her bottom lip stopped trembling.

"I do. Now tell me what color your doggie is. When I go back, I promise to keep a look out for him."

The little girl tilted her head. "Queenie is a girl—not a boy. Her head is white, her back is brown, and her tail is black. If you snap your fingers, Queenie will do a trick."

"Okay, I'll remember that, especially the trick part. I'm Lyndie. It's nice to meet you."

The girl hesitated until her mother nodded. "My name is Abby." She placed a dimple-knuckled hand on Lyndie's knee.

Touched by the alliance, Lyndie patted her hand and

winked. A heavy tap on the shoulder shifted her attention. She hesitated to look up.

Burk stood over her, his expression gradually warming at the scene. "Hey there, Abby-ca-dabby. Can I borrow Miss Lyndie for a few minutes?"

"Sure. She's going to help look for Queenie when we get to go back home."

"That's mighty nice." He put a hand on her elbow and helped her stand.

She tried to read his complex expression. "What's up?"

"As you might expect, news about the wildfire's progress is scarce in these parts. Some area ranchers heard you drove up out of Oklahoma and wondered if you could share what you came across down there."

She walked along with him a few steps. "Sure thing, but brace yourselves. Nightfall will confuse the communication issue further." She read genuine concern on their faces.

"Dawn's reckoning will be an agonizing wait for the landowners, especially the cattlemen. Many didn't have a chance to move their herds like I did. The wildfire came in too fast." He pulled her into the group and kept a hand propped against her shoulder blade. "Gentlemen, here's Miss Sessoms."

"Call me Lyndie, please. I started out in Oklahoma City. By the time the rodeo closed down, word was out that a wildfire had already made it to the Kansas state line. I'd guess that would have been pushing noon."

Several men nodded in collusion, their expressions taut.

"Smoke out on the highway stopped me twice. I crossed the state line on highway one-eighty-three, but couldn't get to Sitka because of cows on the road."

"That'd be Red McMinimy's herd," an older, sharp-chinned man said.

"I turned west onto a gravel road, and then north. That's when I saw my first fatality, a steer burned up against the corner fence."

"Then she found me," Burk added, "half dead and not knowing which way was up."

"We may all feel like that by morning," another man said.

"I won't be able to sleep much twixt now and dawn," the older man replied.

Compelled to offer, Lyndie gathered her courage. "For the sake of the children, maybe we should hold a group vigil after we eat. Someone could share a few words of encouragement, and then we could pray."

"Yeah," Burk replied. "That would give us an opportunity to find out if anyone needs special accommodations. I spotted the Fellows across the way. They're both pushing ninety. The last thing we need is a broken hip from someone rolling out of a cot. What do you say, Clint? Would you ask the Red Cross coordinator if he'd speak a few words of comfort?"

The old rancher pulled at his mustache. "Sure. Give me a time."

"Let's say seven o'clock sharp," Burk replied. "I doubt many more people will stroll in after that."

She flexed a stiff leg. "If that's all you need, I'd like to freshen up a bit." She stepped back with a general nod, avoiding eye contact with her former passenger. Once she found the restroom, the line strung out into the hallway. *Not a problem.* She had until seven o'clock. What kind of a difference could she possibly make until then?

Chapter 3

Burk drank a water bottle empty trying to dislodge the white-on-dry ham sandwich from the bottom of his esophagus. Some added condiments would have gone a long way toward lubrication. A dull ache throbbed from his left temple.

True to her word, Lyndie had produced the ointment from her camper and doctored a couple of spots on his back. That tactile action made him feel more human than he had in ages. The rest fell to him, so he smeared his thumb across half a dozen wounds hidden by his shirt.

As time drifted by, he became less concerned about checking to see if his own house still stood. At least he had his cattle to depend on for future income. Other cattlemen would go sleepless over that unknown variable. When his best friend, Cub Haines, mentioned that none of the county residents west of Ashland had arrived at the evacuation center, the sketchy news added to his mounting worries.

Lyndie knelt by the elderly Fellows across the way, pausing to introduce herself. A friendly exchange followed. Before she left, she stooped to hug Mrs. Fellows.

He tried to counter the reactive sensation in his chest by taking a drink from an already drained bottle. The sides collapsed in a forceful crackle. A hand slapped his shoulder, barely missing a sore spot.

"Easy, Tiger," Cub teased with a short-lived chuckle. "I heard you got brought in by a tall rodeo sideshow gal, so I had to come see it for myself. Zowie—no wonder you have to keep your lips distracted nursing that empty bottle."

"Stifle it—or I'll introduce you by your given name, Jacobi." He looked at his long-time friend and gave his head a shake. "We're really being smashed underfoot in God's winepress tonight. It feels none too good."

Cub stared at the floor. "I don't rightly know how Ashland can dodge this. The fire line goes all the way from Protection to Englewood. Maybe I'm safe up by Clark County Lake, but I wouldn't bet on it."

"What about your dad?"

Cub shook his head as his gaze began to track Lyndie's approach. "Dad stayed put. If the fire spreads that far north, he'll hose down the house and barn, and then take shelter in the root cellar. It's plenty dank down there."

"That scenario adds to the heartburn I'm already having." Burk checked his phone for the time. They had fifteen minutes before the vigil. When he looked up, Lyndie stood off his left shoulder. "Hey, let me introduce you two. Lyndie Sessoms, meet my buddy, Cub Haines."

"Ma'am," Cub replied with a tip of his hat. "Thanks for bringing Burk out of the cemetery. Guess that's a resurrection of a smudgy kind." At that, he engaged his boyish dimples for her enjoyment.

Lyndie scarcely seemed to notice. She grabbed Burk's hand and took a step back. "Can I borrow you for a short minute? I don't want to run out of time."

Burk yielded to her begging tone, stepping away from Cub with one brow cocked for effect. When he turned to Lyndie, she had her bottom lip crimped between her teeth. Not an expert on women, this one definitely had something brewing. "What gives?"

She shifted her attention from a cluster of cots. After

searching his face, her gaze aligned with his. "I want to make an offer to a stranger, but I don't know how appropriate it would seem. I figured I could run it by you first."

He sank right into her baby blues. Sensing a need for privacy, he moved a step closer. At this proximity, he might not have a clear recollection of what appropriate entailed. He studied her flawless features a precious second. Her skin seemed almost translucent in the gym's lights, a total contrast to his burned-up hide. "Go ahead and try me."

She looked over his shoulder for a protracted second, but returned her focus on him. "It's about my camper. Naturally, I'd planned to sleep in there tonight. But Lord help me, Burk. I can't put myself in that kind of comfort with the Fellows in here sleeping on rickety cots."

Somewhere during her explanation, his jaw gaped open. That earned him a tender finger under the chin to guide his mouth shut. His throat proceeded to go dry.

"Anyway, if you agree, I'll offer the camper to the Fellows. I'd like you to come with me, so I'd have both support and help to make it happen. What do you think?"

"That's mighty generous of you—and maybe another reason God sent you our way. I like the idea a lot. Could we tackle that offer right after the vigil?"

She nodded, although she didn't seem to have total resolution. Her cheeks blushed a pretty shade of pink. "Okay then, that leaves me not knowing where to lay my head. Should I try to help Abby's mother?"

Selfish as it seemed, only one feasible option came to mind, aided by his touch-and-go headache. "No, her husband Cody came along, too, so they're solid. Listen, I'm on the wind-down with these trampling bruises, though my skull still feels mule-kicked. Do you reckon we could place two cots head-to-head? That way, if I got bad off in the night, you'd be right there, so I wouldn't have to stumble around in the dark for help."

"Goodness, Burk." She grabbed his shoulders and stared

deep into his eyes. "Why didn't you speak up before now? How bad is it?"

"I can't rightly say. Why don't you test me? Hold up two fingers."

She complied, flashing him a peace sign.

"Good, I see two fingers." He wrapped them in his hand and winked. "That settles it. You're with me—for my health and your well being."

She smiled a bit, obviously relieved.

A metal bowl struck the corner of a food table and made a ruckus. Two ranchers and a Red Cross man waited behind the table. For leadership, they formed a loose posse.

Burk led Lyndie over to join them. On his way, he had a flicker of relief seeing that Gene Shawboro had left the town's perimeter and now sat safe with the other evacuees. He gave the man's stooped back a pat as they passed by.

Gene nodded and suppressed a catty grin when he saw Lyndie.

"Evening folks," the Red Cross man said. "Let me start by saying how much I appreciate everyone's cooperation. I'm the site director. This evacuation site serves both Ashland and Protection, so be sure to greet your neighbor and make a new acquaintance, too."

When Lyndie squeezed Burk's hand, he realized he still had a hold of her. He squeezed back and tore his hand away to rub his neck. There was nothing in the world wrong with his neck short of windburn. Maybe he did have a mild case, at second thought.

"Anyway, you might appreciate knowing that you're released to go back to town at six o'clock tomorrow morning unless worsening conditions warrant a delay. Just leave your cots right where they are. Our volunteers will deal with those after breakfast has been served. We'll try to be timely with that, though our cooks don't like to rise too early."

Clint Hooper took center stage next, his pointed chin poking authority into the program. "Here's a quick word from your town commissioners. We want to thank Gene Shawboro for disking a firebreak around the perimeter of Ashland. If we somehow dodge this threat, Gene, I'm writing you in for mayor this fall." He gestured toward the humble man and numerous evacuees applauded. "That's all from me. I think someone wants to aim a word at the Almighty next." He moved away and sat beside Gene.

Burk shifted to the center, his knees aquiver. At least Lyndie stood with him, which generated some assurance. He looked out over the room and saw confused order. "It struck me that good people stretched in harm's way might want to lift a late plea heavenward. Even though I'll speak the words, my hope is that you'll each feel them in your heart. Please bow with me.

"Dear God above, we beg you to stop the fire and hush the wind to protect your people in Clark County tonight. Keep our losses to a minimum and protect our neighbor's spread with your almighty hand. Calamity makes us mindful of our weakness and your strength. We're flat out asking for your mercy tonight, in Jesus' name, amen."

Several more benedictions echoed from the townspeople.

Lyndie inched him over as though to take command of the program. She gave the slightest smile and locked in on her audience. The reassuring words to "Let There Be Peace on Earth" slowly wafted skyward and hung on velvety notes from the rafters, loud and clear.

After the first stanza, the room fell quiet. For a few moments, the musical invoking of peace held mayhem at bay. Burk stepped away, pierced through by Lyndie's crystalline voice. By the song's end, he could hardly draw a breath. Part miracle, his headache had vanished.

Across the gym, several mothers hugged their children. Mr. Fellows drew his white-haired bride closer. The impromptu singing performance delivered therapy plus. The message to take each moment and live in harmony wasn't wasted on this group, not by a long shot.

As the final note faded, Lyndie raised her arms to praise God and then meekly stepped away.

Burk returned to the table and pressed his thighs against its rim. "Have a peaceful evening, everybody." He tapped his chest about heart level and flung the sentiment across the room. Uncomfortable about being the man up front, he longed to blend into the crowd.

Two younger men crossed his path, their faces grim. Covered head to toe in soot, they apparently had pulled some fire suppression duty. With slumped shoulders, they took their place at the speaking table. "We're here to report on the wildfire's advance. God as my witness, Englewood's done burned to the ground." His face twitched with emotion, and he paused to collect his nerve. "The driver of a big rig got trapped in the fire line along highway thirty-four and couldn't maneuver out. Sad to report the news, but he's gone, too."

Clint Hooper rose to his feet in slow motion. "What about the Guard family? They never sought shelter with us."

The young man braced on the table and shook his head. "The fire department remains out there yet, pumping everything they have on it. I'm not sure it's going to be enough. The Guard brothers got separated trying to fight the fire. Two houses have already burned to the ground at their ranch. North of the highway sits untouched. Your place is in the clear, Mr. Hooper."

Gene Shawboro rose beside Clint. "What about Ashland? Do we still have a town?"

The volunteer fireman lifted his head with a defiant look. "Yes—Ashland stands."

A woman nearby couldn't contain her apprehension any longer and burst into tears. Another gasped when the shorter brother's knees gave out. He collapsed under the table. The Red Cross man teamed with Clint in getting the exhaustion victim laid out for proper care.

An unseen urgency propelled Burk deeper into the gym. He somehow located Lyndie kneeling beside the Fellows. Bending low, he spoke into Mr. Fellows' good ear. "We've got a special place for you both to rest comfortably, sir. Come with us outside in the parking lot, and let's get Mrs. Fellows settled into a quiet place."

"That'd be nice, Crosby." The old man's eyes twinkled, though his face remained solemn. "It's already well past my regular bedtime."

When Burk glanced at Lyndie, her eyes fluttered closed. She looked like peace incarnate, a specter he rarely beheld. "No sir, there's nothing regular marking this day. Not one single thing." He helped the old man to his feet. With Lyndie bringing Mrs. Fellows along behind them, it proved to be quite the exodus.

Halfway out the door, Burk recalled the devastating news about Englewood being burnt to ashes. A real gut check, he wondered if outlying Sitka had fared any better. "Stop the fire, hush the wind," he whispered heavenward into the blustery twilight.

~

Restless, Lyndie shifted to her other side, so the wire mattress supports could poke her left ribs for equal opportunity non-enjoyment. Weak lighting illuminated the far hall where the restrooms stood. Otherwise, the gym remained dark enough to foster sleep, if only she could.

Hadn't she hoped to discover a place like this? Tonight, she'd held a baby, soothed panicked children, helped feed the hungry, deferred to the elderly, and rubbed ointment on an injured man. She'd given an eyewitness account of the fiery enemy and sang to call down a beginning to peace. After taking inventory, it represented a productive start to her sabbatical. If God was pleased, she would be also.

An arm's length away, Burk moaned out of his broken sleep. His cot squeaked in a fit of restlessness. In the distance, a man coughed.

More than ready to be shed of the cot, Lyndie eased her bedding onto the hardwood floor and sat cross-legged beside Burk. Light as a feather, she stroked the base of his neck and softly hummed a reprise of her peace song as midnight came and went. Her head grew heavy, so she rested it on his shoulder.

Sometime later, the room stirred with a general rustle.

"Lucky man," a voice said, hovering over the cot.

She blinked and recognized Cub's boyish grin in the dawning light.

Burk stirred and strummed his lips across her forehead, his hand stroking her hair like a man fingering a skein of spun gold.

She cherished the richness of the moment, knowing the sun would rise to hardships for the day. *Be with us, Lord.* God would have to lend her strength and grace, beauty for ashes, and the oil of joy for mourning. Beyond that eternal truth, she had no earthly idea what the light of day would hold.

Chapter 4

The trip back home held mounting trepidation. Burk assessed the standing buildings. From all indications, his mowed yard had spared the ranch house. All else beyond the closest corrals had been reduced to ashes. Even now, the unceasing south wind tried to scour the black ash covering from the face of the land. The two paired up well—harsh wind and lifeless ash.

Lyndie walked up and stood beside him, her shoulder barely touching his. "You're a fortunate man, Mr. Crosby."

"I'm feeling favored, believe me." He lifted his hat and ran a hand through his hair. The wind played comb without any invitation. "There will be others who need more help than me, so we'll head back into town. I gotta find some hay for the cattle in the cemetery plot, until I can move them out onto the wheat field this evening."

"Let's keep an eye out for extra hay then. I can't keep dragging around this camper, though. Would you let me store it beside your barn for now? I may be able to hook up in town once we see how stable things are."

"Sure. Park wherever you want, and I'll chock the wheels in place."

"Go get your shower, Burk. You need to clean those wounds. I'll deal with the camper."

He nudged her arm with his elbow. "Mighty nice of you to let the Fellows borrow that last night." When he loosened his shirttail, the wind riddled the flannel like Swiss cheese. "Guess I fell the ultimate benefactor of that kind gesture." After a quick glance, he ran up the back steps into the house. Inside, no trace of smoke lingered. The wildfire must have burned past too fast.

Ten minutes later, he could face the day, come what may. With his shirt in his hand, he stomped on a pair of boots and came down the back steps. He found Lyndie peering into an empty dog house. Overgrown grass blocked the entrance.

She rose and gave him an incredulous look. "You don't have a dog?"

"Got that ointment handy?" He planted his palms on the hood of her truck and arched his back. When she brought it to him and began the application, he felt he ought to level on the canine issue. "I need a dog, and even want a dog. Maybe I'm hesitating because a pet can mean so much to you…and then one day, it's gone."

She ran the lubricated pad of a fingertip around a sore spot on his shoulder blade. "The investment is worth the risk, if you ask me. Plus, if you had a herding dog, you might not look like this, trampled and hobbling."

"Hey, I'm not hobbling." He stiffened under her touch.

"You're limping worse than Mr. Fellows last night when we walked him to my camper." She moved to a different spot. The pain soon followed.

"Well, I'm better today. The fire department will likely need all the help they can get. I plan to volunteer for duty."

Her finger hesitated for a second. "I prefer to stay in town and help. If there are more dead cattle out there pinned against fences, I can't stand that horrible scenery." She finished and handed him the tube.

"That settles it. We'll drive into town separately." He took a dab of medication on his index finger and swiped across the worst of the wounds. "Think you can find your way back out to the Crosby ranch?"

She took the ointment and dabbed across his jaw. When she glanced up, her eyes shined a deep blue. "Trust me. I can find my way back."

"Would you mind if I loaded an extra hay bale in your truck?" He pulled the T-shirt over his head in time to catch her nod. "I need your phone number to get a hold of you later." He saw her smile flicker and realized he'd mixed business with pleasure. *Good move*. Plus, it got results.

~

Lyndie's gaze skittered across the Clark County fairgrounds south of Ashland. Overnight, two truckloads of hay had been donated to ease the dire situation. Town officials attempted to get word out to local ranchers. Thinking the windfall might run thin, Burk hastily loaded two bales. She'd just met the director of the nonprofit foundation that supported various local endeavors. Fire recovery likely fell outside of their original purview, but roles could adapt.

"Six fires are still burning, mostly up by the lake," Ken Ray said. "Unfortunately, there's a pesky line north of Protection that nobody's fighting. Have you heard the weather forecast, Burk? We're in for a change."

"What? We finally get a hush to this infernal wind?" He stroked his jaw, stopping short of the bruise.

Lyndie studied the two men. Something went unsaid between them. It put her ill at ease.

"A shift is in the forecast for this afternoon. The wind will swing around from the north. That should back the fire onto the huge blackline it's already set and starve it out. At least, that's the way I figure." Ken shrugged and stepped away to catch a pickup driving into the area.

"I'll call Cub and see what he knows. He's up by the lake. I'll warn him about the wind shift, too. I don't trust it an inch." His lips pulled tight as the arriving truck filed over toward the hay supply to take a free load. "Lyndie, would you like to stay here and help Ken?"

With the Red Cross set up in town and fully functional with its own volunteers, she considered her limited options. When a flatbed truck pulled in full of fencing supplies, she saw Burk's eyes light up. "Sure, I'll stay here and help with the distribution. Should I grab some supplies for your place as they come in?"

"Yeah, take whatever Ken allows. I'll tell him you're covering for my spread when I pull out. I'd better get going. Hope you can find a way to help."

"Take a few water bottles out of my cab before you leave. I'll lock it behind you." She pressed a smile in place to alleviate his concerns.

He backpedaled away from her. "Nobody locks up around here."

"Well, people will be coming and going today. With so much chaos, there's no need to tempt anybody." She flicked her wrist and brushed him away, certain his time could be better spent on the fire line. For her part, she would broker the donated items. She walked up to Ken to get the lowdown on how to operate. "I'd like to volunteer out here, if you can use me."

"Yes, ma'am," he replied. "Let's go unload that truck. It'll help if you know where everything is stockpiled from the start. Then you can direct local ranchers coming to pick up."

"What's your procedure, Ken? Do they have to sign in and prove residency?"

He shook his head with a little laugh. "No. They wouldn't show up if they weren't already in a world of hurt for the supplies. Whoever comes in can have whatever they can load. We'll give supplies away until the donations are gone. Tomorrow, maybe more truckloads will arrive, God willing, and we'll have the opportunity to give it all away again."

Compassion worked deeper in her heart. "Quite a hurting

landscape, that's for certain."

"If they can't get those hot spots suppressed, the devastation will only grow." He whistled to the truck driver and began to give hand gestures for backing the big rig into place.

Lyndie looked west and saw an ashen ridge flanking the town limits. How the town's cavalcade of trim wooden houses had been spared fell as a downright miracle. Her efforts today would springboard off of that impossibility. She could embody the generous hands of God—even if it meant hefting barbed wire spools and fence post bundles all day.

~

Burk took one look at Cub's farmyard and knew the rancher had kindling on his hands. The whole place seemed dry-rotted and dilapidated beyond use. At least Cub had the good sense to crank up the farm equipment and leave it parked in an open corral. His father's beat-up truck sat poised for escape down the driveway. He pulled in and began honking his horn.

Cub emerged from one of the outbuildings, his face smeared with grease. He threw up his hands and wiped his face on his sleeve. "Hey, what gives with you coming out?"

"Answer your phone, for crying out loud. How am I supposed to know if you're okay?"

Cub patted his back pocket and came up empty. "I must have left it in my truck. What's the latest news? I still see smoke in two or three places around here."

"Ken Ray says there are six fires still burning up by the lake. I'm heading over there to volunteer on the fire lines. Can you throw in with me—at least for the morning? Time is short. The forecast calls for the wind to swing around out of the north after noontime."

"What? Exactly opposite?" Cub screwed up his expression. "That means everything that's been spared in the first wave will be in the crosshairs again."

"Ken thinks the burned areas will serve as a blackline and snuff out the fire. Still, the whole situation remains too unpredictable for my liking. The less fire we let meet that wind shift, the better off we'll be. Go get your phone, gloves, and some drinking water."

"Let me run and tell Dad. Want to grab a rake or shovel? You know where everything's kept." He trotted off to the main house.

Burk threw the truck in neutral and stepped toward the first outbuilding, which Cub called the shed. He opened the door and found the hand tools racked up to the right. After selecting a shovel and a hard rake, he grabbed a five-gallon bucket for good measure. This would be dirty, front-line work where he'd look the flaming enemy dead in the eye.

Cub met him in the farmyard after retrieving his phone. "Dad heard on the radio that the game warden had to rescue an isolated group of gawkers trying to witness the wildfire over at Clark County Lake."

"Sounds like he's got more trouble than he knows what to do with. Let's head over there first. We can always detour if we see the fire department working a hot spot." He shoved the tools behind the hay bale and slid behind the wheel.

Cub took the passenger seat. "Where in the devil did you get that hay?"

"At the fairgrounds south of town. Relief donations are already pouring in. Ken said the first hay shipment came from ranchers struck by the Anderson Creek fire last year around Medicine Lodge. They know what it's like to lose the grass under your feet. Let me tell you, I was glad to see it and double glad to take some. I've got to move the cattle out of the cemetery before it gets dark tonight. Lyndie said she'd help me. I've got her truck loaded with hay, too."

"Do tell? What makes you think she'll end up at your place at sundown?" He waggled his brow as if to test him.

"Well, I've got her rolling sardine can in my barnyard, for starters." He tried to stay poker-faced, but a grin surfaced. He pulled onto the blacktop and headed for the lake.

Cub gave a low whistle and pulled his hat brim down. "Do tell. Like I said this morning, you're a lucky man."

A black plume curled on the horizon like an obscene gesture. Burk had every intention of snuffing the life out of its source without the first regret. The more he thought about it, the more riled up he got inside. With no grass, what would the cattle eat this spring? Hardship was one matter, but cutting off a rancher's livelihood rated as despicable in his book. He lived by that honorable book of ranching, and right now, its pages were aflame.

~

The banker looked up at the shy figure standing in his door and recognized the longtime associate. "Come on in. It's been a ghost town around here, what with the fire and all. What can I do for you today?"

"Rumor says you're handling the donations for the Ashland Foundation," she replied, stepping closer.

"That's right. Ken Ray came in first thing and said he expected some state money. The federal livestock aid is capped at a hundred and twenty-five thousand. The fencing costs cap at two hundred thousand. You know, it could be weeks before we see any relief money come in."

She shifted her stance. "Once the smoke clears and we can get our feet under us to explore the damages, we'll assess the magnitude of what we're dealing with. Let Ken know he'll need to start a list of ranchers receiving financial donations. Be sure to emphasize that our entire community stands with the Ashland Foundation."

"Yes, ma'am. I'll be sure to do just that." He raked his fingers down his abundant chin. "Can the bank help you with anything?"

"Just doing my part." She dropped a check onto his desk. "That's to remain anonymous, by the way. Call me Miss T."

When he spotted several zeroes on the amount line, he

stood up to shake her hand. "That's mighty generous of you. I'll rattle an empty can around and see if more of our downtown business partners will join you."

She stared at him a meaningful second. "The ranchers keep this town alive. They need support to bridge their losses, and we need to let them know we have their backs."

"Money talks. That's a lesson from banking one-oh-one."

She started for the door and stopped. "I hope you'll join me, Neil."

He fumbled for an appropriate response when the warning tone went off on his cell phone. Holding a finger up to have her pause, he picked it up and read the message. "Oh, here we go again. Protection just got placed under evacuation orders for a second time in as many days. The wildfire is coming back from the north." He looked up at her, his mouth agape.

"Gotta go protect a highly flammable fort." With a salute, she disappeared from sight.

He picked up the check to verify the amount before depositing it. If that fire came back, they would need a hundred times this amount—or more. Grateful he lived in town, he walked behind the teller's counter to make the deposit.

~

Lyndie quelled her doubts about the unrestrained distribution of donated goods. She'd met twenty or more local ranchers, all tight-faced and speaking minimal exchanges during the donation pickup. Not used to receiving help, it worked against their self-sufficient nature to accept a handout. She tried to make the process as painless as possible. Livestock had to eat. She mentioned her own horse a time or two, so they wouldn't mistake her for a city girl. It sure felt gratifying to fit in.

Darkness had begun to fall as she waved goodbye to the last hay recipient. With the days still short, they didn't have much time left to get the fire under control. Her thoughts detoured to Burk. She hadn't heard from him all day.

Ken strode up from the fencing supply arsenal. "Hey, we're closing the gates at six. You might as well call it a night. I heard the Red Cross set out some hot food. You should pick up dinner for you and Burk on your way out."

"Thanks, Ken. I believe I will. I still have to get my camper hooked up once I get to the Crosby ranch. A shortcut to dinner sounds great. Can I come back tomorrow?"

He laughed. "Anybody gonna say no to that? I don't think so. You cheer things up around here, Lyndie. Thanks for sharing a smile with these guys. They're about as low as I've ever seen them." He shook his head as though to dismiss the admission.

"Tomorrow will be a little easier. You get some rest, Ken. When do you want me back?"

"I'll open the gate at seven, but I doubt there'll be any takers that early. Hard to say."

"Okay. I'll try to make plans with Burk and follow him into town." A shiver trailed down her spine. "This north wind has a nip to it. I'll bring a jacket tomorrow." She waved farewell and headed to her truck.

Before she could get the door open, her pocket pinged with a text. She viewed the number and saw Burk's name. Warmth pulsed through her chest.

Headed home.

She typed a response. *Hot dinner waiting.* Now, she had to make a cozy meal happen while the wildfire raged on the county's perimeter. It would be her last donation for the day. Something told her this particular rancher would be grateful.

~

Aching from head to toe, Burk halted on the back step to jack off his sooty boots and remove his shirt. Like his grandpa used to say at the end of an exhausting day, he was all in. He had enough energy to stand up for a shower, and then it would be meltdown from there. He threw the back door open and strode through the laundry room, headed for a light in the kitchen.

When he looked across the bar, there stood Lyndie, sporting an apron and looking quite at home. "Hey, that's a welcome sight." He smiled and nodded to the bowl in her hands.

"Dinner's ready in ten minutes," she replied. "Go ahead and shower. I'll keep it hot until you get back."

He nodded and strayed back to his bedroom, where he tossed his smoke-filled clothes in a pile. For all the ugly he'd seen today, including dead cattle and barns burnt to the base, he'd come home to a lovely sight. Even so, he had zero energy left for courting a woman. Maybe she could accept him for the ordinary man he was and let it be enough. He walked dead-away into the shower and turned it as hot as it would go.

When he returned to the kitchen wearing his softest cotton shirt and faded jeans, he thought maybe he could go this final furlong. The aroma of fried chicken sent the restoration deeper. He found Lyndie sitting off the end of the bar. A place to her right had been set for him.

"Come on over for a bite to eat." She stood and crossed to the stove where she lowered the oven door. A sheet of crispy chicken and round-topped rolls made it to the bar. After resting that on a trivet, she returned to the stove and brought back green beans and mashed potatoes. "Courtesy of the Red Cross. Ken invited me to partake, so I brought some back for us."

"A little bite of manna." He slipped onto the bar stool. "I'm bushed beyond reason, but we got three of the six fires snuffed out. Praise God and pass the potatoes."

She snickered, sitting down beside him. "I discovered there's a whole lot of unmet need out there. We'd better say grace first, so the Lord knows how thankful we truly are. Let me say it tonight, as I'm feeling pretty strong gratitude over the day."

He nodded and hesitated to close his eyes, thinking the tender scene might go away. As soon as his eyelids shut, he visualized fire licking the sky. That had been his view all day long. He almost missed the velvet touch of her fingers as Lyndie reached to connect with him.

"Dear Heavenly Father, thank you for this first post-fire day and all the gains we had after the losses yesterday. Bless this food to strengthen us for tomorrow's work. Also, impress upon us who needs an ounce of extra grace, amen." She pulled away and reached for her fork.

Burk held his face in his hands. "If you have an ounce of extra grace left, you can use it right here." He tapped his sternum and then reached for his glass of tea.

"All right." She picked up his plate and loaded it with one of everything, including the biggest chicken breast on the pan. She centered the plate in front of him and grabbed his napkin. After a moment's hesitation, she tucked it into his left hand. His fork soon assaulted the mashed potato mound and rose to his lips. "Open up the hangar. Your humanitarian shipment has just arrived."

He shook his head in quasi-disbelief. "You're making this unreal for me, Lyndie." With that, he bit the fork-load and let the potatoes dissolve in his mouth. Seasoned just right, the side dish tasted delectable. He had to have more.

She bent over him, cutting the chicken breast into bite-sized morsels. "Oh. Shucks. I was trying so hard to make it *real*." She hummed a tune and went about her business, rendering the food readily edible. Once she had the roll shellacked with butter, she held it up for him to bite.

He grabbed the roll. "Sit down and eat with me. I'm just tired, not debilitated."

She hummed as she sat down, pulled her stool in, and picked up her fork. "There it is, Lord, my last act of helping for the day." She stabbed a pile of green beans and ate them.

He reviewed his situation as the roll dissolved in his mouth. He chased it with a drink of tea. The chicken breast came under attack next. Salty and moist, he found it more than satisfactory—like his dinner company. He chewed and swallowed, knowing he needed to say his piece before she got too withdrawn for retrieval. "Well, if there's any good deeds left in your bag tonight, I do need that ointment on my back."

She gave a slight smile as she fingered the drumstick on her plate. "Is that so?" She hoisted the drumstick within biting range. "Would there be a pretty please with that last request?"

Burk turned to her, letting his gaze sweep her features. Tired meant honest, and he sure could do honest. "Yeah, there's a pretty hanging on that. A real pretty…even beautiful." He searched her eyes to enjoy the depths of blue corralled there.

She extended the drumstick and offered him a bite. "I'd be happy to, now that you realize that you're neither too tired nor debilitated."

He bit into the chicken leg like a hungry wolf. Between his plate and hers, the platter would be clean tonight before he'd consider dinner finished. After that, he'd allow a short leash on consciousness, ointment treatment or not. He better not look into those blue eyes again, at least not from such close range.

~

Lyndie wiped the ointment from her fingertips and sat back on the trunk Burk used for a coffee table. "I'm not totally unemployed during my sabbatical, which brings up my next concern. I have to set up a temporary broadcasting spot for my Friday night radio show with Western Star. Tomorrow's Thursday, so I truly need to get that established. Any suggestions?"

He sat up and pulled his shirt into place. "You'll need good acoustics. The community room at the library has sound-absorbing panels on the wall. That might be a good start. Tara Daniels is the librarian. She'll go out of her way to help you. Mention I sent you over there."

She smiled at his smugness and twisted the tube of medicine open, seeing another place that needed treatment. After putting a dot on the pad of her finger, she leaned closer and touched it to his jaw. The ointment slid it into place while her finger celebrated the stubble on his chin.

His eyes fluttered closed. "Forgot about that one," he whispered, his words dragging.

"Yeah, just like you forgot about moving those cattle from the cemetery. Let's go look for them at daybreak. If we lower the tailgate on my truck and strew the hay, I bet they would follow us to wherever you want them to go."

He floated back against the overstuffed sofa. "Sounds easy."

She stood and leaned over him. "As easy as sending you off to la-la land." With one puff, she sent his boat toward a far horizon and then let herself out the back door. The camper would be climate controlled by now, as the north wind had brought March's chill back in no uncertain terms. She couldn't wait to sleep in her own bed.

Chapter 5

Given the early morning hour, Burk found few quality supplies lying in the mounds of donated items at the fairgrounds. He'd beaten Lyndie to the site, as she'd gotten waylaid on Main Street looking for a decent cup of coffee. He kicked around a used fence post too crooked to reuse. *What are people thinking?* He needed straight, sturdy posts, about twenty miles worth.

Another truck pulled into the staging area with hasty aggression. It came to rest just behind his truck. Suddenly, a line of demand had formed. The driver hopped out, covered with soot from head to foot.

Burk barely recognized his best friend. He'd obviously been through a bad situation. When the whites of his eyes grew too large to ignore, he had to say something. "Morning, Cub. Did things get hot out your way?"

"Don't even say the word *fire* to me. I've stricken it from further use. It overtook our outbuildings just past midnight, crept around and started licking the main house by one o'clock. When the sun came up, our ranch was gone—the whole lot of it—except the equipment left standing in the wide open."

"Where's your dad? Is he okay?"

"He packed up a box of his stuff, threw in his banjo, and

drove out without a word to me. Boom—left me there to watch the homeplace burn to ashes. He didn't even look back once."

"Maybe he couldn't stand to look back. I'll ask Ken to keep an ear to the ground in case someone locates him. You're welcome at my place tonight, unless you've got other plans."

"Thanks, Burk, but you're too far south. I need something closer. I'm going by Cousin Heath's house to see if I can stay over there. At least he's right in town."

Burk gestured to the piles of fencing supplies, depleted though they were. "Tell me what kind of donations you'd take, and I can pull some aside for you."

Cub shook his head. "Better let me look at 'em myself. I brought the truck in thinking I might make a haul out this morning."

"It's really picked through right now. The Red Cross has some clothes you could wear. Look, I'll have Lyndie pull her truck in line for you while you go get cleaned up and have some breakfast. Check in with Heath and see if that's going to work. The offer of my place still stands. You have to go about this logically, Cub. Rome wasn't rebuilt in a day."

He wiped across his face as if to collect his thoughts. "Okay, I'll be back within the hour. Watch for pipe gates in addition to the fence wire and posts. I need a corral up by nightfall at the very least. Thanks for helping me think through this, Burk. I'm half crazy and the other half desperate right now." He flung his frame back into the driver's seat and soon had the truck turned around, headed for town.

In less than a minute, Lyndie's truck approached down the gravel road. He considered what it might look like having Cub thrown into the mix back at the ranch house. That would sure put an end to his private dinners with the attractive camper resident, but survival never toted personal convenience on its back. Besides, if they were working on something beyond acquaintance, it would happen no matter if his sooty sidekick hung around or not. She didn't seem all that interested anyway.

Her truck crept onto the lot, so he motioned her over to the line to keep his promise. He'd scarcely gotten her aligned when a flatbed rig rumbled down the road. As it turned into the fairgrounds, he could see the emblem for a feed and seed store on its door panel. *Shout hallelujah.* More fencing supplies had arrived. He spotted half a dozen red pipe gates latched to the load which fostered a little yip of momentary delight.

Lyndie slid out of her cab, balancing a paper coffee cup in her hand. "Hey, what's the jubilation all about?"

"I'm celebrating my way up from the ashes. Cub got burned out last night. He's gone to town to get cleaned up. We're loading your truck for him right now. I hope you don't mind."

"Not at all. Let me get this truck of donations pulled in where we want it. Ken's downtown at the Red Cross station getting interviewed by every newspaper in Kansas." A little smile lit her face before she took a sip.

Standing close enough to smell the vanilla in her coffee, Burk studied the morning sun on her hair as it left a wheat-colored halo. The horizon shrunk to just the two of them for a few precious seconds. "Listen. Even if Cub needs to crash at my place, I want you to know it won't make any difference to me. You're still welcome out back." He brushed a toying knuckle across the tip of her chin.

Her gaze skimmed his as she gave a sideways nod. "Thanks for saying so. It never hurts to have an extra set of hands around when you're dealing with wayward cattle."

"I'm glad you're here," he replied, his voice a bit husky with the admission. The trucker laid on his horn for service which about earned him a vanilla latte right in his shirt pocket. He steadied the cup and hooked her elbow. "Let's go get those pipe gates unloaded. That's two for Cub, two for me, and two for the next fortunate Clark County resident who has the good sense to pull up in line." As they walked side by side, the unloading task became an inconsequential means of spending the morning together—at least until Ken arrived.

~

Thinking the library looked seventies vintage, Lyndie walked up the entrance sidewalk and into a spacious atrium. The roofline lofted in a peak to accommodate the glass-topped segment between two brick buildings. She saw bookshelves to the right while walking by overgrown indoor plantings. Inside the next door, a quiet atmosphere hung over even rows of books, as if to hush a thousand voices from reading the stories out loud.

She caught the attention of a student-aged assistant behind the counter. "Excuse me, can you tell me if Tara Daniels is in today? Tell her Lyndie Leigh Sessoms has a question for her."

The girl's eyes sparkled. "Yes, ma'am. Hold on a second. She's in the back. I'll let her know you're here." The courier let out a faint giggle as she raced through the office area.

In less than a minute, a distinguished-looking woman with a solitary stripe of gray in her bobbed hair came forward. "Hello, I'm Tara, the head librarian. How may I help you?"

She placed her hands on the counter, palms up. "Maybe I shouldn't try hiding in such a public place." A sheepish grin followed the admission. "I'm looking for a suitable location to broadcast my Friday night radio show. I'm Lyndie Leigh Sessoms with Western Star Radio."

"Are you in Ashland for long?"

She nodded. "I took a leave of absence from the rodeo circuit right before the wildfire hit, hoping to find something more significant to accomplish with my life. This week, I'm volunteering with Ken Ray at the donation distribution site.

What an eye opener. If I can portray that level of need over the air waves with a local broadcast, that might put the community in a favorable light across the entire nation."

The librarian dusted off the counter. "I'm afraid radio work falls outside of our mission. We're all about books and children's literacy."

"I was told by Burk Crosby that you had a room with acoustic panels on the walls. That might be a good fit for what I need. Think I could take a look?"

"Come right this way." She led back through the atrium into the second wing.

Lyndie dodged the craft tables and scanned the room's perimeter. Burnt orange panels glared back at her, but they seemed to take the harsh edge off the brick walls. She clapped and it sounded almost muffled. A pin could drop incognito in there. "This is amazing. Do you think I could set up my transmitting equipment for Friday's show and give it a test run?"

"I'm afraid my technical abilities end at the computer keyboard," Tara replied with a smile. "The space is yours. We close to the public at five o'clock on Fridays, so you'll have your privacy. This room would be available for setting up any time after four-thirty, when our after-school program adjourns. We let the children browse the stacks for the last half an hour before their parents come. That way the reading nook gets some use—after their homework is done."

Satisfied the space would be a feasible option, Lyndie nodded. "Thank you for working with me. My broadcast time is from six to seven. I plan to have someone drop in for an interview and make updates from the community."

"I'll whip up a sign to let our patrons know to listen in. I think everyone has an interest in how we're represented to the rest of the world."

Lyndie ran her thumb over the studs in her leather belt. "I love being in this little town, Ms. Daniels. Something about the realness of hurting from the devastation makes everything seem more genuine. If a broadcast can help, I'll sure do it."

The woman folded her hands and gave her a long look. "These ranchers are an independent lot. Add headstrong to that assessment on rare occasions. But the utter desperation of what the wildfire left won't allow for pigheaded independence right now. We've got to pull together in this recovery, forget the temporary hurt that came with the losses, and think about tomorrow."

"I like that speech," Lyndie replied with a smile. "Be careful, or you'll be my first guest to interview."

Daniels gave her a good old-fashioned shushing right over the counter, followed by a wink. "Librarians belong in the background, Lyndie. Thank the Good Lord folks like you step up to the microphone, because that would be torture for me."

"Glad to do it. Say, one last thing. I hoist an antenna from my camper to transmit the radio signal. Is there a door that leads to the back parking lot? I probably should check that out."

"Oh, right. You likely parked off Main Street today. Head for the atrium and bear right at the glass door. If you miss it, you'll be standing in our staff break room which doubles as a kitchen. That's been getting plenty of use lately, since we're helping make meals for the burned-out victims."

Lyndie shook her head in sympathy. "Cub Haines and his father joined the ranks last night. Thank you for your time today. I'll see you Friday around four-thirty to start the setup. I hope that seven o'clock wrap-up time doesn't pose a problem for you."

"If a conflict comes up, I'll have someone from our friends group watch the building for me. You'll have help, one way or the other." A rash of giggles bubbled up from the reshelf book cart. "And yes, your celebrity status will be a novel occurrence around here, so expect some random appreciation now and again."

"Never disappoint an audience," Lyndie quipped, pointing her finger in the air. She fired it at the young assistants hiding behind the cart and turned to leave. Retracing her steps, she walked into the atrium and found the glass door to the parking lot. Once outside, she thought the day had turned a bit chilly. A dragging noise led to a crash behind the dumpster gate nearby.

When a dog yelped, she had to investigate the commotion. A black tail led to a brown back. Eventually, a white head emerged. "Oh, Queenie. What have you gotten into? Come here to me, you mischief maker." She clapped her hands and got no response. Exasperated at the little mixed-breed scamp, she knelt to better set a trap. "I need to get you home, so Abby won't stay worried. Come here, girl."

When she remembered to snap her fingers, the dog fell into a well-rehearsed circus move by circling and planting its back haunches. Lyndie lunged to scoop up the wanderer and got a successful hold on its scruffy neck. A quick glimpse at her tags revealed an address on Fifth Street. One-handed, she unlatched her belt and pulled it free. She slid the leather strap through the collar and locked the buckle. She now had full possession of a hound and couldn't have been happier. She welcomed a brisk walk to Fifth Street, headed for an overdue reunion.

~

Burk watched as the bulldozer buried the last trace of the burned-to-a-crisp mobile home. He'd driven out to Englewood to help a volunteer troupe salvage the remains of the tiny outpost. The fire must have severely scorched the earth here. Even paint stripes along the highway had buckled and peeled off, a true phenomenon. The scene redefined carnage. It unnerved him a bit to see humanity's feeble influence reduced to such a worthless pile of ash and rubble.

A truck pulled in shellacked with red dust from grill to tailgate. Gaunt-faced, the driver seemed only faintly familiar. Drawn to him, Burk stacked the cinderblock he'd salvaged and headed toward what used to be a stand of trees. Only hulking stumps remained. Within steps, he could put a name on the dejected face. "Hey, Rodney. How'd the Gillian family make it through the wildfire up in the northern county?"

The man shook his head once like slinging off a vile threat. "Didn't make it—mostly. The family's safe. I tell myself that's all that matters. Once the wind swung out of the north, we had no time to react at all. The herd's half-gone, I wrecked my ATV maneuvering in thick smoke, and lost my cell phone. My eleven-year-old had to drive the pickup leading our cattle to the wheat field under the presumption I was a goner practically all afternoon, since I wouldn't answer his panicked calls." He drew a long breath and blew it out. "To top it all off, I can't find my blue heeler. Chip was already down to three legs, so I guess his luck finally ran out."

"Donations are pouring into the fairground, if you can get by there. The fencing supplies are coming in daily. You ought to ride in and get your fair share, Rod. It's not much, but it's a start. They have volunteer groups that'll come out and help the landowner. Some young bucks came in off their spring break from out of state. The Mennonite Relief group and the Methodists have sent in crews, too. I glimpsed a skid steer unloading, so they didn't come empty-handed. A man's got to reach out for help every now and then. I believe this is one of those rare times."

"If I could work past the devastation, maybe I could function and make some decisions. I'm so low right now, I can't figure out how to get back up again." He eyed the ashen tree trunks and tried to spit, to no avail.

"You don't think your grandfather or mine had it easy, do you? Where would we be today if they'd given up? I say it's time to give the next generation something to admire about us. It won't be hard to spot the gain, since many have nothing but bare ground to start from."

"Are you burned out, Burk?"

"No, sir, by the grace of God, I saw the fire coming in time to split the herd and get some green grass between the cattle and the wildfire. My mowed yard ended up sparing the ranch house. I'll need to reset the fences like everybody else, but I'm volunteering these next few days, wherever the most need exists."

He worked his lips and fired up the truck's engine. "Guess I'll go to town and see what the fairground supply holds for me. I might as well start with a drop in the bucket. Much obliged for the pep talk. If my granddad could carve a working ranch out during the Great Depression, then I guess I can take a turn whittling something out of nothing."

"That's the spirit. Look for Lyndie Leigh Sessoms from Western Star radio. Tell her Burk said to be generous with the donated supplies." He winked to authenticate the insider's tip.

"Will do. Say, if your fence pliers wander up to the north county, we'll be setting that stretch between us and the Guard brothers tomorrow. That's four days of work, right there."

Burk held his hand out as the truck jerked into reverse. "Count on me. Hey, try to get those Methodists to come out. I'm kinda fond of their equipment."

The man clamped a bony hand in his. "I bet you are. Keep us in your prayers. My wife is as uncertain as she can be."

"Will do. Be strong and courageous, like the Good Lord told Joshua."

The truck backed out in a slow withdrawal. Rodney leaned out of the window. "I don't think Joshua had any wildfire to deal with, back in the day."

"No, just heathens armed to the teeth. You never get to pick your enemy."

"Apparently not." The drawn-faced man disappeared behind the dust-covered windshield.

Burk watched his exodus, heartened that he'd turned toward Ashland. He pulled out his cell phone and sent Lyndie a text, hopeful she'd continue his salvage mission to help reclaim one of Clark County's most despondent victims.

~

Riding toys spattered the front drive of a modest gray house with red shingles. Lyndie tried to encourage her canine friend, but was slowed by perpetual sniffing at the corner of the lot. Several dogs barked from the alley nearby. She'd not visited this section of town yet and found it darling. Similar to Main Street, the residential street seemed twice as broad as necessary for two-way traffic.

As she tried to coerce the dog up the sidewalk, a woman came through the side garden gate. She recognized Abby's mother from the gym in Coldwater. Leading the escapee, she gestured to the far end of her belt.

The woman's hands clasped over her mouth to trap a tiny squeal. "Please, stay right there." She backtracked through the gate. "Quick, Abby, come see who's paying us a visit. You won't believe her surprise."

The little girl appeared in the gate opening, an old wooden spoon in her hand. Her lips pressed into an inquisitive circle, until she saw the dog. "Queenie has come home. You found my Queenie!" She ran toward her beloved pet, dropping the spoon as she came. Soon the two tumbled into an inseparable huddle on the brown lawn.

Lyndie stood in silence, letting the reunion strum across a few heart chords. What the fire had spared registered beyond precious. It made life richer.

The mother stepped closer. "Where was she?"

"Behind the library, pulling pizza crusts out of the garbage bin. I surprised her by coming out of the back door to check the parking lot for my radio broadcast Friday evening."

"So you're Lyndie Leigh Sessoms? I'd heard you were

helping out, but it's good to put a name with a friendly face. Thanks so much for finding Queenie."

"You're most welcome. Maybe you could spread the news about the radio show. I hope to publicize the community's needs, so the hay and fencing supply donations don't dry up. I'll be glad to add anything else to the most-needed list."

"Cody says the men are running low on ammo. They're mercy-killing the more severely burned cattle so they don't suffer." She shifted her stance, looking uncomfortable with the topic.

"That tops my hard-to-request list, for sure. With so much suffering out there, I don't know how the men can stand it. I'll stick with extracting confused mutts from the town's dumpsters."

"Amen, sister. It's good of you to be here, Lyndie. I mean it. Most people would have avoided the scorch zone. My name is Mandy Collier."

The little girl gripped the far end of her belt. "You're Abby's new friend."

"Guess we'd better deposit this troublemaker in the backyard," Mandy said.

A text pinged from Lyndie's back pocket. "It sounds like duty is calling me back to the fairgrounds. I'd better get going." She unclipped her belt as the girl held the dog's collar.

"Try to come to church on Sunday. We go to Community Church, if you'd like to see a friendly face down the pew."

"That sounds amazing right now. When the world goes topsy-turvy, only God can set it right again. We all could use a strong dose of ordinary this week." She waved and headed back to Main Street, lacing her belt in place. At the corner, she remembered the text and pulled out her phone. Burk had sent a message.

Double bless the man in the burgundy truck.

How hard would that be, given that any supplies

remained? She had new fodder for her prayers, and she let loose on the assignment with fervor. Before she got to her truck, she'd started singing praise songs at the top of her lungs.

Chapter 6

Burk waited face-down on his sofa. The request he needed to make rolled around his mind like a hamster wheel that squeaked with incessant urgency. With the Gillian fence job located so far north in the county, his strategy to borrow accommodations made logical sense. Whether Lyndie would regard his notion the same way remained to be seen.

The back door slammed closed, marking her return. He crimped his eyelids shut trying to make his sudden dependence vanish. It occurred to him to be a bit more attentive before springing the proposal on her. He had more energy tonight to interact for some unknown reason. The hot meal prepared by her hands earlier may have been a contributing factor.

Buttons on the microwave played like a calliope in the background. Having her knocking around the kitchen struck him as soothing. They'd built a fairly reliable bridge with friendship, though that structure would be duly tested tonight. Impatient to close the gap between them, he rolled onto his side. "Can you please come in here a second?"

Her footfall echoed off the tile floor, until she leaned over the sofa. "Are you sore tonight? No wonder. You probably did too much lifting with that salvage work in Englewood."

He nestled right into her caressing gaze. "I'm somewhat rested now. That story struck me as heartbreaking. The volunteer fire department had a split second to choose between the two towns, so they opted to keep a solid vigil over Ashland. Tiny Englewood went up in smoke."

"Wow, that truth pokes my heart, too. I hope to find some way to portray that anguishing human element to my listening audience on Friday night."

He reached up to her and rubbed his palm across her forearm. "You will, Lyndie. Your on-the-air charm keeps your audience listening."

The microwave dinged, so she pulled away. "Careful there, Mr. Crosby, or someone might mistake you for a devoted fan."

His chuckle muted as he shifted onto his stomach again. He'd take this medicine if it kept the loudest protesting body part at bay. At least he could bear it for a while, for her sake.

Lyndie knelt between the sofa and the trunk. "Okay, sore guy. Lift your head and let me get this compress situated."

He complied with a slight groan, eyeing her at close range before looking away. When the hot pack came in contact with his jaw, he saw stars for a few seconds. The effect toned down right away and soon bordered on tolerable therapy.

Lyndie unzipped her jacket, took it off, and laid it on the carpet. She nestled back into the padding and glanced up at him. "So, you have enough old-fashioned in you to listen to the Western Star radio broadcast each week. Why does that almost seem reassuring to me?" A small smile traipsed up her questioning expression enough to make her eyes dance.

He tapped the hot pack to one side. "Well, maybe it helps extend our friendship across the radio waves." Though he cocked one brow, he doubted the subtle look of interest would deliver well around the plaid hot pack squished against his face. At least his jaw felt better.

Lyndie let out a willowy sigh. "Radio waves only

transmit one way—which can be a big problem. Ever since I've been here, life's been extremely two-way. I'm hooked being on the donating end of things, let me tell you. After Friday's broadcast, I plan to ask Western Star to step up with a donation for the Clark County fire victims."

He could hear the determination in her tone. Such earnestness moved him. "Guess when you're at the lonesome end of a one-way radio broadcast, there's not a lot of room for human interaction of the romantic kind."

She looked away as her chest rose and fell with a labored breath. When she glanced back, her eyes glistened with unshed tears. "If you're asking whether I have a boyfriend or not, my answer is—I don't even have a life. I go from one performance to the next, riding my horse and singing. That's how the show goes on. She's the Sweetheart of the Rodeo, but no man's sweetie." A tiny whimper chased the admission. She turned her head when the first tear rolled.

Unable to stay apart, he dropped his hand down to her and brushed a shirt button with his knuckle. Searching for neutral territory, he found the hip pocket of her jeans and set his grip on its rim. "When you took a sabbatical, you must have been looking for something more. One thing I know, God honors those who actively seek his will with an earnest heart. Can you tell me what you're looking for?"

She smeared a tear from the corner of her eye. "I'm searching for real life that isn't a show. That's what I flat-out love about Ashland. People are so genuine here. They speak their minds. When they hurt, you can see it. That makes me care and draws me out. I want that kind of interaction. I need that community fellowship. That's the two-way radio broadcast I crave, if that makes any sense." She gestured with one hand, waving toward him.

On a hunt, his left hand swooped and captured hers. He tucked it beside the hot pack where he could nuzzle it with his chin. He held her with his gaze and sensed the frailty of the moment. "That might have been our gain, since you've been such a good fit in the wake of the disaster. I'm glad to hear volunteering benefits you, too." Unable to restrain himself, he brushed his lips over her fingertips.

"I hope you can help me," she said in a whisper. "Help me find the words to speak during Friday night's program, so that others can relate to the devastation these ranchers are facing. I need more stories of overcoming hardship to share with the audience."

Captivated by the woman lying on his living room floor, he took a few seconds to soak in the vision. Framed by wavy hair that turned lighter blond under the sun's direct influence, two mesmerizing blue eyes now looked up at him with transparent receptivity. He exhaled and gave her a weak smile. "Funny thing, your request for help, as I seem to have one of my own tonight. Maybe the two can mingle."

"Possibly. Go ahead and ask—but I sure hope it doesn't have anything to do with Cub coming to live here."

He laughed, as her comment landed as far off the mark as possible. He locked his thumb around hers and caressed the back of her hand. "No, it's not about Cub. It's about convenience. I've been asked to join a fencing crew in the north county to put in a line between two major ranches for Rodney Gillian. I wanted you to think about this trade. Let me borrow the camper rig for four days to get the job done, while you stay here at my ranch house. We'd swap out, like you did with the Fellows the night of the evacuation."

She looked away a long minute. A breath seemed to catch in her throat. When she looked back, a crease marked her brow. "Excuse me while I try not to get emotional over this."

His midsection tightened. "It's asking a lot, but trust me to take care of that camper like it was my own." He tucked her hand into the base of his neck to offset his quickened unease.

Her eyes fluttered closed which released a solitary tear that trickled into her hairline. "The camper is inconsequential for the most part. It does hold an antenna I'll need for Friday night's broadcast. We can take that off in the morning, no problem."

"Where's your trouble with the swap then? Tell me, so I can set it straight."

"I wasn't in such a hurry to have this time of day turn solitary—the time we typically spent together. It feels so authentic, forfeiting our shared time hurts a bit."

In all his buildup to ask for the favor, he'd not thought of their separation once. He growled at his own ineptness, momentarily forgetting her hand remained tucked against his neck. Again, honesty proved his only way out. "Too many other folks out there are in a desperate way for me to put myself first. If I drove out to the Gillian ranch and back daily, I'd be getting home at midnight anyway. When I thought of the camper swap, I meant to put an end to the coming and going—not an end to this." He squeezed her hand and flattened it against his chest. The contact warmed to the touch.

"Here's the deal. I want a phone call every night. Tell me stories about people in the wildfire and how they escaped. Tell me what you've done to restore the damage. Bring me stories America will want to hear, because I plan to share them Friday night on my broadcast. Those are my terms. Take it or leave it." She smudged out a tear while her shoulders shook.

"Beholden as I am, I'll take it." He sat up and pulled her hand to lift her off the floor. Now a lukewarm nuisance, the hot pack dropped between them.

She stooped to pick it up off the sofa cushion. "I'd better go. Knock on the camper door at seven, and I'll go over the specifics with you. You'll need to hook up your electrical in the Gillian's yard, if that's possible. Maybe I'll write some steps down and post it inside the door."

"I appreciate it. There's enough going on in my head without worrying about barracks."

She glanced up at him, her expression less certain than before. "Protect your weak spot." She stroked his jaw line right over the bruise.

"You're not even close." He pumped some bluster into his tone. Any coward could hide for four days, though it seemed a mighty thin strategy with her back at the ranch house alone.

~

Lyndie recommitted to the work of the day, though the morning's crushing farewell had hampered her efforts thus far. She'd chased the fire to find real life, not a real live man. Though she'd prefer to separate the two, both man and burned land somehow fused together in her mind with an unbreakable weld. She glanced up to find a pickup hightailing it in her direction.

Ready to be distracted, she stepped abreast the fence post pile and noticed it had been picked over. At this meager accrual rate, the weekend distribution was bound to suffer. Tonight's broadcast needed to make a difference. She'd started jotting down some notes to get specific stories correct. Maybe the day would reveal a few more heart-rending tales of survival.

Cub walked up from a pile of corner posts. "Hey, Lyndie."

"Hey there. You're up and at it early today." She shoved her hands into her back pockets and gave him a lukewarm smile.

"Well, that's my strategy for staying in town with my cousin. Looks like I've outrun the supply wagon this morning. Maybe I'll hang out a bit after I load a couple of corner posts."

"I could use the company, since it looks like Ken got stuck in town again."

His expression knit with worry. "Where's Burk today? Has he already come by and loaded up some hay?"

"No, but thanks for the reminder. I'll take some back in

my truck tonight. Burk's gone to help the Gillian family reset their fence line with the Guards. He took my camper and plans to stay out there for the duration."

He shook his head. "That guy could hatch a scheme every minute, given enough latitude. Anyway, the radio just reported rain in the forecast for the weekend, God willing. That would snuff out the rest of the perimeter fires. Rain doesn't make for good fencing weather, though."

"Rain? Talk about a blessing straight from heaven. I'd hate for it to spoil the weekend repair work, but the good outweighs the bad on that forecast. I don't know what you're looking for, Cub. Tell me if you see something here on your list to load."

He scanned the piles of supplies until his gaze came back to her. The coy smile he sent her didn't say friend-of-a-friend. "Maybe just the pleasure of your company, Miss Sessoms."

"That comes with a penalty, so I'll tell you right up front. I'm dedicating my Western Star broadcast tonight to Ashland's recovery from the wildfire. I'm collecting stories of man versus wildfire, and I'd like to hear yours."

Cub tipped his hat which set loose a straight shock of sandy-blond hair. "I've got the time if you do." His steady gaze spoke of heightened interested.

"Go get your corner posts loaded first. I'll meet you at your truck." She gripped her pocket flaps, determined to listen only. Cub held no appeal for her—except he was best friends with a man who did. With only one of those men around today, she still needed a story for her show tonight.

"Business before pleasure then," he replied with a tiny wink. He turned and got right to the task. A laden lift earned a grunt.

Lyndie exhaled and kept her distance. They should have a supply truck by nine o'clock, and Cub could be on his way again. She bent to straighten several new fence posts that had been left from a complete bundle. *Where in the world is*

Ken? She could use a chaperone out here.

~

Burk would try to describe this wide open desolation to Lyndie later this afternoon, but words might not paint the full picture. Flat expanses of high plains stretched as far as the eye could see. On occasion, a run-off gully led to sheer cliffs where a red-dirt canyon would yawn below. The land up here drained into Clark County Lake, a wonderment in its own right having been hand-dug by the CCC laborers back in the forties. He always held the steep canyons to be severe, like the surface of the land couldn't decide whether to yield or resist weathering through the ages. A twenty-five-foot drop represented a capitulation of a different sort, maybe a hardheaded compromise between plain and valley. Dramatic in its drop-off, the closest canyon had caught his eye more than once already this morning.

At rough count, Rodney Gillian had two dozen men out here on the job, all volunteers. A team of fence demolition workers led the march, complete with the little skid steer being used to pull up fire-weakened posts. Huge balls of rolled-up barbed wire began to dot the landscape. Burk took it as a positive sign of progress. That particular picture would paint well on the radio, so he'd be sure to mention it to Lyndie.

He killed a boring minute unrolling new wire to let his thoughts wander in her direction. She'd been most helpful showing him around the camper earlier, though lacking some of the usual sparkle in her eyes. Why it mattered to be forthright stirred around in his mind as the midday wind began to pick up. He didn't have any personal time for girlfriend attention, at least that's what he kept thinking. One glance ahead indicated this fence repair job would go on forever, not a week or even a month. The latest damage estimate placed over five hundred thousand acres in the burned total. Every linear foot of it would need new fencing.

He pulled the old-fashioned spool cart up a slight incline

as one of the red canyons drew closer. After kicking a dried yucca stem from his path, he grabbed the plant's thick stalk and heaved it over the nearby ledge. A choked whine echoed up the canyon wall in protest.

Never one to ignore an animal in pain, he dropped the cart handles and abandoned work for something more merciful. Approaching the ledge, he recalled having his rifle in the truck, should the situation call for that brand of mercy. His gut clenched when he toed the edge, a combination of peering into the unknown and the straight drop to the canyon floor. A carcass flinched on a ledge not four feet beneath his feet. The singed head of a dog lifted to meet his gaze.

Heartened, he shrugged out of his flannel shirt, knotted the arms into a loop, and hung it around his neck. "Hold on, boy. I'm coming for you." With a couple of sturdy roots for handholds, he lowered over the rim. Barely enough room for his boots, he leveraged his arms under the scorched animal and tucked it into his makeshift sling. As he worked back up the ledge, Burk muttered a prayer of thanksgiving for one more life spared from the killer wildfire.

At ground level, two men from the church group stood braced to give him a hand up. The dog lifted its head as though to regard the helpers. Weak, it didn't keep vigil for long.

Burk slapped his palms into theirs. "Heave ho, guys—on two. One and two." He punched a boot toe into the cliff face to add leverage as the men hoisted him up onto the plain. The ground felt remarkable under his back, but the squirm against his chest melted his heart. Once he rolled to his knees, the men helped him get to his feet. "I think Rodney might be looking for this fella. Be back on the fencing job in a short five minutes."

With his arms cradling the distressed animal, Burk broke into a trot. Most of the men worked strung out between his spot and the corner post where a double gate was being set. He soon spied Rodney's brown cowboy hat and aimed straight for it. From nowhere, happiness bubbled up and gave him a midstep boost. The dog made a couple of guttural groans and licked at his chest. "We'll get you some water real soon, boy. Great job hanging on." He shifted a hand up the sling and caught the dog's head, rubbing its ears.

Rodney glanced up from his post-setting job and locked his gaze on the delivery. A second later, the tamping pole dropped from his grip. He took a step or two that looked mechanical.

Burk halted an arm's length away. "I heard something down in the canyon and found this survivor on a ledge about four feet down."

Another man walked up to witness the exchange. "Probably saved his life, that ledge."

Rodney's cheek flinched, though his face remained stoic.

Burk widened his stance and drew a breath. "I believe God is trying to let you have your dog back, Rodney. With him being out there for three days without food or drink, I reckon that counts as a miracle."

This time the landowner swallowed down some emotion and reached for the dog.

"Sturdy stock, those blue heelers," the other man added. "A lot like us ranchers."

Burk shrugged out of the sling and surrendered the whole package to Rodney. "It's almost lunch break anyway. Why don't you run to town and let Doc Hartner have a look at him? You could stop by the fairgrounds and bring us more fencing supplies back, too."

Rodney gave a cursory nod. "Get my truck door open, will you?"

"Be more than happy to." He turned to locate the truck. Renewed by the turnabout of fate, he sprinted to the burgundy club cab to get the job done. When Rodney slipped up behind him with his precious load, Burk could see his work shirt had become entwined with the animal's limbs. "Just keep the shirt as padding."

Rodney moved in slow motion, loading his beloved pet. As he straightened, he began to unbutton his flannel shirt. When he looked at Burk this time, his eyes were full of appreciation. "Here, borrow mine. Wind's coming up."

"Much obliged. He might lap some water on your way to town. We've got this west fence well in hand. Would you want us to turn along the north flank when we get to the upper corner?"

He extended the over-shirt to Burk. "The north flank would be dandy. If we can enclose this pasture, I can move what's left of my herd off the wheat and start hay-feeding."

"I noticed the donated hay starting to stack up out at the fairgrounds," Burk admitted with a wink. He shoved an arm into the borrowed shirt sleeve and let a stingy grin chase his comment.

Rodney moved around to take the driver's seat. Once he'd settled in, the dog attempted to sit up and ride shotgun. The man bit his lower lip to stop it from quivering as he reached for a water bottle.

"I'm calling ahead to request your hay allotment, so remember to stop by the fairgrounds." Burk tipped his hat with finality. He eyed the walk back to his workstation, thinking the distance rather inconsequential, recent gains considered.

~

The banker watched two of his oldest customers enter his office. Perhaps they would start living on their retirement fund today. They weren't getting any younger. He took to his feet as the husband settled his wife into one of the leather guest chairs. "Well, look at the time. Guess I'll have to say good afternoon. I don't know where this day has gone, but it's half over."

"You always were one to be exact on things," the old man quipped. He sat with a grunt.

"I hope I can talk you into a scheduled withdrawal of your retirement fund at long last."

The old man held up his hand. "We're here to take a lump sum of that and donate it to the Ashland Foundation. We heard about the lumber yard's donation and didn't want to be left out."

He slid his side drawer out to retrieve the foundation's register. At quick glance, they'd received four donations since the fire, ranging upwards from five thousand dollars. These were no ordinary times, for sure. He fingered the bank's withdrawal form and slid it across the desktop.

The old man took possession of the slip and squinted. "Just to make sure, there's no penalty for using this fund, am I right?"

Humored, the banker leaned across the desk. "Your penalty period ended over twenty-five years ago. I think you can operate in the clear from here on out. In fact, I encourage it."

The old man brushed him aside with a bent-fingered gesture and proceeded to write out the withdrawal amount in jittery longhand.

A pinch of the unfamiliar kept the banker from taking his next breath. He thought he knew these folks, had lived down the street from them for over forty years. Something had changed about their perspective. Perhaps it had been the wildfire, or the desperation left in its aftermath—a non-crimping thought that moved more than the decimal point around.

~

Not Cub again. Lyndie waved to the driver of the exiting burgundy truck who had managed to load three hay bales. After checking her phone for the time, she strode toward Ken. She had to set up for tonight's broadcast, which left little time to entertain Cub. Not that she wanted to, but he seemed to downright expect it. As his pickup turned into the short line for fencing supplies, she stayed focused on conserving the clock.

Ken zipped up his vest and looked skyward. "Overcast.

Maybe we will get that rain after all, doggone it. I hoped that precipitation could hold off until Sunday."

"Ah, but what did Jesus say? The Sabbath was made for man, not man for the Sabbath," she countered. "Are you afraid of losing a workday to the weather?"

"Sort of, I guess. I thought traffic here might pick up on Saturday, as ranchers from further out finally come to town for some supplies. I heard we've got a truck coming in from Meade after a community-wide donation drive ends Saturday at noon."

"Oh? That should be an interesting truckload." She glanced over and saw Cub strutting over like a peacock. "Listen, Ken. I've got to get going in the next five minutes. I need to set up for tonight's broadcast from the library. Do you think you can cut me loose?"

He started to answer when his cell phone rang. He fished it out of his shirt pocket and took the call. "Ken here." His mustache twitched a time or two as he listened. "I see. Thanks for letting me know. Goodbye."

When Cub started to speak, Lyndie stiff-armed him back into silence. She nodded at Ken.

"Gene Shawboro suffered a massive stroke this afternoon. He's inbound to Greensburg's Hospital. It's looking rough for him, right now." He blinked as if trying to process the news.

"Good Lord," Cub said. "He practically saved the whole town single-handedly."

"Now, who's going to save Gene?" Ken asked.

"Only the Good Lord," she replied, helpless to stave the loss. She'd have to tell Burk when he called later. Until then, the bad news would sit like a rock in the pit of her stomach.

"I've come back for a second load," Cub added. "Got any wire?"

"I'm leaving to set up my broadcast. Let Ken help you." She turned and took lengthy strides to her truck, ready for a setting that didn't evoke such deep need. For the first time, she sensed the energy draining from her. "Shore me up, Lord—and be with Gene. Remember what he means to this town. Be mindful of Ashland, Kansas, and please don't pass us by, amen."

By the time she made it onto Main Street, the tears arrived. She pulled in at the library and noticed the rain. That development would make getting the antenna up a little more interesting. She needed a distraction at this point. Radio might be a good one.

Chapter 7

"**I'm telling you,** I didn't think Rodney was going to take the dog from me at that point." Burk's voice rose, pepped by the after-hours interview. "I don't think he'd ever touched a miracle before—one with a singed hide at that."

"That's a great story, my fencing friend. It definitely goes on the air tonight," Lyndie replied. "Tara's been great, just like you promised. She's given me a list of activities around town, regular stuff that proves the town still has a pulse. Looks like the high school basketball team has a game Saturday night, and they've decided to play. I thought that showed gumption."

"Go Blue Jays." Maybe he should receive the news indirectly like this all the time, as she cast a pleasant aura of appreciation around it. He heard a metallic click in the background as the conversation lagged. "I probably should let you go since you're counting down to show time. I may have to sit in my truck to listen in tonight."

"Oh, there's a radio in the camper right over the microwave. You haven't explored too much in there, I'm sure."

"No, Rodney's wife brought out a spread for us at nightfall—venison stew and biscuits."

"Burk, before time runs out, I have one more thing to tell

you from town news."

When her voice softened, it put him on edge. The burned-up prairie sat quiet beyond the camper's stoop, making him yearn for a coyote's howl. "Okay, I'm sitting down."

"I'm sorry to say the news is about Gene Shawboro. He suffered a massive stroke this afternoon. The last Ken heard Gene was being transported to the hospital in Greensburg for treatment."

"Dear God, no," he managed, though the air had been knocked from his chest. He tried to refill his lungs, but got pain instead of relief.

"I'd hug you if I could. Listen, I have to go. Pray for Gene. God could restore him just like he's restoring the prairie. I'll talk to you in my famous one-way broadcast style here in less than fifteen minutes. I…wish you were coming home tonight, Burk. I miss you. Goodnight."

The click of disconnect seemed deafening against the hollow night. The tenderly spoken words of promised hugs and being missed swarmed his consciousness as he stood to go inside. The camper offered no relief, as pictures of Lyndie's rodeo act spackled the walls.

He found the radio, called it to life, and sent the tuning dial into search mode for the right local station. The bad news about Gene gnawed at him as he weighed the day's gains against the losses. Funny how life could feel like one foot in the grave at any given moment on the backside of catastrophe. There would be no pulling themselves up by their bootstraps from this. No, the chasm proved too deep. Exhausted, he dropped to his knees in an attempt to pray his way out.

~

Standard routine for the show, Lyndie started out with a live performance for her radio audience. To help set the tone from Ashland, she laid out a somber rendition of "The Streets of Laredo," keeping it slow and rich. Truly a lament from a cowboy, she didn't have much trouble visualizing one in particular. Tonight, he would be sad, so part of her sympathetic heart would be also. From the dimly-lit atrium, Tara walked in and perch on a bench by the door. She nodded in that direction as the song wound down.

Settling her earphones into place, Lyndie checked her notes to ready the broadcast intro. "Evening, everybody. This is Lyndie Leigh Sessoms welcoming you to Friday night's Western Star show. I'm broadcasting from tiny Ashland, Kansas tonight—which certainly lived up to its name over the past week. Many of you have heard about the sweeping wildfire that took Clark County by storm. Well, yours truly followed along the coattails of the fire line and stayed through the week to help extend disaster relief to the ranchers. Tonight, I hope to share some of the hardships and the victories since the fire, but first, here's a word from our sponsor."

She cut the feed to a recorded message and took a breath. Only when a shadow moved did she notice Tara standing by her table. Glancing at her timer, she still had forty seconds.

"We all admire your bravery for standing in the information gap to represent these ranchers." Tara paused and took a breath. "This is our way of life, plain though it is. Nothing will honor them more than flat-out truth, so don't feel you have to embellish anything."

"No, ma'am. I can hardly bear to speak the harsh truth as it happened, so embellishing is beyond me tonight. I'm about to get real with my radio audience, which rarely mixes with entertainment because heavy and light don't go together."

"Perhaps, on certain occasions, they do," she replied, stepping back into the shadows. She returned to her seat by the door, her slender figure blending with the quiet.

"Inspire me, Lord," Lyndie prayed as the timer ticked shy of ten seconds. With eyes closed, ashen prairie reappeared across her mind's eye. At least the black ash had all blown away. Bare dirt came easier to take.

"I'm welcoming you back so I can paint a picture of western Kansas for you at home. The land sweeps in slow rises as far as the eye can see, covered in short bunch grasses that have been bleached by winter and trodden by cattle. The pastures are expansive to the point that you barely notice the barbed wire fences separating them. And the herds, oh my, the herds are large, the cattle uncountable. They breathe life into the landscape. For every herd, rest assured there's a rancher in the background, looking after its well being.

"On Tuesday, a riddling wind brought a wildfire out of Oklahoma across western Kansas. Too fast to fight, ranchers struggled to move cattle onto anything green. Some made it onto sprouted wheat fields. I saw a herd inside a cemetery for a refuge. Tragically, many of the cattle couldn't be secured into safety. Left in the pasture to fend for themselves, they expired in the direct path of the wildfire, pushed up against the far fence. Those not dying right away became the first point of urgent business. It's sad to say, but the need for mercy-killing grew so prevalent, the locals have run out of ammunition.

"Cattle losses are still being estimated. Because most large operations didn't have a number for spring calves yet, they've been left out of the headcount for damage estimates. With the fire so hot, the fences are weakened beyond salvage. Wholesale replacement has begun. For a large operation of thirty thousand acres, the linear fence replacement equates to a hundred miles. Imagine how much wire a four-strand fence would take, if you can. It boggles my mind.

"Yet the picture here remains far from bleak. I have stories for you of heroism in the face of catastrophe, of split-second decisions that determined survival, of separations within families and the opportune meeting of strangers. But first, let me paint this redemptive picture. Inside the burned perimeter of Clark County stands a square untouched by the ravages of fire. Some credit the volunteer fire department, while others attribute its protection to the saint who disked a firebreak around the town's perimeter. I offer you this explanation, that the Lord Almighty drew a box in the sand and rebuked the wildfire from entering. As the librarian here so aptly put it, Ashland is a Christian town, founded by people of faith. As such, we have this unscorched center of operations to work from and minister to these hurting area ranchers."

Her host stood and exited the room as Lyndie cued up the next sponsor spot. She glanced at the recording of Burk's conversation. Instead of rehashing his fencing report and the finding the three-legged dog, she decided to play the recording and allow him to tell it firsthand. Not only would it give her voice a break, the audience would appreciate a straight-talking messenger reporting in from the field.

A tiny worry that she hadn't cleared it with Burk made her hesitate to cue up the tape, but she pressed on, a bit out of sync with tonight's change of venue. She would lead with her arrival in the area, share stories of other families, mention the wind reversal, and Cub's all night fight for survival. After that, she'd return to Burk's report.

It all fell in place so smoothly, she shrugged off her apprehension and tried to get each component slotted to save time for the donation request at the end. Her closing song tonight would be a hymn. "Amazing Grace" popped to mind, and she scrawled the title into the program's rough outline. It would be a show to remember. She'd make sure of that.

~

His shoulders throbbing from the low work of rolling out wire, Burk shifted on the bed and hung his chin off the edge. Lyndie's singing had fallen like medicine on his body aches, a real lifeline tonight. He'd appreciated her description of the Ashland area, thinking she had a real knack for rendering the land.

If the rain held off, he'd put in a full day up there Saturday for Rodney and wait to see what Sunday brought.

A day of rest would be welcomed. Four days seemed too long to be away from his spread anyway. He hadn't even considered how his cattle would get more hay.

He almost missed the transition in broadcasting as a man's voice came over the air. If he hadn't picked up on the choice of words in the first sentence, he wouldn't have recognized his own voice. Insecurity leaked down his spine in a chill as his recounting of the day broadcast out to millions of listeners. While he sensed the merit of the direct message, he couldn't shake the shock of being exposed like that. Ranchers only knew private—knew it and preferred it.

By the time his little recorded recitation had run its course, his teeth grated together in slim forbearance. They would talk about this when he got back home. Yes, airing his phone call would be a one-time thing, and then like the wildfire, it would be snuffed out. Once again, he fell into the suppression business, trying to get his life back under control. When Lyndie sang "Amazing Grace," it did little to sooth his bristled hide. They needed boundaries for this new friendship, such as it was. He fisted a pillow under his stiff neck and tried to drop off to sleep.

~

Missing the morning sun's golden gleam over the fairgrounds, Lyndie approached the open canopy Ken had erected to ward off adverse weather. Late from stopping to deposit the hay bale to Burk's cattle, she found one donation delivery had already arrived.

Ken worked to get the bottom row of creosote posts aligned. More waited to be added to the pile. The air hung heavy with humidity, though the rain held off.

Lyndie grabbed a pair of leather gloves and stepped over to join him. "Even though they've just been burned out, ranchers will go right back to these wooden posts, won't they?"

Ken straightened and gave her a nod. "This is the way their fathers fenced, and their grandfathers before that.

Besides, only every other hole would be set in creosote posts, so they still have metal posts alternating. A lot of good that did them in this wildfire, though. Too hot.”

She hummed in agreement. “Did you listen in for Western Star last night? I hoped you might give me some feedback on whether I hit the final donation plea too hard.”

“I heard the broadcast all right. The whole time I told myself you were talking about some other town, it seemed so idyllic. Good people, bad fire, and the aftermath left behind. Then I began to realize you were right about everything you said. I guess when you’re smack dab in the middle of catastrophe, the picture’s none too glossy. Thanks for your perspective, Lyndie. Standing on the outside looking in adds objectivity that lends the situation more credence.”

She smoothed her tongue across her teeth, deciding what to say. Handing him a creosote post, she took a stab at it. “I appreciate your candor, Ken. I’m trying really hard not to come across as the visitor standing on the outside looking in. Maybe I should see the mayor about gaining citizenship.”

He laughed and motioned for another post. “The mayor is my brother, Cal. I’m sure he’d take you in a heartbeat. It would help if you owned property in town. That’s the major deciding factor. Once you’re a taxpayer, they have to claim you.” A dual-wheeled pickup drove in and honked its horn. Ken motioned the driver over. “Here’s the first I’ve seen of the Guards. Their place burned badly, two houses, all the outbuildings, and five hundred genetically-bred Angus.”

She glanced at the metal fence post pile and saw bare ground. “Wish we had more.”

“To answer your first concern, I thought your donation plea was just right.” He gave her a wink and took the next post. “It’s out of our hands. We can only distribute what’s been donated.”

“And pray a lot,” she added. With just enough time, she flashed a grin his way.

The truck driver walked up beside the barbed wire pile and looked around. "I don't know how this goes. It's my first time here. Things have been rough out our way this week."

Ken offered his hand. The man took it and gave it a hardy shake. "We're mighty glad to hear your kinfolk made it out okay. Garrett Guard, let me introduce you to my helper, Lyndie Leigh Sessoms from Western Star radio."

The man appeared lost for a brief moment. He gave his hat a slight tip in her direction. "We appreciated your touching message over the radio last night, Miss Sessoms."

"Please, I'm Lyndie around here—and I'm glad to help out. Thank you for listening to the broadcast. Could you tell I was talking from the library's activity room?" She eased a smile into place.

"No, but when I heard Burk Crosby tell his story, I figured you were somewhere nearby."

"He's held up in the north county helping Rodney get the fence line up between your spread and his," Ken said.

Garrett shook his head. "I can't figure out how you got Crosby to open up like that. He's about the most sequestered rancher in the county. I mean, the man's private to a fault."

"Ain't you got eyes in that balding head of yours, Garrett?" Ken replied. "She's using her feminine wiles on the poor guy."

She chuckled and dropped another post into place. "Well, I did rescue him from the cemetery looking like an ash heap and brought him to town for medical attention. Too bad we got evacuated straight to Coldwater."

"Tell me, do I need to sign up to be eligible here? I see something I want." Garrett stomped a boot on the first creosote post and cocked his brow.

"We're on the honor system out here," Ken replied. "I recognize just about everybody anyway. If you make it here, you can have a truckload of whatever we've got."

"We hope and pray more will be on the way," Lyndie added. "By closing time, a community-wide collection from

Meade should come in."

"I'd like some metal fence posts, too, but let me start with these. I'll pull up." Garrett stepped away to retrieve his vehicle.

"We really need that next truckload of donations delivered pronto," she said under her breath, scanning the horizon for some sign of its approach.

"Yep," Ken replied. "Unfortunately, it doesn't take folks too long to forget the stricken and go on about their carefree lives."

She shot a finger directly at him. "You don't see me raising a white flag, do you?"

He snickered and shook his head. "No, ma'am. I don't."

Lyndie grabbed two posts at once as the truck pulled up alongside. She didn't know what to make about Garrett's comments regarding Burk. Since he'd rolled out the welcome mat to her, he hadn't seemed all that reclusive. Maybe that explained why he still lived out there by himself, unattached and—from all signs—not looking. Like she'd told Ken, she didn't want to be an outsider. If Burk didn't see her as one, then impinging on his privacy fell as a non-issue. She already faced enough problems without making up any hypothetical ones.

~

Burk pulled the camper onto the blacktop as the rain drummed the hood. Somehow, they'd gotten in the full day of fencing, but with the weather so stormy, Rodney had called off the work crew for a Sunday reprieve. From his shoulders down, he was mighty glad for the break. He could shift his focus to his own cattle with what remained of the weekend.

A glimpse at the dash told him the fairgrounds would be locked up by the time he made it to town. No need to drag the camper through the mud out there anyway. Since his hay shed had plenty of empty space, he thought about backing in to lend the tin can some shelter from the deluge. He could still run a power cord to get the electric hook-up accomplished.

He'd made it to the outskirts of town before Lyndie popped to mind. As he tried to decide what to do about dinner, lights from the high school parking lot distracted him. From the looks of it, the whole town had come out to cheer on the home team. Thinking a mild diversion might do him some good, he signaled for the turn. Seeing the parking lot filled to the brim, he pulled in behind the country-style convenience store and parked. After setting his hat in place, he braced for the mad dash into the gym. He jumped from the cab and ran like a crazed man.

Once under the front awning, he stopped to make an assessment. The puddles in the paved lot had cleaned most of the mud from his boots. His jeans had gotten wet, but they weren't soaked through. He slung the rain off his hat brim and wandered inside.

The smell of popcorn lured him over to the concession stand, where he found Cody chaperoning members of his wrestling team. "Hey, I'll take one of those."

Cody released his half-nelson choke hold on the glass cabinet and extended an overflowing box to him. "Glad you could make it, Burk. We weren't too sure about going ahead tonight, but Barrett Guard finally made the call to stick with the schedule."

"The coach is always right. I'll take a bottle of water, too."

"That'll be two dollars," the stocky student at the cash box said.

He shelled out the money and snagged his water bottle, turning to head inside.

"Oh, Burk," Cody added. "I heard you on the radio last night. Pretty entertaining stuff. We'll have to get you on the school's talent show playbill this spring."

"Ha," he said with extra heft. "I don't think so." He waved and set his sights on the closest entrance. When he got to the door, he noticed the hush inside the gym. The English teacher on duty locked her elbow in his and ushered him into the gym. The lights went dim except for the center medallion, where the singer stood to deliver the national anthem. He blinked to be sure. Lyndie straightened at the microphone, ready for service once again.

A recording started that seemed less familiar and she began to sing "America, the Beautiful." The moment froze in time. Deep, rich notes resonated across the hardwood floor.

Upon the phrase "amber waves of grain," it occurred to Burk that he still had his wheat crop coming up strong and vigorous. With this rain, it would grow even faster. He had to get the cattle off that field—the sooner, the better. In seconds, the song's crescendo bore the nation's name, and he heard the crowd singing for the first time. That melding of her voice leading theirs began to leave an impression, a healing mix of unrehearsed harmony.

The lights went back up, and the English teacher punched his arm with her extended palm. "Three dollars for the gate, please."

An arm reached past him and delivered the bills. "I've got this," Cub said with a grin. "Let's go watch some basketball. Hope I haven't missed the girls' game. They're scrappy."

The teacher stepped back into position. "No, you're both right on time."

"Have you heard yet, Burk? It rained down on the fairgrounds today."

"Cub, turn on your windshield wipers, for pity's sake. It's raining across the whole blame county." He eased into the gym and started looking for a seat in the risers.

"No, I mean donations. They poured in—maybe triple the amount they had before." He flexed a goofy grin. "I had to come back twice myself."

He looked at his friend to gauge his honesty. "Is that

right?"

"Yeah. Lyndie filled her truck up for your place. They plan to open at one o'clock tomorrow after church, so anyone who's come to town can carry a load back. It's a real heyday, if you'll excuse the pun."

He paused to let the plentiful response seep through his half-miffed attitude. When he glanced at Cub, he wore a monkey-like expression. "Guess I have to excuse the pun. Consider the source." He waited a second for further effect, and then laughed.

"Ha, ha. That Lyndie sure knew how to get the word out over the radio waves last night. You didn't ruin the show too bad yourself." He winged him in the side and stole some popcorn.

Burk spotted an empty space not too far from the team and headed for the steps up to it. He almost didn't see Lyndie until she bumped his arm. Popcorn showered the scene. The way her expression morphed from surprise to elation really worked him over. "Let's head up here," he said, struggling not to put his arm around her. To make matters worse, Cub stole the popcorn box and shadowed them up the bleachers. He gestured down the fourth row and guided her in.

A tenuous arrangement, he removed his hat and sat down, wishing the game would start and end their awkward meet-up. While Cub jostled about and shook a few hands around the vicinity, he settled his hat between his boots and ran his fingers through his hair, trying to remember if he'd even brushed it that morning.

Lyndie turned toward him, and the space separating them evaporated. "Good Lord above, please help me. I'm left breathless, Burk. Having you drop in just made my day."

Her admission came delivered on the press of feminine lips against his chin stubble, a combination for which he had little defense. His thumb found her delicate jaw and guided her into striking distance. The game official blew his whistle about the time his lips made landfall on hers, an illegal move he lacked any restraint to stop. The trespass lasted more than a few delectable seconds. By the time he looked at the court below, the score stood four to two.

Lyndie shifted closer until her hip aligned with his on the bleacher. "Good Lord above," she repeated under her breath. She held her hair to one side and started fanning her neck.

"Have some of your popcorn," Cub insisted, shoving the box back into his possession.

Burk took the snack, only to find three-quarters of the contents gone. He'd eat this and go back for seconds. That would guard him from further romantic interaction, a feeble plan at best.

Chapter 8

Lyndie couldn't remember the last time she'd sat through a church service accompanied by organ music. For some reason, it seemed to fit Ashland, plus lend reverence to the service. She'd sat on the pew with Cody and Mandy, which gave her Abby for company part of the service. To her right, Burk sat with his attention focused straight on the speaker.

With so much alternate standing and sitting in the order of service, her form-fitted dress had worked its way higher on her thighs. When Abby left for children's church, she managed a timely tug that gained more coverage. She caught Burk stealing a glimpse of her knees. *Where are my longer dresses?* Living in a camper definitely had its disadvantages. Still, a person couldn't be that space conscious.

The choir began to sing a benediction, so she bowed her head. Maybe Ken had solid advice. She needed to own some property in town. That would give her more space and a sound studio for the show. She couldn't stay parked behind Burk's ranch house forever. The choir began to file out as the organ pumped a few boisterous notes.

Mandy leaned over and patted the back of her hand. "We

want to have you guys over for lunch. I have a big beef roast in the oven and lots of vegetables inside the roasting pan. Please say you will."

Burk leaned forward, expressing keen interest. "As long as we're in line at the fairgrounds by one o'clock, I'm all for it."

"Great," Cody replied. "That settles it. I can show off my new back deck."

"Do we need to get Abby?" she asked, thinking they weren't exactly ready to head out.

"The baby first," Mandy replied. "Then we stop for Abby. She doesn't want to be the first one picked up. We've been duly notified." She made a face that stretched her eyes wide.

"Wow. There's a lot more to this parenting thing than surface stuff," Lyndie quipped.

"We get a Christian parenting magazine once a month," Cody said. "Even that doesn't cover every scenario. The general rule is to act out of love. That makes it hard to go wrong."

Burk let her lead down the aisle, but followed closely behind. "Looks like you get to see your rescue dog."

"Oh, you're right. Maybe Abby and I can walk Queenie while Mandy gets the rolls heated. I'm suddenly in the real estate market and would like to look around town."

His eyebrows arched. "Is that a fact?"

She nodded at a teenager who seemed to be staring at them. "Yes, Ken said it would help me obtain citizenship to Ashland if I owned some property in town. I can't stay plugged into your farmyard forever. Plus, I need a studio for my radio work."

"I'm relieved to hear you're planning to stick around." He gave her a quick wink before turning to shake the pastor's hand.

"Happy to learn your place made it through the fire, Burk," the pastor said. "That must have truly been a help-me-God moment for you."

"I prayed while I herded the cattle, but some of that was muttering about their lack of cooperation, as I recall. Pastor, this is Lyndie Leigh Sessoms, who drove up from Oklahoma to help when she heard about the wildfire."

The pastor extended his hand to her. "Nice to meet you, Lyndie. My daughter has been telling me all about your rodeo show. She's an up-and-coming barrel racer, though her mother wishes she wasn't."

She nodded as she shook his hand. "Most teens lose interest and begin to chase the next fad. Only the good ones stick with it. Barrels can be hard on the knees."

He laughed. "Yes, she's already found out that truth. Keep up the good work at the distribution center. We look forward to having you back in our congregation."

"I appreciate that. Please continue to pray for the area ranchers. We see lots of desperate faces while waiting in line for a fair share of donated materials."

"I promise. We've still got a long way to go."

Burk's hand claimed the small of her back. She led down to the curb and turned to look at the church. The rain had stopped for now, and the town seemed snuggled into a background of soft gray.

"Your faith looks beautiful on you, Ms. Sessoms, not to mention your fine singing."

She turned to him and gave him an earnest look. "I hope you won't mention it, at least to the choir director. I'd like to be able to worship as part of the congregation, so I can commune with God in a more spontaneous manner. You won't give me away, will you?"

He touched a knuckle to her nose. "You give yourself away, Lyndie Leigh. Nobody else holds notes like that."

"Guilty as charged. I'll make it a point to tone it down a notch from the pew."

Burk laughed and slapped Cody on the back. "Here they are—our impromptu hosts."

"It's like a border crossing in the children's department," Cody replied, wiping his brow. "We drove because of the rain. Let's meet over at our house in a minute. That way you'll have your truck handy to go get in line."

"Doesn't that seem weird?" Mandy asked. "I mean, two weeks ago, who got in line for anything in Ashland?"

"It's a sign of the times," Lyndie said. "We try to load fast, but there's only so much space." When Burk gathered her to his side, she followed in step.

"I might be getting a little hungry," Burk admitted.

"What? Two hot dogs at the game last night didn't hold you over?" She spiced up her dubious look for his benefit.

He opened the passenger door of his truck. "You're talking about defensive food. Today I'm eating offensively, though Cody can put me to shame. He's going to make a jolly old man someday."

"At least tall men carry their weight better." She aimed a poke at his shirt placard, but he dodged and closed the door. Suddenly, the outing took on the appearance of a small-town date. She glared at the padded console between them while he walked around. With a little lift, she rotated it out of contention and rescued the lap belt for the center seat.

Burk got in and reached for his seatbelt. His gaze halted on her knees again and then slowly climbed her frame. His expression held a hint of surprise. "I didn't even know it did that."

"What?"

"The console—how it rotated out of the way like that. Don't think I've put it in that vertical position before."

"Good to know," she replied, letting the admission fortify her position. "I thought the occasion felt a little date-like, having lunch with friends. I wanted to maintain the spirit."

"Watch this next part," he said with a glimpse to the rearview mirror. He shifted into reverse to back out of the space and leveled his arm behind her back. When he turned to see out the back window of the cab, he trapped her in a most romantic predicament.

Her gaze searched his features and found the playful spark in his eyes. "Hope you like what you see."

He hovered for a few extra seconds after the backing job had ended. With a whistled exhalation, he pulled down the lane, headed for the center of town.

Lyndie fought the attraction with a quick diversion. "Could you drive me down Sixth Street, and then back around to Fifth? I'd like to see more of this neighborhood."

"Sure thing. We're not in any hurry."

"I think I'm going to like this spirit-of-dating thing." She ended with a touch of smugness in her tone.

"My console and I couldn't be more surprised." Though he tried to seem aloof, his hand slipped from the wheel and alighted on hers, another date-like move.

The truck passed a huge house with wrap-around porch and made the turn onto Sixth Street. Box hedges ten feet tall blocked most of what seemed like the original carriage house for the adjoining mansion. A break in the hedge revealed a Cape Cod style structure topped with a gambrel roof. By all appearances, no one had lived there for some time.

Lyndie pointed across his chest. "Okay. That house really gets my attention."

"Interesting, yes, but can you imagine trying to heat such a big box in winter?"

"Sound logic. You're good for counterbalance."

"Of course, I am. Is now a good time to ask for help with the cattle this afternoon?"

"Are we fencing?"

"At a minimum, we're putting in a gate. The rest depends on the rain."

"Is this how ranchers rest on Sundays?"

"Pretty typical, I'm afraid."

She gave his hand a squeeze to let him know it didn't matter. They were together rebuilding the ranch. She'd call that move two steps in the right direction.

~

Burk parked the truck as the waiting line trailed out of the fairgrounds onto the road. Impatient to get home, the delay grated his nerves. "This backup is horrendous."

"Let's go see what we can do," Lyndie replied. "We've only been loading from one side, but if we clear away some shipping pallets, that would open the other side. I think Ken would be on-board with that."

He leveraged his door open. "Sounds like a must-happen to me." He walked up the snaking line, stopping to shake hands and greet other ranchers. As he approached the head of the line, he noticed Cub hadn't come in yet. That landed like a relief.

Two men hefted fence post bundles into the bed of a rusted-out Ford. When Ken looked up, he appeared exhausted. "Hey, are you two coming straight from church?"

"No, Cody had us over for lunch. Looks like you could use another hand here. What do you say we open this distribution lane up on both sides, Ken? That would keep things moving as the ranchers help themselves. You should really be overseeing, not loading."

Ken wiped his face. "I can't help but pitch in. If you see a way to open this up, I say go for it. With both sides available, we could unload the donations when they come in without disrupting the distribution."

"That would sure help," Lyndie said. "We don't want the line to seem so long that the folks in back think they're not going to get anything."

"Which is exactly what I thought when we drove up," he added. "Everyone should receive a reasonable truckload of supplies, to make it worth their time. Let me get going on clearing these pallets to open up this far side."

"I'll get you some help." Lyndie promised. "Sorry I'm not dressed for lifting today." She drifted back down the line of trucks.

Ken slapped the rancher on the back to signal a full load. The man nodded and got in his truck to pull away. The empty space soon filled with the next recipient.

Burk hefted a shabby shipping pallet and dragged it to a new location further away from the loading area. By the time he returned to repeat the process, two fellow ranchers stood waiting to help. "Thanks, guys. Anything along this lane needs to be moved clear. These pallets can be stacked for tighter storage. Space might become an issue in the near future."

"Donations are pouring in from out of state now," Ken replied.

A young rancher with a tight expression stepped out of the cab.

Burk motioned toward the next pallet and his assistants took over. He stepped toward the pale-faced rancher and extended his hand. "Burk Crosby. I ranch on a spread near Sitka."

"Tommy Downing from Protection. We got hit pretty hard when the wind shifted out of the north. My outbuildings were old, so I'm looking forward to rebuilding if the state funding comes in for disaster relief. Protection is struggling to get its relief organization set up. You folks in Ashland are two steps ahead of us."

Ken stepped into the conversation cradling a bundle of posts. "Got to keep loading. We were fortunate to have the Ashland Foundation already set up coming into this, but it wasn't our original mission, not by a long shot."

"Still, it allows you to receive private donations," Tommy replied. "Our hands are tied."

"Let me ask around at the bank tomorrow when I stop in," Ken said. "They may have a way to hold that account for Protection while a nonprofit gets established. Our donations are being funneled through the bank to us." He gestured to a clipboard hanging from a makeshift pole. "We're contemplating starting cash payouts later this week to Clark County ranchers."

Loading post bundles two at a time, Burk hesitated at that news. "The families who lost their homes should top that list, Ken. Their needs are more urgent."

Ken lifted the clipboard and indicated several names denoted with the letter "H" in the margin. "I thought along the same lines. Good to gain your input, though."

"Can I get some wire?" Tommy asked.

Burk stepped down to the barbed wire pile. "How much, Ken?"

"I've been doling out a dozen spools per load." He hooked the clipboard back in place and shrugged his shoulders.

"Look at this line today. We'd better cut back to eight." Burk gave the rancher a weighted stare. "Can you check back by here the first of the week, say Monday afternoon?"

"Sure thing. I need more fencing supplies, but I can get started with what I have here."

Burk nodded as two more men stepped up to help clear the second lane. He tumbled the wire spools into the truck bed until they'd reached the maximum. With a final word of appreciation, the man got in his truck and pulled away.

"There goes another moderately happy customer," Ken quipped in the interim. "At least the price is right." He walked around the newly cleared area and picked up a bent nail.

"Listen, about the distribution, Ken," Burk began. "I'm not sure having cash money out here is wise, especially the amounts you'll be handing out. I think you should let the bank do it. They already have security measures in place."

"But the ranchers needing the money come out here." Ken pocketed the nail with a shrug.

"What if you handed out vouchers for the money? I don't think folks will mind stopping by the bank on their way out of town, especially for a withdrawal they don't have to cover from their own account. You could use color coding to distinguish between the regular donations and those for ranchers who lost their houses. That way the sums wouldn't have to be written out, just have them pre-printed."

A truck pulled up along the fence post pile, so Ken responded by lowering the tailgate. "I like that idea. Let me talk it over with the banker in the morning. Spread the word that monetary donations start Monday at one o'clock."

He looked at the foundation director with one eyebrow cocked. "If you're hauling cash out here, I'll have to come post a guard." He grabbed the first bundle of fence posts to load. "I was hoping to start my own fencing tomorrow, which would be my preference." He held his stare a meaningful extra second.

The driver got out and greeted them with a terse nod.

"Okay, no cash out here," Ken agreed. "We have to check for county residency anyway, so that adds a twenty-four-hour waiting period from the time they get on our list. We might look at midweek instead."

Burk saw Lyndie approaching with two more helpers and noticed the extra lane had almost been cleared. "Well, no two ways about it. Lyndie sure knows how to get results."

"That woman is a multiplier, reaching out from her radio broadcast like that. We're fortunate to have her involved." Ken turned to get the man's name added to the clipboard list.

Burk stepped past the fence post pile and scoured the new lane for any signs of blockage. It looked clear and ready for use. As soon as the last two helpers heaved a large pallet off the gate pile end, he motioned for the next truck in line.

Lyndie nudged his shoulder. "What can I do next? Want me to direct the trucks into both lines?" A close-lipped smile chased her question.

"Let's go ahead and divide into two lines to get off the road for now. Could you go down the line and have the drivers alternate right or left? That should look like slow-motioned mayhem while it's going on, but the end result will be worth it. Anyone pulling up after that can simply choose a line."

"I'll move your truck up when I get out to the road. Are the keys in it?"

He glanced up past his hat brim, a grin inferring his answer. "Don't think you're about to figure me out, Miss Sweetheart of the Donation Line."

She turned to get busy with her assignment, but her gaze lingered over her shoulder a few seconds. Her dress hem tapped the back of her knees as she headed for the second truck in line.

Ken stabbed at his boot toe with a bundle of posts. "Are you going to help—or are you too moon-eyed to be any good?"

Burk redirected his attention to the matter at hand. "She's a help and a hindrance, all at the same time." He shook his head like he couldn't help it.

"Only to you," Ken replied. "He wants a pipe gate, too."

"I'll get the man a gate then." As he strode down to the pile, the first truck pulled in and occupied the new lane, a glorious sight. Another truck nosed in behind it. In a wink, they had arrived at maximum efficiency. Now, they had to keep the line moving. He jerked the gate into compliance and let it rest on the shoulder of his nicest Sunday shirt. Agreeable to work until Lyndie drove his truck into the loading area, he put his all into the job, as unto the Lord.

~

The rhythm of their fencing work offset the occasional drizzle. Lyndie saw another side of Burk in the process. Built for ranch work, he conducted it masterfully. She tried to catch on quickly and anticipate his need as old posts were pulled and new ones set next to the former spot. When he lifted the post pounder, his shoulder muscles bulged with power. Repeated contact with the metal posts held the ring of progress. Soon, they had closed the gap between corner posts. "What now, boss?"

He flipped a finger down her hat brim and a few drops of

accumulated rain spattered off. "Now, we roll out some wire so I can stretch it. This is going to be a four-strand fence, so if the weather holds, we'll repeat the process four times. Once I get the bottom strand tightened, you can unroll the next length of wire. Otherwise, they'll get tangled up while on the ground."

She stepped closer, taking advantage of his full attention. "No tangling up allowed. We have to keep it systematic."

He tugged at her chin strap. "The heavy rain will return, so we'll break then."

"Let's see how much we can get done," she replied with a tease in her voice. "I saw you had a dozen eggs in the fridge. Can we make breakfast for dinner tonight?"

He rubbed his right shoulder. "That sounds remarkable. I'll show you how to roll out the wire before I get back to pounding in the remaining posts." He put his arm around her waist and walked back to the starting point. In one fluid motion, he laced the wire spool onto an old iron cart and unlatched the end of the barbed wire. "Keep your gloves on, for sure."

Duly warned, she held up her hands and wiggled her fingers as a sign of compliance. The supple leather of her gloves seemed protective enough, though the sleeves of her waterproof jacket might prove somewhat less durable.

"This is your station." He held up the handle extending from the front of the cart. "I'll attach the wire to the corner post and then you can set out. Stay as close to the post line as possible while letting out the wire. If it hitches on a barb, stop and clear the snag. You'll know if you're hung up or not."

She had to ponder *hung up* because her attention had already been hitched on a barb, so to speak. Stealing another look into his mottled green eyes only reinforced her condition. Instead of being at the distribution site helping the community, she'd opted for time alone with a particular rancher. Though entitled to a day off, she still felt the internal wrangle. She twisted her gloved hands around the cart's rod and tried to shake off the unbalanced feeling.

Burk tugged at the wire. "Giddy-up, little pony."

She glanced back to see that he had the wire fastened in a loop around the corner post. As he walked by, she admired his long stride. "I'll be up there in a few."

He trailed a hand behind. "I'll be watching and waiting for you."

When he rubbed his achy shoulder again, she knew that would be her job later, after breakfast-for-dinner had been served. Uncertainty birthed at the thought of being together in his house alone. That kiss in the gym may have changed the rules a bit.

The cart wheels clanked as she pulled it through a low spot. Not willing to wish the kiss away, she vowed to keep up her guard. The camper would be her refuge, and she would seek it at the first hint of affection. The moment she ruled out the possibility, she wanted a second kiss more than ever. The cart lurched to a halt. *Great.* She had to give the wire her undivided attention, a hesitation of the pokey kind.

Chapter 9

Lyndie welcomed Tuesday with whatever it would bring. When the gates closed Monday, only hay bales remained. If some weekend drives would deliver, they'd be in business again. The community collection from Meade had lasted only a day. She sighed, staring at bare ground.

Ken walked up, making quick work of his morning inventory. "Before I forget, Leslie and I want to have you and Burk over for Sunday dinner after church. We still plan to open up over here around one o'clock for a couple of hours. That way the ranchers could leave town fully loaded. Do you think you can fit in a home-cooked meal?"

"That's gracious of you, Ken. May I give you a tentative yes? I'm sure Burk would like to, but I hate to speak on his behalf. Let me ask him tonight." Hearing a vehicle rumble up the road, she glanced over the same time Ken did. The law had arrived.

He spat while kicking a fence post too crooked to use. "Smells like trouble."

"That's no way to start the morning. Are you friends with the sheriff?"

He winced and shook his head. "Not that I haven't tried."

The car pulled onto the fairgrounds and made a menacing cut right toward them. "I'm now squelching the urge to run and hide in the stack of hay bales," Lyndie quipped.

"You and me both. Something tells me I don't want to hear what the good sheriff has to say." He spat again and fiddled with his shirttail.

The car crept to a dead stop outside of the closest loading lane. Two polished boots appeared under the door panel. Muscular and tall, a uniformed man strode toward them, his demeanor all business.

Ken tipped his hat in slow motion. "Morning, Sheriff Waller."

The lawman's steel gaze shifted from Ken to her. "Is she official?"

"Volunteer—but official, yes. This is my distribution site assistant Lyndie Leigh Sessoms. She's been on duty since the first day."

"All right then. You both should know. Someone called in a claim over our tip hotline. A fellow drove into Englewood offering to sell discounted fence supplies out of the back of his truck. Not getting any takers, he headed south into Oklahoma."

Lines at the corners of Ken's eyes deepened. "You don't suspect he was marketing donated supplies after picking them up here for free, do you?"

Lyndie's jaw dropped at the prospect. Their loose system of non-registered distribution now carried a backlash of alleged abuse. Vulnerable to being taken advantage of, the notion made the skin crawl across her shoulder blades.

The sheriff's expression remained flint-like. "That makes the most sense to me. Protection doesn't have the same setup. Theirs is much more controlled. You're handing out supplies willy-nilly, which might explain why your stocking area looks depleted like this."

Ken squared around, placing his hands on his hips. "Donated fencing supplies don't do anybody a bit of good sitting out here in nice, neat piles. In case you haven't noticed, there's a world of severe need going on across Clark County. Our ranchers are scrambling to replace miles of fence line to keep what's left of their herd separate from their neighbor's."

Unable to stay out of the conversation any longer, Lyndie took a half-step closer to Ken. "I've seen nothing but cooperation and shared effort by the ranchers. Most of them have either hired crews or host volunteers working daily to tear down damaged wire and resurrect fence lines. Nobody has the time to sit on a street corner, peddling goods for profit."

He squinted at her rationale. "I thought about that, too. Have you distributed supplies to anyone who's not someone local that you recognize?"

"I haven't," Ken replied. "Even if I had, I wouldn't have any regret over it—not with the depth of despair we've been addressing. If there's someone taking advantage of the free stuff to profit from it, that's on them."

"No, that's on *me*," Waller replied. "Once they cross the line of criminal intent, I have to make it my business."

Lyndie evaluated the distribution process and couldn't come up with a rectification to save her life. With Ken so adamant against registration, that left little room to operate. "I don't know what more we could do from our side, short of registration or somehow marking the separate loads."

"It may come down to hiding a marker for tracing," Waller replied. "For now, keep your observations general. Maybe you could notice who loads up more often."

Ken kicked at the dirt. "That's ridiculous. Not only does that turn our good-natured generosity into stingy suspicion, it condemns the larger spreads for needing more supplies. If Garrett Guard drives in four times today, I'm going to fill his truck every time."

With the two men at loggerheads, Lyndie could barely draw a breath. She launched a silent prayer for wisdom in the moment. A big rig rumbled up the road and slowed to take the turn-in. "Sheriff Waller, you'll have to excuse us. It looks like we have a load of donations arriving. At a minimum, we need a description of the peddler's truck to provide any meaningful surveillance from our end. It's our job to give it all away—"

"And that's what we intend to do," Ken added. He exaggerated a gesture to signal the truck driver to take the far lane.

Waller pointed an accusatory finger at Ken. "You have a siphon—not a poor peddler. If *he* found a way to bilk the system, you can bet there'll be others." He lowered his arm and took a step toward his vehicle. "Once you sober up to your civic responsibilities, then we can get serious about a resolution." His gaze swept both of them before he retreated to his patrol car.

Ken nudged her shoulder as he stepped to the rear of the semi. "He's got some nerve, lecturing me about civic responsibility like that."

"God knows your heart, Ken." She looked up to see a couple of vans bearing the Red Cross emblem. When they parked, half a dozen strapping young men wearing purple T-shirts began to wander toward them. "I heard it's spring break week here in Kansas. It appears we're getting some Wildcat power this morning."

"Count on K-State to send some good ones." A hint of a smile reset his expression.

"Time to shift back into generosity mode. If something seems out of the ordinary, I'll make note of it. All else registers as total giveaway. I'm more than happy to do it."

"Attagirl, Lyndie." Ken waved to the students as the truck driver slid the rear door open. "Where are you hailing from this morning?"

"Wichita," the driver replied. "Farm Bureau teamed with the local John Deere dealership, Prairieland Partners, for this drive."

Ken scratched his head under his hat brim. "What's in all

these cardboard boxes? I'm not recognizing the packaging."

"These are fence clips, boxed by the gross. We thought the donor might have gone overboard, but who's to say what's excessive. We had the space, so I brought them."

"Sweet, sweet, sweet," Lyndie said in a sing-song voice.

"We haven't had the first fence clip before now," Ken added. "This donation falls like balm on a sore spot this morning. We need to get the word out."

"I'm on that," Lyndie quipped, set to text the good news.

A broad-chested student stepped up to Ken. "Sir, we're from the Agronomy Department at K-State. The Red Cross thought you could use a little support out here early on. We're scheduled at the Guard's ranch this afternoon."

"Good to have you, fellas," Ken replied. "We've got to get this truck unloaded so we have something to give away today. Each item has a set spot, so take note of the system that splits the two loading lanes."

Lyndie surveyed the supply line and found a location for the new item. "Hey, Ken. Let's put the boxes of fence clips down here." She tapped the ground with the toe of her boot.

Ken pulled off his cowboy hat and made a sweeping motion that encompassed the open bay of the truck. "Let's get 'er done, young men. Exertion is fair payback for volunteering, and we've got a truckload of opportunity for you guys."

She smiled as purple shirts began to swarm the heavy load. Concentrating on the phone's keyboard, she took great pleasure in spreading the word. One rancher in particular needed to know. *Load heavy with fence clips arrived. Want a few boxes? Spread the word.*

She hit send to mark the shift back to giveaway mode. Next, she'd send an announcement to the library, where Tara had an e-mail distribution list for the county's ranchers, as well as a vast network of Facebook friends. A savvy grassroots effort now touted social media prowess. Getting the word out was vital—and they were positively killing it.

~

Behind the counter, the banker had used the slow morning to reiterate several procedural points to the tellers on duty. After all, he didn't want the hardship birthed by the wildfire to ricochet into a run on the bank's holdings. A sharp throat-clearing from the lobby redirected his immediate attention.

"Got a minute for me in private?" The client stroked his pointy chin, seeming a bit uncomfortable with the wide open atmosphere of the lobby.

"Certainly. Please join me in my office." Nodding at the newest teller with tenure of only five years, he stepped around the restricted access and led the local rancher back to his grand desk. He loved that desk, as it had guarded him from desperate clients that needed to beg money, or ask for extensions on loans. Part of his immunity system, its massive flanks helped him remain distant, but fair. "Here, take a seat. I don't suppose you're in town for no reason."

"That's right. A self-employed man always has plenty to do." The rancher eased into the chair, but looked uncomfortable despite the tufted leather.

"I think that Hackman land you were watching dropped off the market, last I heard." He clamped his hands together while his elbows propped on the desk blotter. A land loan might just perk up his morning, if the rancher had an itch to invest in more dirt.

"Yeah, that bunch was too flighty for me. Once the estate settles and they see nobody's standing in line with an offer, maybe the price will drop into the realm of reasonable."

"So what's on your mind this morning? I trust I can help you with whatever it is." He flashed a standard-issue smile that didn't last.

"I'm here about the wildfire."

"Oh? I just read the news this morning. State officials are naming it the Starbuck Fire."

He fidgeted at the moniker. "Not for coffee, I hope."

"No, not that at all. It's for the fire chief of some Podunk little town in Oklahoma who first reported the fast-moving fire line to the state to get some suppression assistance. Chaz Starbuck claimed the fire outraced him because of the wind. That's why he called for re-enforcements. To dispatch a plane, they had to label the fire, so they put his name on it."

The rancher looked down at his boots, letting the information steep in his kettle.

"Hey, I heard the fire department kept the blaze off your place. What a stroke of good fortune—you're right across the highway from the Guards' spread. They didn't fare as well." He rocked forward in his seat to better commiserate.

The client rubbed his chiseled chin and looked him in the eye. "A man can't get passed over by calamity like that and not be changed. Many lost everything that night. Through the meet-up of wind, fire, and water from the fire department's tanker truck, my ranch got spared. I came in to let the rest know I feel for their loss." He tugged at something in his pocket, producing a paper. "Here's a check for the Ashland Foundation. I didn't want that distribution of funds to start without my five cents added to the pot. If it means one more rancher can rebuild a shed, it's well worth any delay I experience in expanding my operation."

The banker leaned forward and accepted the folded check. "How about we walk to the front teller together and make sure this gets to the foundation?" He rose, holding the check prominently to keep the issue at the forefront.

The rancher stood, seeming taller than before. "Word's out that the distribution is coming by week's end. Maybe you could speak to Ken about that and convince him to move it up a day, so nobody drinks up their donation in a Dodge City saloon over the weekend."

"Good point. I'll start the conversation when he drops by this afternoon." He led back into the lobby and fingered the check open. *Well now.* The pot had definitely deepened. No doubt some Morton building salesman in an outlying county would be poised to strike it rich.

~

Burk rested under a bare-branched cottonwood tree, ready for lunch. Trays of bagged meals had arrived with a brigade wearing purple T-shirts. The fencing team had dropped down the western fence of the Guard's expansive ranch. That formidable boundary would set the boundary for the Krier ranch's open range to the west. Right now, it stood only two strands tall.

A relief worker passed through the group, which now numbered upwards of twenty. Men nodded as they accepted the milk-white bags containing their lunches. With the wind absent, the day had warmed up considerably for mid-March.

"Excuse me, sir. I understand you are Burk Crosby."

He looked up to see one of the spring break students studying him. "That's right. Can I help you?"

"No, sir. I'm here on delivery duty." A sheepish smile broke across his round face. "We worked the distribution site at the fairgrounds this morning. They kept us plenty busy. We had an absolute blast."

"My friend Lyndie has been worried about running out of supplies over there. Did they have a truck come in?"

"Not one truck—three. We got to load up about twenty ranchers during our shift. What an honor. We shook hands with each one and then sent them on their way fully loaded."

He nodded his approval. "That should keep Lyndie happy."

"Oh, yeah. She'd bust out singing right in the middle of helping load a truck. I'd say she's plenty happy." The young man tried to wink, but it came out more like a troubled squint.

"She reminds the rest of us how much we have to be grateful about."

A genial relief worker interrupted to hand him a lunch bag and proceeded down the way.

"Yes, sir. I believe you might have one more thing to be

thankful for. Remember? I'm on delivery duty." With an impish grin, he produced a plastic-bound wad from his back pocket.

Burk recognized the gift in an instant. He held out a palm and received the package with a jangle. Bless her heart, Lyndie had sent him some fence clips.

"Well, I'd better get back, or my friends will devour my lunch for me," the student teased. "I'm Max, Mr. Crosby. I'd be honored to work alongside you later, if that's how things fall with my assignment."

"I sure could use a helper, so let me come look for you when they crack the whip to get us going again."

"You bet." With a nod, he headed off to a gang of purple camped out near the vans.

Burk gave the wrapped clips a playful toss, pleased to be the object of her special gift. When they landed, he noticed the inked-on handwriting for the first time. Intrigued, he turned the package to read the message. *Hooked on you.*

He chuckled at her pun, fingering the bent-in hooks on the row of clips. Their friendship needed more serious consideration. No question, he needed to ask her out. Maybe they could leave the fire damage behind and see what they had in common beyond smoldering ashes and flesh wounds. That would be a true compatibility test, one he was most definitely up for.

He opened the lunch bag and extracted the sandwich. The meat had a reddish tint, possibly ham. Though he checked the bottom of the bag, no condiments lurked under the chips. Nothing fancy, the sustenance would keep him going. His thoughts left unguarded, the steaks at the Stagecoach Stop came to mind. *Yes.* Dodge City would make an ideal date destination. With visions of Lyndie sitting across the table from him, he began to formulate a foolproof plan.

Chapter 10

Twenty minutes ahead of departure time, Lyndie had a notion to cook some bacon and eggs in Burk's kitchen. This day—a Wednesday—would be unlike any other. She clomped down the camper's steps in her cowgirl boots, determined to kick life into high gear.

Without a cloud in the sky, western Kansas seemed to go on forever. The vista south of the Crosby ranch enticed the eye with a cascade of gentle ridges descending into Oklahoma. As she approached his back porch, something about the nearby pasture snagged her attention.

She widened her path to take in the scene. Where bare dirt had maintained the lunarscape of nothingness, detectable fuzz now covered the land. Lyndie gasped, clapped a hand over her mouth, and broke into a run to retrieve her host.

Unable to block it, a laugh rippled up her throat. The ordinary day assumed newfound significance, as the prairie lived again today. She burst through the back door without knocking, an unruly guest. "Hey Burk—come out here. You've got to see this!"

When she rushed into the kitchen, he stood shirtless by the bar, sipping from a brown coffee mug. Her enthusiasm collided with the sight of his bare chest, arresting her in a tippy standstill. Bewildered, she lost her direction.

Unaffected, Burk sipped his coffee and gave her an interested look.

She looked at the floor. "Really, get dressed. I have something amazing to show you." The kitchen grew steaming hot.

He grabbed a faded blue T-shirt from the kitchen chair. "You're riled like a whirlwind this morning. It looks good on you." He raised the mug in a toast before surrendering it to the counter.

"You wouldn't even recognize a hurry-up if you saw one." Hanging a smirk on the comment, she stomped back down the hall. Before she could turn the doorknob, he managed to eliminate the distance between them.

"Maybe if I hang close enough, some of your enthusiasm will rub off on me." He tugged at her hair in a mischief-laden move. Reaching around her, he turned the doorknob.

"I'd count on the caffeine in your coffee, if I were you." She shoved the door open and practically skipped to the fence she'd help build last week. Today, it seemed a minimum component that ended where the ground fuzz began. Once Burk had joined her, she gestured to the spreading pasture. "Ta-da. You have grass again."

Burk shifted at the declaration, squatting until he sat eye level with the fence's second strand. His gaze roamed from south to north. Next, it froze on her. "I have grass again." Satisfaction permeated his voice.

"The weekend rain brought the prairie back to life." To connect with the miracle-like apparition, Lyndie leaned between strands and brushed a hand over the sprouts, a tactile picnic. "Ooh, you should feel this sensation."

Not hesitant in the least, Burk slid above the bottom wire and readily knelt in the pasture. "I'm a rancher—with grass."

"Would you look at that? Thank you, God, for the gift of green. Only your almighty hand can bring such a widespread blessing like this."

He caught the sleeve of her flannel over-shirt and tugged

at it. "Come in here with me. The grass feels amazing."

She flattened onto her belly and shimmied inside the enclosure. After sniffing the fresh growth, she laid her cheek against the blades to feel the earth's velvety cover. "I never thought I'd see grass as a luxury, but it sure looks like one today."

He shifted to lay flat beside her. Their gazes soon collided. "I want to ask you out, Lyndie. Can you think about that for a second? I mean out—like on a date. Dodge City has a great steakhouse. We could stroll along historic Boot Hill afterwards to see if Marshal Dillon is still on duty."

She rolled flat onto her back to let the offer filter down to her heart. A change of scenery that didn't come with a coating of ash or a heap of recovery tasks seemed dreamlike. Her hand roamed the tender sprouts until it found his. "A date truly sounds nice. Thanks for asking. Finding the time might be an issue, though. My radio show is Friday night, Saturday is the busiest day for distribution, and we go to Ken's for lunch on Sunday after church."

His fingers locked around hers as if tying an unspoken claim. "Thursday night will be ours then. Let's plan to leave here by five o'clock. It's an hour drive to Dodge City." His thumb rubbed across her knuckles.

"Okay, Thursday night I have a date." Just saying the words set loose a tremor of excitement. She'd come to Kansas to discover a life with more texture and found it in the wake of a burn-out. She pulled his hand along with hers to brush the flat-topped grass sprouts to absorb the resurgence for their gain. "Want me to cook us some breakfast?"

His chin nudged her shoulder. "I thought you'd never ask."

She snickered and broke free, rolling under the fence wire to get domestic in the kitchen. Though it seemed an inglorious start for the day, she intended to carry her newfound happiness along. The more ordinary, the better.

She glanced at the Western Star decal on her camper, occupying a space that existed about a million grass blades away from celebrity.

~

From the truck window, Burk could sense the emotional toll the wildfire had left in its devastating wake. As the fence crew was transported further into the interior of the Guard ranch this morning, they passed the charred foundations of two houses. Nearby, a barn lay in shambles, partially burned and caved in like an eyesore on the desperate horizon. Barely able to cope, Garrett Guard glanced away as they rode past the carnage.

Burk elbowed the armrest, wishing he could escape. He'd been restless since asking Lyndie out before breakfast. Change lurked on every canyon precipice. Scars marked the landscape from freshly dug pits used to bury massive numbers of dead cattle. Garrett had more than his share. *Is there nothing left untouched in Clark County?* As soon as the truck lurched to a halt, he threw the door open. A breath of fresh Kansas air would do him good.

The workers began gravitating toward a stack of new fence posts lying near a dozen spools of barbed wire. Burk recognized a few volunteers from the crew at the Gillian ranch last week. Clint Hooper had also joined up. If the occasion presented itself, he'd ask about Gene Shawboro's recovery.

Garrett cleared his throat. "Thank you men for being here today. Though it might seem like a drop in the bucket, if we can get this section in, I can take my breeding stock off the winter wheat."

"You'll appreciate that move come July," Burk assured him. "We're here to get you back in the ranching business."

The landowner shook his head. "I can't see that far ahead, but tomorrow is a far sight better than yesterday. I keep walkin' and talkin' about ranching, even though half my family is homeless. The wildfire sure has been a gut-check on what matters most."

"Today we'll help the cattle—because they can't help themselves," Clint said.

Burk stooped and picked up a fence post. "You set the line location, Garrett. I see traces of the old fence line, if you want the new one to match up."

"Let's move it a yard further out." He soon stepped off the adjustment.

"I'll unroll the wire," Clint added. "That leaves the post pounding to the younger men."

"What category does that put me in?" a man asked.

Burk turned to find Rodney Gillian standing with the rest of the crew. When the reserved man touched his hat brim in greeting, Burk understood the nobility of his act of reciprocation. Time was a precious gift. Ranchers helping ranchers would heal the wounded shortgrass prairie, one generous act at a time.

"Get some help laying out posts, Crosby," Clint ordered. He hoisted the first wire spool to load it.

Burk glanced around to assess the crew for helpers. An unseen force bumped the back of his knees, knocking him off-balance. The wiry body of a blue heeler circled his feet, its uneven three-legged gait spiked with vigor. "Hey now— it's Chip! It looks like he's back to full-force ornery."

With a yip, the dog parked between the two men and stared at its owner. Clint chuckled and slung the wire spool toward the roll-out cart. Several others picked up posts and then paused for further direction.

"Looks like you've made a new friend," Rodney said, tamping down a grin. "Heelers tend to be loyal to a fault."

A rogue idea struck from out of the blue, but Burk sensed such a deep agreement with the notion, he overrode caution to render it. "Tell you what. I sorely need a herding dog. If you mate Chip this spring, I claim a puppy from the litter."

Rodney's mouth fell open at the request.

Clint leaned into the conversation. "Red McMinimy

hired a fence builder out of Hoxie. I saw him at the fairgrounds with a good-looking merle heeler riding on his flatbed. I'm pretty sure it was a female. She's plenty territorial, too."

"Is that so?" Burk asked. "Those two need to meet up. Since I live beside the McMinimy ranch, Chip can come visit me to better accomplish the rendezvous."

"Up to you," Rodney replied with a shake of his head. "I can hardly plan for such extracurricular pursuits."

Burk pushed a post toward him. "Stand back and let a three-legged dog teach you how to go about living again, Rodney. When I saw my newly sprouted grass this morning, I realized that life is precious."

Garrett strode out seven paces and dropped a post. "Start right here."

Burk claimed a post in each hand and followed, feeling the strength of the land under his boots as he went. By fall, he'd have a ranch dog on the hearth once again. A tail thumped his jeans. When he glanced down, he found a salt-and-pepper escort leading the way.

~

Money would start to leave the bank soon, which always made him uneasy. The banker paced behind the desk, wishing his office had more space. Now wasn't the time to appear irritated over trivial matters, so he had to control his demeanor.

Miss T tapped a pen on her notes. "The Clark County Proud dot com money will transfer to your bank this afternoon. Watch for it in the form of a PayPal payment. Come sit down, Neil, and I'll read out that amount. You'll need to double check it for accuracy when the sum arrives."

Her words fell with no-nonsense confidence, guiding him back to the desk. "Of course, I understand this part has to be conducted with utmost accuracy. Should the federal government try to track the dispersal later—"

"Then our impeccable records will hold up under their

scrutiny." She raised both graying eyebrows as though to test him.

He fumbled the pen, but finally got it in his grip. "Please go ahead. I'm ready."

Her shoulders rose and fell with an inhalation. "You may think you are ready. Here's the total—two two nine, nine five two. Now, you read it back to me."

He stared at the six figures as numbness began to arrest his dexterity. The paralysis spread up his arm and crossed his back in a shiver. Aware that local donations to the Ashland Foundation already in the bank would run the total well over three hundred thousand dollars, his lungs began to constrict in his chest.

"Neil? Are you stonewalling me on purpose?" Miss T slid to the edge of the guest chair. "Please read the Clark County Proud number back to me."

"Two hundred twenty-nine thousand, nine hundred fifty-two. Would you like to inspect the Ashland Foundation's total to date?" He adjusted the ledger in front of her without waiting for a response.

She read through the line items that detailed incoming donations for the past week. Systematic as usual, she noted each donation exceeding one thousand dollars for a personal expression of thanks.

"Ken's all set to run the distribution Thursday and Friday. We'll have the vouchers printed up this afternoon, now that I have the total." Seeing that she had finished her list, he retook the ledger and slid it into his desk drawer.

"Your bank is going to be busy."

"Well, I hope some of the money is deposited right back into personal accounts." He wiped his forehead and couldn't feel his fingertips.

She stood and stared at him a long moment. "Maybe you should diversify into the fencing supply business."

"It's a little late for that. We'll be ready." He'd committed, now he had to mean it.

~

Lyndie swiveled on the bar stool, sure she needed to talk, but hesitant to say too much. Queenie turned circles around her ankles before disappearing around the bar into the kitchen. A pan slid onto the counter below. "Burk asked me out on a date. He's taking me to a steakhouse in Dodge City tomorrow night."

Mandy turned with a can of refried beans in her hand. She settled the rim under the can opener. "I think you two were heading for that. It can't be all work—even when there's so much to do." An electric hum filled the kitchen as the can rotated a full circle.

"I worry that he'll default to picking up supplies or something extra to justify the trip. Why do I let myself sabotage a carefree date with such an undercurrent of distrust?"

Mandy leveraged the spoon like a crowbar. "Has Burk ever given you any reason not to trust him?"

"No, he's been open and honest. Maybe I'm the weak link." She covered her face with her hands. "Please don't get me wrong. I really want this date."

The cook lined the rectangular pan with beans. "Have you thought about what you're going to wear?"

"Not once. I have a closet full of show costumes and a dresser stuffed with jeans."

A jar of salsa popped open. "I wouldn't go the jeans route if I were you. Burk might misconstrue that as permission to shift back into work mode, if the opportunity availed itself." She spooned the salsa over the bean layer.

Lyndie squeezed her eyes closed. "You're so right. I have a dress I splurged on for my birthday. It's clingy, but it might work."

"There now, you're one step closer to being ready. Wear some unreasonable shoes, too."

"Not my red boots?"

"Definitely not. Burk is small-town comfortable. Any

showgirl look will strike him as over-the-top. He likes *you,* Lyndie—not the Sweetheart of the Rodeo."

She exhaled and gripped the edge of the bar. "Okay, it's my wrapped bodice dress with my wedge heels. This feels good, like I'm getting some traction. Thanks, Mandy. I needed some coaching."

Her hostess leaned across the counter while the browned ground beef drained over the sink. "Pray before you leave, and then have a fun first date."

Lyndie slid to her feet. "Let's call that some carry-out advice I can count on. I'd better get moving on down the trail. Mexican food sounds good for dinner tonight. Thanks for the inspiration."

"You're welcome. I'm excited for you and Burk. Let's catch up at church on Sunday."

She nodded and walked toward the front door in a decidedly improved frame of mind. Queenie tried to follow her out, but she snapped her fingers, and the mutt planted its haunches. "Good dog. Now, if that trick would only work on a certain rancher, I'd have more control over this date."

As she patted the dog, she realized she could only control the way she looked. Even that depended on whether her curling iron cooperated or not. The dog whined when she stepped through the doorway while dinner and dating battled for top priority in her mind. *Oh, how I love small-town life.* A streetlight flickered on, so she picked up her pace.

Chapter 11

Burk grabbed his leather gloves and hastened to join the others. Brisk this morning, the fencing effort seemed like a perpetual challenge. Every length of fence looked exactly like the last, a chink in the monotonous repetition of his day.

Garrett Guard paced up to the group in a display of misplaced vigor. "Good morning, gentlemen. We've got to hit it hard this morning, as I'm dismissing the team at one o'clock. You may be aware that the first round of monetary distribution will take place at the fairgrounds today, so at least half of us should make an appearance."

Two men behind him murmured something akin to a complaint. Burk guessed they were hired help. He nodded at Garrett to acknowledge the handy break. After all, his name would be listed on that registry, and he definitely intended to pick up his allocation.

"I see that Clint's not here yet," Garrett continued. "I respect that and hope he's in town getting his voucher. That leaves the wire cart unmanned. Crosby, can you take the lead there? I'll put my men on the fence posts today."

"Count on me," Burk replied. "Rodney may be in town, too. I think Ken plans to start the distribution to match the bank's hours of operation. We may get some reinforcements after that."

The ranch owner nodded. "Let's see what we can get stretched out and clipped up with a half-day effort. I'm much obliged for everyone coming out today."

Burk headed toward the wire spools to load the cart. He stooped, slid the spool onto the central axle, and capped the rig with the second wheel. When he stood, he spotted another caravan of volunteers headed toward them, their equipment a dead give-away as to their identity. "Hey, Garrett. Looks like you get the Methodist disaster relief team this morning."

"Hail to the skid steer," he replied in a buoyant tone. "I'll put them south of us tearing out that old fence line. That will clear the way for our next project."

"There you go. That sounds like a plan." Burk gave him a half-cocked grin, thinking the man had finally crawled out of the rock-bottomed pit that despair had dug.

"You fellas get to fence building and let me work in with them," Garrett replied. "Destruction matches my mood today anyway." Though he lacked any facial expression, his gaze held some mischief as it swept the crew. Turning back, he strode out to intercept the newly-arriving volunteers.

A fence post thumped the ground. Burk guided the cart just inside the post, ready to start. He hadn't gone twenty paces before the wire hitched on a barb and then fouled around the axle. "Curse the man who gets in a hurry," he muttered. After fiddling with the wayward loops, he got the line straightened out again.

Seeing the horizon stretched before him, he took a deep breath. His thoughts wandered to his date that afternoon. It better not hitch up like the wire, or he might not end up with his goal—Lyndie in his arms exchanging a few breathless whispers. That dream escorted him over the next quarter mile, until the last inch of wire cleared the spool.

~

After a period of trial and error, Lyndie believed they had finally struck upon the most efficient plan. First, Ken informed each rancher of his eligibility for the monetary dispersal and helped them load their fencing supplies. She stood at the last stop along the loading zone, safeguarding the Clark County Proud vouchers, while manning the clipboard.

At last possessing a modicum of registration, she had an alphabetical list of forty Clark County ranchers that could be checked off one recipient at a time. Ken had capitulated to her request to have the men show a photo ID, so she could match the rancher to the name on her list. The handsome rancher that had asked her out this evening wasn't far down the list, seeing his full name "Burkett N. Crosby" printed for the first time.

They had exactly forty vouchers. Each one came numbered like a check with the identical amount on each one—seven thousand five hundred dollars. Intended for immediate relief of their most pressing issues, she sensed the well-aimed distribution fell at the right time. Maybe that reflected her perspective as an outsider. She really needed to find time to shop for some property in town.

After processing the first handful of participants, they had learned it worked best if Ken joined her for the actual bestowment. One senior rancher, Mr. Krier, broke down upon receipt, so instead of her regular spiel about heading straight to the bank to safeguard his allotment, she had to play emotional nursemaid. Once the old-timer managed to regain strength in his feeble legs, Ken loaded him back into his truck, the voucher tucked into the chest pocket of his work shirt.

Lyndie glanced up the line and caught a friendly wave being tossed from the cab. Her reaction clouded with mixed feelings. Cub Haines had arrived like clockwork for his load of fence posts, wire, and hay. She waved back while Ken met up with the energetic rancher. In an earlier capitulation with the sheriff, Ken agreed to the restriction of one visit per day during the monetary dispersal, so as not to confuse their recordkeeping. She prayed Cub wouldn't buck at the constraint, as harmony remained essential to the process.

Glad Ken had volunteered to establish the caveat, she took a deep breath and checked the clipboard for Cub's name. She located a joint listing divided by a slash for Byron and Jacobi Haines. Since many local ranches represented generational family operations, she noted several other joint listings, guessing they were father-son cooperatives.

The sound of post bundles clattering into the truck bed shattered the relative peace of midmorning. She remembered how Burk lamented the unreliability of Cub's father, disappearing in and out of the area which left the brunt of the rebuilding on his son. Mindful of his situation, she would still require Cub to show his photo ID. Protocol that lacked follow-through became weak words etched on paper. That would not be her downfall. No, she played by the book.

Once Ken closed the tailgate, she slipped her hand into the lock box and pulled out a voucher. The men strolled up to her station to complete the distribution's exchange. Her pulse hitched a notch.

"Lyndie will take care of you from here, Cub. I need to take a quick break before the next truck rolls in for service. Remember to load your hay." Ken turned to her and tapped two fingers on his hat brim. "Be back in five."

She focused on her customer. "Hey, Cub. How's it going up at your place?"

"Well, it's moving a slow breed of forward. I got the tool shed rebuilt Monday, so I have some shelter now." He eased closer as though to share a secret.

"That's good. You can always add a lean-to for quick shelter to protect your tractors. She pressed the voucher against the clipboard and held her ground.

"Looks like you're playing the Sweetheart of the Distribution today." A catty grin chased his toying tone.

When his hungry gaze swept her from head to toe, Lyndie sensed the need to stand on protocol. "I have your name on my list, Cub, but I still need to see your photo ID.

Those are the rules for release of funding to all Clark County ranchers. I hope you don't mind."

His eyes crinkled in a squint beneath his hat brim. A thin-lipped grin flattened to birth an objectionable groan. Still, he reached for his back pocket and then flipped open his wallet in compliance, holding it for her to read.

"Thank you, Mr. Haines." She made the obligatory check beside his name and recorded the voucher number. "On behalf of the Ashland Foundation, I'm delighted to bestow this cash voucher for your immediate use." She pushed a smile into place and handed him the slip of paper entitling him to a fair share of the donated funds.

Cub reached for the voucher and took possession. He snapped it back at her. "Any strings attached? I don't know how this works."

"No—no strings attached. Take this to Neil Goering at the bank. You can deposit it into your account, cash it out, or any combination of the two."

With a slight hesitation, Cub finally examined the print on the voucher. A high-pitched squeal caught in his throat. Next, he crouched and sprang into the air like a kid. "Yee-hi!"

Once his boots had settled back in the dirt, Lyndie gave him a pat on the shoulder. "Today's a happy day, for sure. Now go straight to the bank before you lose that thing."

"Yes, ma'am." He shook his head as if to clear it. "This is my down payment on a brand-new modular home. I plan to order one in Pratt this weekend."

"That sounds perfect for a rancher hot on the comeback trail. Good luck, Cub." She extended her hand as a farewell gesture, but he wouldn't take it.

"Maybe now *I'm* the lucky man." With a spirited swoop, he wrapped her in a hug that seemed to extend well beyond the bounds of casual gratitude.

She pushed his shoulders back, wedging the clipboard between them. "God bless you, Cub—now get out of here."

She laced plenty of emphasis on the last part to make sure he knew she meant business.

He backed away, allowing the voucher to flit in the morning breeze. "Say you'll come out to see the new house once I get everything in place." He climbed onto the truck's running board, waiting for a response.

Determined not to offer him any hope outside the realm of proper friendliness, she realized a neutralizer had to be inserted into the meet-up. "I'll come by to see your new house all right, whenever Burk has a free minute to take me up there."

Ken stepped between them. "Adios, Young Bear Haines. Now roll out so we can keep this line moving. See you again Friday—and not before."

Cub smirked, adjusted his hat, and slid into the cab. Soon, the engine revved. The truck lurched forward, causing the top post bundle to shift lower with a clank.

Lyndie resisted waving goodbye as a final indication of non-interest. As Ken took inventory down the line, a question popped to mind. "Hey, what's with the 'Young Bear' name?"

"His dad Byron always went by 'Bear' so the son becomes 'Cub' or 'Young Bear' to us locals." Ken shrugged his shoulders. "Old habits die hard."

She dropped her chin, reflective of the encounter. "I didn't see his claustrophobic hug coming until it was too late."

"Use the clipboard like a shield." He crossed his arms in front of his chest while a tiny grin brightened his expression.

"Who knew I needed a bodyguard?" Most of the ranchers remained too down to try any shenanigans like that. Leave it to Cub to breach the good faith barrier. It wasn't that she didn't have affection to give—because she had plenty. If she could unleash some tonight, there would be no further doubt as to the identity of the lucky man she preferred in her proximity. She sighed and daydreamed about the date while in a lull for the next truck.

~

Grateful the one o'clock hour had arrived, Burk straightened and flexed his shoulders, tight from the stoop the wire cart required. Once the barbed wire spool ran out, he backtracked toward the vehicles. Empty, the iron cart clanked behind him.

The skid steer soon led the other work team up toward the vans. He'd be surprised if Garrett released them on their way so early. The Methodist relief crew had earned a reputation of being quite capable for this fence replacement work. Maybe they could negotiate a return later in the week.

He made a mental note to pick up some hay along with his voucher when he swept through the fairgrounds later. With any good fortune, he'd run into Lyndie out there for a quick infusion of magnetic draw. He'd drop a hint as to how much he looked forward to their date this evening. Her immediate reaction might speak volumes, so he'd pay attention to get the right read on the matter. She represented the focus of his distraction, he didn't mind admitting.

The lead volunteer with the Methodist team had Garrett engaged in a lively conversation. Burk ditched the cart beside the full spools and walked toward the loose huddle of workers. Nearby, the skid steer bucked up the ramp and halted midway of the trailer. From all appearances, work would cease at the Guard ranch with ample daylight left, marking this as quite a red-letter day.

"I can't rightly express how much this means to our family," Garrett said, "for your group to lend a hand like this." He removed his hat and wiped a sleeve across his forehead to mop his sweat. "We've always believed in paying it forward within our community, but we're in such desperate need of assistance since the fire, the shoe has to fit on the other foot this time. It's mighty hard to get used to receiving help…mighty hard."

When Burk sensed the seasoned rancher had begun to

falter, he stepped beside him. Their shoulders bumped in mutual support. Should Garrett grow too tongue-tied to ask them back, Burk would do the asking for him.

The head volunteer stepped forward. Several others entwined their elbows along the flank. "As spokesperson for the Methodist relief team, we count it our distinct pleasure to join you in your reconstruction efforts, Mr. Guard. In truth, we've been trying to draw this particular assignment going on ten days now."

Several men from their group chuckled. The last man patted the speaker on his shoulder. Instead of being exhausted, the entire bunch seemed to gain their second wind.

"Because of the extent of your losses here on the Guard ranch, and in affirmation of our call to spur one another on toward Christian love and good deeds, I hereby present this check for five thousand dollars to be spent as you deem best for the recovery of your ranch." The leader produced an oversized bank draft from his jacket pocket, held it by the corners, and made the bestowment with a slight bow.

The workers began to applaud while Garrett stood slack-jawed, staring at the check. One man stepped out of the line to take pictures with his phone. From the trailer's platform, a horn tooted in celebration of the generous act. After a few speechless moments, Garrett found the fortitude to accept the benevolence offering.

Though the entire scene proved to be rousing, the recipient's humility caused a lump to form in Burk's throat. *Mighty hard* comprised the understatement of the year from a man living with his brother's family, victims of a total burn-out. By every measure, all eyes were on the Guards, Ashland's largest operators. The recovery of their ranch proved critical. He shuddered as the skin crept up the back of his neck.

"May God bless each and every one of you," Garrett said in a meek voice. "Please carry our thanks back to your church members. We're about to get a foot up on this recovery, Lord willing. I admit reliance on others is new territory, but the Almighty's a patient teacher. Looking back, I wonder if I've somehow forfeited other blessings by acting so independent. A trouble shared truly lightens a load. Today, I stand a little taller in that knowledge. Thank you from the bottom of my heart."

Burk started the applause, nudging Garrett's shoulder in camaraderie. "If you'll excuse us now, I believe Mr. Guard might need to make a deposit at the bank this afternoon." A grin tucked into one cheek at the admission.

After a wordless walk back to their trucks, he offered Garrett a quick handshake and jumped into his cab. The fairgrounds south of Ashland beckoned to him, a lure he lacked any power to halt. Once he accomplished his own banking task, he'd head for home, toss hay to the cattle, and then devote himself to some sprucing up for the date of a lifetime.

Chapter 12

Burk couldn't stop looking at the woman in his passenger seat. With traffic nonexistent west of town, his focus shifted to the immediate situation at hand. Lyndie's dress held her frame like shrink-wrap, fueling his distraction. On heightened alert, he may have let the conversation lapse over the last few minutes.

He leaned closer, trying to eliminate the space between them. "Forgive my not mentioning how incredible you look before now. I'm still trying to shush the battle between feast and riot from here to there." He gestured from his eyes to his heart in hopes of completing the delivery.

She crossed her ankles which skimmed her hemline above one knee. "Thank you, Burk. Tonight feels special, so I wanted to do my part. It's been an unforgettable day so far with the voucher distribution. Never thought I would be able to feel the wind under my wings that lifted the Clark County ranchers out of hopelessness. It turned me into a parasail, aloft in the upward momentum."

He reached for her hand and ran a finger over her knuckles. "Glad you could join the sky-high club. I sure walked on a few clouds today."

"We had an episode of turbulence right at the end, but Ken's wisdom prevailed."

After checking on traffic, curiosity got the better of him. He gave her a quick glance. "Was the problem anything you can talk about?"

"Oh, we were down to the fortieth voucher ten minutes before shutdown when two old-timers pulled up at the same exact instant."

"Two slow-moving tortoises crossing the finish line."

She smiled enough to birth a set of dimples. "The first man snarled and stamped his foot, demanding his allotment. The second humble saint kept shaking his head and staring at the ground. My, oh, my—it was a first-rate standoff."

His brow hoisted into his hairline. "Did you find both men on the approved list?"

As she angled toward him, her gaze gained intensity. "Yes, in fact, they both were legitimate. Once Ken called down the snorting-mad guy as Bear, the resolution out of the tight spot came to me in a flash. Cub had been through the distribution line earlier and had already claimed the Haines operation's allotment. Ken surrendered the last voucher to sweet Milt Enoch and offered to escort him to the bank—which he did."

"At least you could trust your handy checklist to keep matters straight."

"I had to show Bear the check mark by Cub's name before he'd believe me. Talk about outright stubborn."

"Cub claims he's been behaving erratically since the burn-out. No question, those two need to communicate more." He slowed the truck, spotting the road marker up ahead.

"What's this?" Lyndie's gaze traced the landscape unfolding beyond the vehicle.

"Stop Number One on our enchanting date—St. Jacob's Well." He turned the truck north onto the access road. The land rose and fell to wall in the Little Basin surrounding them.

She unbuckled and perched on the edge of her seat like a

little kid. "I can't see anything yet. Tell me what to look for, Burk."

"Water has always been a rare commodity out here. Knowledge of a permanent water source has been passed down by oral tradition starting with the Native Americans. Folks making the passage westward from pioneers to horse thieves have used this spot ever since."

"So what am I looking for? An oasis?" She diverted her imploring gaze to him for a few protracted seconds.

The prairie sky had an immediate rival, as her eyes had deepened in intensity. The need to have her closer pulsated in his ears. "Come over this way."

She shifted against the console and scanned the land through the windshield. "This doesn't look right over here. The slope seems higher on your side."

A sliver of guilt riddled him for misleading her. "No, call that a personal request." He skimmed her close-fitting sleeve with a finger. "The solution hole will appear on your side."

In the twitch of a deer's tail, she shifted back to her window. A curled lock of hair flounced free and soon decorated her front neckline. "There, I see another sign coming up."

"It marks the parking lot where the trailhead starts. Listen, I may have to assist your climb down, as those shoes aren't meant to wander off the pavement."

She flexed one ankle in response, causing her shapely calf muscle to bulge. The shoe's wedge heel banked one way and then the other. She sighed, but resumed her vigil. When the wispy top of a willow tree crested above the slope, she bolted upright in the seat. "I see it!"

He guided the truck into the parking area, relieved to find no other vehicle in the lot. They had the remote spot to themselves. That would only serve to heighten the intrigue. "Please hold up and let me get your door. A Living Water Monument awaits our inspection."

He slid out in a hurry, knowing he had waylaid a

curiosity conniption ready to happen. When he got to her door, she practically poured out onto the prairie. The shoes proved tippy at first contact. "Here, lean on my arm for stability. If the climb down gets too tricky, I'll carry you the rest of the way."

"Let me give it the old rodeo-girl try first. I'm so excited. Thank you for thinking of this." She squeezed his arm to chase the exclamation.

Tiny black lines of makeup rimmed her eyes, swept on occasion by alluring lashes that were impossible to ignore. He pulled her hand against his ribs and headed for the top step. The attachment boasted an unanticipated bonus as her silky dress brushed his bare arm.

"I see the open water of a pond beneath the willow. This gets more intriguing by the moment. Plus, it's so blissfully quiet here." She maneuvered the top two steps before the trail turned more rugged. "Okay, excuse the adjustment, but this dress just has to give." With brief warning, she balled up the hem in her clenched hand, freeing her legs for the steep stride down.

Burk continued to lead by a step while feasting on the newly exposed scenery. When she stumbled on a crumbly stair, he reinforced her traction with his other hand. Unable to walk like that, he made certain of her balance before releasing her elbow.

"Thank you, Trailblazer. It looks like the path levels to dirt up ahead. I'll be better equipped for that terrain."

"No complaints," he quipped, motioning for her advance. From there, he'd allow her to lead so her curiosity could be fed unhindered.

Several dragonflies skittered across the pond's surface as they approached the permanent water source. A vocal blackbird surrendered the willow tree for their private use. Giant bulrushes poked at the sky. Peace took up residence here. He exhaled in anticipation, hoping their addition wouldn't break the tranquil spell.

"Do you think we're the first ones here today?" Lyndie stepped toward him, her gaze searching his face.

"We're likely the first ones this week." He slid his fingers through hers, so they could experience the pond side by side. "Now for the moment of truth—we let the pond dwellers know that we're here." He tugged her hand as he knelt by the water's edge. Once she'd joined him, he traced a finger over the water in an arc. "Legend holds that the fish are blind—but they aren't."

Seconds passed in pleasant silence. Lyndie's gaze seemed to explore every inch of the haven. When her hair fell forward with her lean, she tossed it back behind her shoulders making the curls dance. The shore suddenly held a show.

Burk nudged her elbow. "There." He nodded to the left. "Our first inquisitive resident." A flash of glinting sunlight gave away the surfacing fish. "A long-eared sunfish."

Her demure exclamation came followed by a quiver down her arm. "He's looking at me."

"Must be a male," he said under his breath. His attention now had to divide between the unassuming fish and the woman at his elbow. Their mutual reactions became equally fascinating. The sunfish swam away, only to loop back again, angling its body to better regard them.

Lyndie snuggled against him. "Would you look at that? He's not afraid of us—not in the least." Her words seemed to travel through a vacuum.

"Guess the wariness somehow wore off over the years." A moment of eye contact at close range became a heady wander. He shied away, returning his gaze to the pond in time to see a second fish approach.

Lyndie made a musical humming noise. "Perhaps the wariness grew unnecessary, so the burden of flinching could disappear. They don't regard us as a threat anymore. That could make this the most honest place on earth." She shifted on the sandy bank until her knees were submerged in an inch of water.

All the sensations began to build a head of steam that expanded his chest. Her hair cascaded as she bent forward, drumming his arm with sensuous curls. The scent of bottled flowers soon followed. A third fish made an appearance, gawking wide-eyed at the visitors.

Lyndie rested her hand parallel with the water's surface as though to caress the division that separated them. The third fish flicked its tail and swam closer. In seconds, it nibbled at her knee. When she looked up, her eyes held misty wonderment. "So precious…so unbelievably precious."

The approach of a second fish prompted Burk into action. He couldn't allow this moment to be all fish. Choosing his initial point of contact, he covered the hand holding up her dress hem and gave it a squeeze. "Lyndie?" His whispered tone hooked her immediate attention, leaving him a split second to advance or retreat.

She glanced down when the second fish began to nibble her other knee. To her credit, she returned her attentive gaze, squaring to face him.

"If this is the most honest place on earth, then it's only fair for me to make my contribution." He tilted his head in search of the rest. A prayer came to mind which lent him some resolve. After weaving together a wordy preamble, he tossed it from consideration. Instead, he traced her jawline with a fingertip, a satiny smooth juncture. "I didn't plan for this…didn't dare dream of it…didn't even see it coming." He shook his head, but kept his gaze locked on hers. "I'm falling in love with you. To deny what I'm feeling would be like disobeying God. I'm not a man who could do that."

"No, you shouldn't." She angled her head, which buried his wrist in bouncy locks. "This feels like one of those lavish gifts that scripture promises. Below the water, it bears a nibble—"

"And above the water?" He teetered on the brink of violating her space. Seeking a hint of encouragement on her part held him back.

A faint hitch of one shapely brow seemed to frame the intensity of her gaze.

Despite the gentlemanly promise he'd made while staring in the mirror shaving, there would be no waiting for the cloak of evening for intimate expression. With his pulse echoing in his ears, he stroked his thumb down her graceful neck and collapsed the space separating them. He gave her his version of a nibble, until she pressed for more. The reward came with instant gratification, a mesmerizing exchange.

Lyndie pulled away with a throaty giggle. "They're tickling me, Burk. What a sensation."

Abandoned too soon for his liking, he straightened and tried not to let on. "Well, we can stay here as long as you want."

She bent low, blew a breath across the water, and laughed when the sunfish retreated. It took mere seconds for them to regroup for the next encounter. "I want to stay, for a bit longer anyway." This time, when she glanced up, her blue eyes held an invitation.

He skimmed her shoulder to alight his grip on the nape of her neck. Her satiny hair bombarded his senses. A bolder approach, the next kiss bore no resemblance to the nibbling fish. As she melted into his arms, he took full possession, a claim that perpetuated for some duration. By the time he finished, her neck had stained with a reactive flush. "You're even more beautiful up close, a view I'd prefer to have more often."

Without a word, she rose to her feet, blew a kiss to the fish, and started up the path.

Unsteady, Burk stood, brushed off the knees of his jeans, and stole one last look at the wide-eyed residents. "One of us is doing all the talking," he muttered to his sound-dampened audience. Sensing he'd fallen too far behind, he hit high gear to catch her.

Up ahead, Lyndie's calves flexed in a regular rhythm as she crossed the dirt path. Instead of assaulting the first stone step, she hesitated. The dress hem crimped in her grip, until she dropped it back in place.

Burk used the pause to accomplish a major league catch-up. He eyed the willow as they prepared to depart the lower sanctuary. If this stop served as any indication, the remainder of the date would possess a trace of testy, no doubt about it.

Lyndie turned around upon his approach. Her palm came to rest above his shirt pocket. "About your request for the close-up view more often…I think I'd like that." She smiled and it crinkled her nose.

"Sorry," he replied with a shake of his head. "There's no room for *like* in that offer." He gestured up the trail, confident in his denial tactic.

Her countenance fell. Reacting in a knee-jerked break-away, Lyndie bunched up her hem and took a giant step up. For some reason, her advance froze right there on the stone step. When she turned around to face him, her expression gradually softened.

Overhead, the blackbird returned to the willow, a flash of red on its wings. All else remained blue-sky background that surrounded a captivating woman who happened to elevate his pulse. His refusal to enter this trepidation solo threatened to end their date early, but he knew they had to walk into this together—or not at all.

"Burk, I'm sorry. I wasn't being fair or honest back there. Here's the truth—I don't know what I'm doing." She flailed her arms in the air, looking vulnerable. "I so want it, though—your special attention, your gentle touch, and your close-up looks. Please give me some time. Don't make me question my feelings."

Her earnestness carved a swath right through his hesitation. Love couldn't be forced into expression, which he would readily concede. When she bent down to reconnect, he wrapped her in his arms and captured a trembling earthquake. "All I ask for is your heart," he whispered against her neck.

She pulled back as if to examine his intentions, first with her searching gaze. Next, her fingertips traced his face in exploration, pausing where the trampling wound had healed. When her lips eventually fell on his, the supple quest lacked the rigor of an uphill climb.

Afterwards, he loaded her onto his shoulder with a rowdy whoop and stair-climbed to a higher heaven. The date would live on, much to his extreme enjoyment. Maybe he'd begun to unwrap the package, and he sure liked what he saw. *No, not liked.* There was no room for like, as something much better awaited—and he didn't mean the prairie's upper deck, although that level was mighty scenic, too.

Chapter 13

Another piece of juicy steak melted in Lyndie's mouth. She didn't choose steak too often, but when she did, it needed to be great. This particular choice cut of tender grass-grazed beef had not disappointed. Even though Burk had ordered a larger T-bone steak, he'd all but demolished his rancher's special. When she speculated that romance might be revving his appetite a notch, her neck heated. "My goodness, you sure are hungry tonight."

"Yeah, I skipped lunch to snag my voucher. After I drove home to deliver the hay, I decided to line up the next section of fence posts. Guess I'll get caught up someday."

"Want a bite of my rib eye? I'm getting full."

"You bet, but try to save a little room for a treat up on Boot Hill. We'll walk around some first." He leaned across the thick-shellacked tabletop.

She stabbed a generous-sized piece of meat and delivered it into his gaping mouth, earning a wink. The act of sharing somehow multiplied into an inner glow that began to filter through her body. She finished two green beans, put her fork down, and reached for him.

His hand soon covered hers in a gentle show of affection. He drained the tea from his glass and locked his gaze on her. The hubbub of the restaurant crackled into a sizzle as a hot platter passed, balanced in a waiter's hands.

The atmosphere suited her mood. "What did you think of me at first, Burk? I'd really like to know." She infused her gaze with some playfulness to encourage him.

"That one's easy. I doubted you were real. It wasn't until I saw you talking to the Fellows at the evacuation site did it dawn on me that you were actual flesh and blood, not an angel of mercy." He raked his fingertips across the top of her hand as if still trying to prove it.

"Talk about tough decisions, giving up my camper that night was plenty hard. Even though I knew it would bless the Fellows, it really tossed me out into the no-man's land of the open gym."

"I didn't let you float out there without a tether for too long, did I?" He gave her a knowing look, lowering his chin.

"No, as I recall, you did not." The admission caused her to blush. "I didn't get much sleep that night until I gave up on the rickety cot and sought the floor."

"The way I remember it—when I woke up, I was your headrest." His eyes twinkled under the pendant's light.

She feigned a defensive air. "Well, Mr. Crosby, you had moaned in your sleep a time or two. I merely put on my nurse's cap and tried to ease your burdens. Consider my head resting on your chest more like a compress in the hands of Florence Nightingale."

His fingers threaded through hers. "I believe I may have taken undue advantage of your proximity by stroking your hair when I woke up." His voice fell to a whisper. "Hope you didn't take any offense at that."

She smiled, cherishing his belated honesty. "No offense taken. Too bad the tender moment couldn't have lasted, but Cub seemed bent on throwing a bucket of cold water on it."

Burk laughed. "He didn't believe you were real, either—plus, it vexed him to no end that you noticed me first."

"Yeah, I think he's still trying to touch me at every opportunity, but not to try and prove I'm real." When his eyes grew wide, she felt an explanation might be in order. "Cub doesn't miss a chance to throw a hug around me."

"Really?" He looked dumbstruck. The dining room got quiet.

"Take today, for example. He wanted his voucher *plus* a substantial embrace. I thought I would have to stomp his boot to get loose."

He gave her a piercing look, one that didn't speak of relinquishment. "By all means, stomp Cub's toe as needed." He kissed her hand as if to seal the threat.

As she watched, one thing became clear. If she wanted another match-up with his lips, she had to get the table out from between them. "Let's go for that stroll along Boot Hill. I'm ready to get moving, all of a sudden."

He motioned for the waitress, but kept her hand trapped on the glossy tabletop. "You're my guest tonight, so dinner is my treat."

"Thank you, Mr. Crosby. I do think that you're making a remarkable recovery."

The waitress stole his attention by popping the padded cover onto the table. He squeezed her hand before letting go. After tucking two twenties into the bill, he stood and came around to her seat. As he pulled out her chair, he touched his cheek to hers. "You're welcome, Florence. Please be obliged to resuscitate me as needed the next time I catch the hoof end of a steer."

She rose, giggling against his shoulder. When she reached back for her purse, she remembered she hadn't brought one. Yes, she traveled light tonight, floating on the arm of a capable rancher who had nothing but special attention for her. The walk along Boot Hill wouldn't last long enough to hang on his clasping arm. The evening was young yet, and she hoped to find a way to extend the date.

~

Only the sarsaparilla floats had been on Burk's to-do list. The slow dancing somehow happened afterwards as inviting music played overhead. For added privacy, he led Lyndie into a nook where an ice machine whirred nearby. Though the décor lost its Wild West authenticity back there, at least they had the space to themselves. With her face tucked into his neck like that, privacy became essential.

The first song faded. A few notes of the next one played on his heartstrings a bit. When she hummed along, he wanted to encourage her. "Go ahead, sing along if you know it."

Her palms drifted up from his shoulders until her fingertips caressed his sideburns. "Shenandoah, I long to hear you," she sang in a breathy whisper. Her gaze turned liquid about the time it collided with his. "I'm in love with the Kansas prairie, Burk, so help me God. And I can't seem to separate you from it, even if I tried. Oh, what's an Oklahoma girl to do about that?" She gave her head enough of a shake to launch a plump tear down her flushed cheek.

He trapped the tear in his lips. Salty admission never tasted so good. He pressed her closer and held on for dear life. If they could keep western Kansas under their boots, they just might have a chance. "Go ahead, love the land, Lyndie." He refused to give anything else away, except the kiss that he thought she needed. Good thing he had one waiting on standby.

~

Worried about the refrigerated food, Lyndie tied off the tops of the plastic bags riding beside her. Though Burk had first mentioned the option, she'd been the one most eager for the late-night shopping spree. With the Red Cross scheduled to pull out of Ashland on Friday, they needed to be ready for meal prep on their own. From the middle seat, she kicked off her shoes and warmed her toes by the truck's heater.

Burk nodded at something ahead. "This town is really hopping for a Thursday night. By comparison, Ashland rolls up the sidewalks at sunset."

"Except on the nights of home basketball games. It sure didn't take me long to discover where the action happened."

She laughed, wondering if he'd dare mention their first kiss, accidental though it seemed.

"Yeah, I really liked that last home game."

"Oh, I heard some rodeo gal switched out the national anthem for a song easier to sing."

"With a voice like that, she can sing whatever she wants." In seconds, he jammed the brake pedal. An old clunker pulled out in front of the truck.

Lyndie instinctively braced behind his shoulder and checked the roadside establishment, a low-rent bar with a flashing beer sign. "Give him some room as he's probably had a few."

Burk seemed to bite back a reply. His grip tightened on the wheel. More space soon separated the vehicles.

The outdated truck began to weave in traffic. An opposing vehicle fired off its horn and then veered onto the sidewalk to avoid collision. Undaunted, the impaired driver tooled along.

"He's going to miss the traffic light ahead, I guarantee it."

"Wish you were behind the shoulder harness right now," Burk said. "Think you can slide over there without too much trouble? I mean, just until this situation clears up."

Lyndie saw the merit in his request and fumbled with her seatbelt latch. Once freed, she picked up three grocery bags and placed them in her lap as she took their spot on the far seat. In a matter of seconds, she had complied with his plan for ramped-up safety.

A growl rumbled up Burk's throat. "If he does miss the light, I may have to pull him over. Someone could get killed driving like that."

"Or even worse, kill someone else." She released the grocery sacks and reached for him. Her palm came to rest on his forearm. "Father God, please see our predicament and let Burk know how to remedy this situation for the best results, amen."

"I appreciate how you keep your faith ready like that, Lyndie, no matter the circumstance." When the truck ahead lurched, he backed off further. A muscle in his jaw tensed.

She read the road signs and tried to get her bearings. Something looked familiar. "Isn't this our turn to head back east to Ashland?"

"Yes, it is. Our happy wanderer likely needs to make the same right-hand turn, as the lane straight ahead is just for local traffic. This could get ugly fast, but if I lag behind too far, I won't be in much of a position to help."

Lyndie began to lower the food bags to the floor. "I trust your judgment, Burk. It looks like your front bumper would match up to his rear one, if you have to get persuasive."

He pressed his lips together, and his gaze softened. "What else did you notice?"

She pulled the console down in preparation for impact. "That this thing adjusts pretty easily. That you've been positively charming on our first date, and that you shaved prior to picking me up." She waited for him to glance at her before letting the grin break free.

"Great first date," he replied. Within seconds, he had to veer left out of the lane. The rusted tub of trouble in front of them mistimed the turn up ahead and ran aground, wrapping its front grill around the streetlight post with a loud metallic crunch. "It figures he'd default straight to self-destruct. Let me get us over to the parking lot. I'll go lend a hand."

With his plan leaving her behind, an objection caught in her throat. She glanced back over her shoulder as the truck bumped up the curb and found safe ground. After Burk cut the engine, she grabbed for his arm. "Be careful out there."

He winked and slid from the cab. Once he'd checked traffic, he broke into a run. The traffic light changed overhead and bathed everything in an eerie shade of guilty red.

Wondering what she could do, her gaze fell to the grocery bags littering the floorboard. Maybe those could ride inside the toolbox straddling the truck bed. Plus, it would be cooler for the refrigerated items. She threw open the door and began tying off all the bags. When she stepped outside, the dry night air smelled strongly organic. "Always essence of cattle around here," she muttered. "Welcome to the Wild West." Lifting the first load, she maneuvered the groceries toward the back, unlatching the toolbox with her thumb.

Satisfied with their placement, she returned for another load. A can of black olives rolled away when she hoisted a heavy bag. "Burk wants you on his pizza, little guy. Get back in this bag." Fighting her loose hair, she recaptured the runaway and cinched the sack. After she'd placed the remainder of the load in back, she ventured a glimpse at the scene across the street.

Burk stood by a shorter man, gesturing in her direction. The man tried to get back in the wrecked vehicle, but Burk denied him access. Soon, the driver capitulated with his head hung. Burk led him across the intersection and ended up on her side of the vehicle. "Lyndie, I think you remember Bear Haines from earlier today."

She swallowed the repulsion coming up the back of her throat. "His head's bleeding, Burk. Shouldn't we wait for the authorities to get him some medical help?"

"I'm afraid we can't do that, as Mr. Haines here has been doing more than a little imbibing this evening. Get in, Bear." He handed him something to blot his head.

"What about my truck?" The man locked his knees, demanding an answer.

"I'll have Cub drive the diesel out and tow it home tomorrow. Now, let's get going." Burk held the man's arm until he managed to climb into the cab. His other hand found the small of her back as he slammed the passenger door. "Come sit beside me."

She tried to match his gait. "What about leaving the scene of an accident?"

"Nobody got hurt here," he replied under his breath. "If

they want to press charges on an old man who couldn't see too well at night, we'll have to risk it." They crossed the truck's grill in silence.

Seeing no easy way out of the predicament, Lyndie clamped her mouth shut and hitched up her dress to climb inside the cab. She slid under the steering wheel, shoved the console back, and tried to fit the lap belt, staying as far on Burk's side as she could manage. The small space began to reek of alcohol. Pressing her eyes closed, she felt the vehicle go into motion as the date's intimate ride home became anything but private.

The light changed and Burk floored the accelerator to head east along the highway. "Get Cub on my phone for me, will you?"

Lyndie opened her eyes to find his cell phone hovering over her thigh. She took possession and brought up his contacts, taking an ounce of comfort when she spotted her name on top of the list. She found Cub's name and tapped the screen. With the call underway, she handed the phone back to Burk.

"Thank you. It's only an hour's drive."

Their disgruntled passenger harrumphed from the far side of the cab.

She exhaled, wishing they could transport the drunk some other way. Sometimes life could be terribly inconvenient—and this rated as one of those times. A text pinged and she had to fish for her phone in the crack of the seat. Ken's name came up on the screen.

Closing distribution center Friday. Intake only. See you Saturday.

The news broke like an emancipation proclamation in the otherwise tight moment. She'd find something worthwhile to do with her time, starting with the rancher beside her who always put his own work last. Except for her radio broadcast, she had her Friday free. *What a gift.*

"Cub, I'm over at Dodge City doing some late-night

shopping," Burk said into the phone. "Guess who I came across wrapping his hood around a light pole? Yeah, it's your father."

She could sense the shame on the other end of the line. Staring ahead, she tried to watch how the old man responded. She couldn't detect any reaction at all. *Call that a double shame.*

"Are you at Heath's house tonight? I need to drop Bear off in Ashland wherever you are. He's…incapacitated. You know, straight from the bar."

Lyndie stared out at the expanse of highway ahead and memorized how the prairie seemed to shore up its flanks like some immoveable force. The innocent land forever held the righteousness of its Creator. Humankind managed to smear that perfection, a continual fall from grace. When the drunk beside her belched, she cringed.

"You'll have to come to town for the truck tomorrow. It might gain a ticket on the windshield by then. I suggest that you come early. Plan on towing it, so bring the diesel."

Trying to not fidget, she toed the back strap on her shoe and shucked it off. The second one came off easier. Her toes found the heat vent which brought her the first bit of comfort in minutes. Now playing the role of a physical barrier between the sop and the savior, she had to insulate herself from total alienation.

"That's not my problem, Cub. You can go through the distribution center after the tow errand. We'll be there in forty-five minutes. Have the porch light on for us." He dropped the phone in his lap and took the wheel in both hands. The vehicle steadily gained speed.

A quiet minute passed. Lyndie turned up the radio volume to help break the tension. In the dark cab, a groping finger touched her right thigh. Naturally reactive, she jabbed an elbow into the ribs of the passenger, causing him to gasp. In a split second, she felt Burk's arm stretch across the top of the seat behind her head.

"Don't make me have to stop and sober you up the fast way, Bear. You won't like it, I can guarantee that. If you can't keep your hands off Ms. Sessoms, you'll leave me no other choice. Do we understand each other?"

The man harrumphed again, wresting away from Burk's grasp. He shifted toward the truck door and rested his head on the window. In half a mile, he began to snore.

Burk's right arm settled across her lap and tugged her over closer to him. "I'm so sorry that happened."

Drawn to him, she rested her head on his shoulder. "Drunk or not, I couldn't let him."

He planted a kiss in her hair and kept his arm across her lap as if guarding his territory.

"Ken texted me. He closed the distribution center Friday and gave me the day off. Would you like first dibs on my volunteer services?"

"Yes, ma'am, I would. Could that start with a private breakfast-for-two?"

Grateful for the familiar request, she nuzzled into his shoulder. Somewhere in the night, the cramped situation lost its sting. A song on the radio gave the glory to God. From where she sat, that would be a difficult gesture, but if she reached down deep enough, she could thank him for both the good and the bad, plus a first date split smack down the middle by both elements. When the next song cued up, she sang along in a whisper.

After a long refrain of wheels humming on the highway, Burk straightened in his seat. "There. See the lights of Ashland ahead? Heath doesn't live far off the main highway."

Lyndie sat up and rubbed her eyes. She recognized the lights of the gas station and the hospital from the perimeter road. As they slowed for the town speed limit, she saw a sign on the vacant lot up ahead. "For sale—two acres."

"That's an abandoned apple orchard planted by a school principal and his teaching wife. Guess the family's finally clearing out their estate, as they've been gone for some time now."

The idea of an apple orchard pleased her immensely. "Since it sits right down the street from the new hospital, wouldn't the land make a fabulous park?"

He gave a dry chuckle and patted her knee. "Sounds like you need to set up an appointment with the Realtor. I'll loan you my phonebook—after breakfast finds my table."

"Ooh, you drive a hard bargain, Mr. Crosby. I might be two acres away from becoming a citizen of Ashland. Hope that development doesn't sit crosswise with you."

He slowed the truck and turned right into the residential district. In half a block, he pulled to a stop. "There are quite a few things around this town that need more looking after, with that apple orchard being the least of them." He unbuckled and tugged at her to do the same.

She managed to grab her shoes and slide them on before her feet hit the pavement. The idea of her camper sitting under an apple tree hit a cozy chord. She just might be home at last.

140

Chapter 14

Between making Lyndie work like a hired hand all morning and watching her chock his ancient crock pot full for a late dinner, Burk could hardly say no to her request for lunch together in town. Once she trotted off to the library after they ate, he would step into the bank to check on some money matters. After Thursday's disbursement, he imagined the display on the wall for the Ashland Foundation's fund drive would be zeroed out to nothing. Too bad that voucher had been a mere drop in the bucket for most of the area ranchers' needs.

When he saw a flatbed truck pulled onto the shoulder of the road where his property met with the McMinimy ranch, he slowed the vehicle. A dog shot from the jobsite and planted its feet so rapidly, gravel sprayed. The red heeler barked incessantly, raising a ruckus. He read the incredulous look on Lyndie's face and realized he needed to catch her up. He reached across the console and took her arm in his hand. "I forgot to tell you—I might be getting a dog."

Her eyebrows shot up as her gaze skittered to the sentinel and back to him. "What?"

"A puppy really, which is why I need to talk it up with this fencing contractor right now." He threw the truck out of gear and turned off the engine.

A stocky man with bowed legs appeared alongside the parked truck. He called down the dog as he peeled off his flannel shirt. His face leathered from years of sun exposure, the smile only lasted a faint second. "Nice day, ain't it? I'm Conroy Nichols out of Hoxie."

"Burk Crosby, Mr. Nichols. This is my spread to the west. We've been neighbors to the McMinimy family for three generations."

"I've been admiring the fencing on your cemetery there on the corner. They sure don't make fancy iron railings like that anymore." He tipped his hat back, which made him squint.

"Good morning, Mr. Nichols. I'm Lyndie Leigh Sessoms. Who is this lovely creature?" She knelt as if to test the dog's receptivity at being approached.

"That's Babe, my pride and joy. Sure would be lonesome out here without her, but I don't know if she'll let you get close enough to touch. Heelers are slow to make friends."

Burk widened his stance. "How might Babe feel about making a canine friend? There's a reason I'm asking, so hear me out. God let me play a small part in finding a missing male blue heeler for a local rancher who got hit pretty hard by the wildfire. To help keep Rodney's chin up, I asked for a puppy from Chip's line. Any dog that could survive three days on a canyon ledge with nothing to eat or drink deserves to have his bloodline perpetuated."

"I can't argue with that," Conroy replied. He lifted his hat and let the wind comb through his reddish-brown hair.

"Come here, Babe," Lyndie said in a cotton-soft voice. "Come let me rub your ears." She beckoned to the dog and held out her palm.

"If she moseys over, try not to touch her haunches," Conroy replied.

Ears flattened, the dog took a couple of tentative steps on stiffened legs. After one final step, it planted a dry nose in

Lyndie's palm.

"Good girl, Babe. Let me love on you a little this morning." Lyndie's musical tone seemed to charm the dog into cooperation. The hackled fur even smoothed along its spine.

Conroy nodded to the far side of the road. "Are you thinking to hire out some of your fence work? I'm waiting on a couple of bids to come back and could start your spread next, if you want. That might make it more convenient to put the two dogs together."

Burk sensed a touch of favor shine on his far-fetched scheme. "That's kind of what I had in mind—for getting the dogs around each other. Of course, Rodney would have to be willing for the loaner on Chip, but I think I could talk him into the deal. I'm not going to be able to catch up on my fence replacement by myself, not in a month of Sundays. Want to come by later this afternoon, say five o'clock? I'll take you around so you can give me a fair quote on the job."

"Much obliged for the chance. I could even start by Monday if you've been stockpiling supplies. Otherwise, I'd lose a day or two gathering materials." When the dog pulled away from Lyndie and bumped its owner's leg, he raked his fingers through its merle coat. "Her mother was half Hanging Tree. I'm talking top of the line."

Burk squatted to get a closer look. He liked everything he saw, especially the way Lyndie connected with the dog. "What about the father? Do you know his lineage?"

"Nope, only that he worked quick," he replied with a slight wink. "Most of the dogs out our way are some type of herder. When I'm repairing an occupied pasture, Babe really can keep the cattle off of me. You've never seen a better heel nipper."

Lyndie gave the dog's head a pat and then moved beside him. "Mr. Crosby needs that kind of protection. He nearly lost his life to a trampling steer during the wildfire."

Burk's expression eased with a tilted grin. "That old

pioneer cemetery almost had a modern-day addition, but it sure spared part of my herd. We've been through the flame's hotspot around here. The longer you stay in Clark County, the more incredible fire stories you'll hear."

"I plan to tell a few more tonight on my broadcast," Lyndie confessed. "Tune in to Western Star's show at six and you'll hear me share accounts of the first voucher distribution."

"You gotta watch her," Burk warned, his grin growing. "She'll make you part of the show if you're not careful." He threw an arm across her shoulders to better represent his claim.

She stuck her chin into the breeze undaunted by his tease. "If this dog link-up transpires, you can bet I'm telling that story. There couldn't be a better symbol of resurgence than a nearly-starved three-legged dog becoming a proud papa."

Nichols crammed his hat back onto his head. "What? That male's three-legged?"

"Yes, but he's strong as an ox and ready to live. I'd bet the missing limb won't make any difference, once we get the pairing lined up. If you stage out of my barnyard, they'll have the run of my backyard plus the upper pasture. Lots of rendezvous opportunities there." He released Lyndie's shoulder and stepped toward the truck.

"I'll clean out the doghouse," she offered, heading toward the passenger side.

"See you at five o'clock, Mr. Crosby. Let me mull over the rest twixt now and then." He tipped his hat and turned back to the job at hand.

Burk started the truck and jabbed the accelerator. His stomach had already rumbled a time or two. For his future comfort and well-being, they needed to make a beeline to town.

"Now I've seen a new side to you, Burkett N. Crosby. You're a bit of a behind-the-scenes schemer, planning a puppy out of nowhere like that." Lyndie stared straight ahead, seeming unwilling to accompany the comment with any direct eye contact.

"If I see something superior worth having, then I want to make it mine." Deciding to clam up for the next few miles, he'd leave her to simmer on that.

As the bridge to town came into sight, her hand wandered past the console in search of something. She finally added a little persuasion of the blue-eyed kind. A dimple appeared on her cheek, adding to her capitulation.

He dropped a hand from the steering wheel, found hers, and gave it a squeeze. "I might need some help housetraining a puppy, say around September or so."

"Maybe I could lend a hand, if I've got my apple cider made by then. Turn down Main Street and let's see what our lunch options are."

"Hey, there goes the Red Cross headed out of town." He pointed down the highway before turning left onto Main. A convoy of vehicles all pulling trailers straggled up the road.

"Aim for that purple monstrosity across from the library there," she directed. "That would make my trip in to see Tara a short one."

"Wishful thinking." He pulled alongside and read the flowing font on the panel truck's side. "Wrappers on Wheels? What in the world?"

"It's called a food truck, Burk, and it contains your lunch. Pull in, as I'm more than ready for a sandwich that has some flavor." She abandoned his hand and unclipped her seatbelt.

Since he'd already knocked her off balance with the puppy idea, he felt the compulsion to comply. Stealing a glance at the dashboard, he saw time had already slipped past one o'clock. "My stomach's too empty to argue at this point." He toed the front bumper toward the curb and cut the ignition. Grabbing his phone, he hurried out to get her door. On the way, he spotted a short redhead passing by the ordering window inside the food truck.

Lyndie soon slid out at his beckon. "Text Cub and have him come join us for a wrapper." She winked and touched her hair like an actress in a shampoo commercial.

Sensing someone else being a little behind-the-scenes, he chuckled and typed out the message. With any luck, Cub would be halfway from Dodge City tethered by a chain to an unpredictable father. After he sent the invitation, he searched the menu for whatever had the fried onions smelling up the parking lot. He could slay that menu item, especially if it had a link sausage attached. After a few uncertain seconds, he spied the German wrap and knew he had to order one.

~

Glad she asked to have the cheese melted, Lyndie bit into the wrapped Reuben and savored the flavor combination. Though the tailgate's lip dug into the back of her knees, the lunch had all the makings of being memorable. A light breeze blew right up Main Street. Except for a car pulling into the trading post, downtown seemed quiet for a Friday. They needed a picnic table along this main drag, maybe on the corner where a tree could provide some shade.

Cub fidgeted to her left. "Man, this jalapeno sauce is killing me. Good, but killer. I'm clearing out my sinuses."

"Your old man could have used a dose of that sobering last night." Burk tucked in a fried onion and bit a couple of inches off his sausage wrap.

"Yeah, he snored the whole way home," she added. "I'm glad he slept it off, although I've read not to let someone with a head injury pass out like that. Guess I considered that cautious act the lesser of two evils at the time."

Cub looked quizzical and flounced a long dill pickle spear in his grip. "I'd say the light pole might have been the lesser of two evils, too. Anyway, it wasn't hard to pull the truck off and get it home. Glad Heath could help me."

Burk cleared his throat. "Hey, I didn't get one of those."

Lyndie traced his gesture and noticed the pickle spear. After searching her wax paper wrapper, she found she didn't have one either. Cub must have received a special favor. She glanced up and caught the food truck owner staring their way, her hands busy tidying up the napkin dispenser. She smiled and looked over at their lunch guest. "Cub, it seems you're getting some special treatment. Can you go order me a lemonade? Maybe you could make some casual chit-chat with the redhead while you're up there. You know, ask her where's she from and that kind of thing."

He stopped chewing as if to clear his mind.

She pulled out a dollar from her pocket. "Introduce yourself by your Christian name first, and then add Cub. That gives her a choice to express her preference…which is quite important."

The man seemed dumbstruck. "A lemonade?"

"Just place the order and let her do the rest. Think about it, she's trapped inside that thing. You might brighten up her day with a little well-aimed masculine attention. Easy does it, though. You need to make a good first impression, friendly—but not forced."

He snapped the money from her grip and sauntered to the ordering window. The attendant appeared in a heartbeat. Cub slid the money toward her and placed the drink order. His hand propped on his hip as he leaned against the overhang.

"You're not the least bit ashamed of yourself, are you?" Burk took a long sip from the straw in his tea. One eyebrow raised and lowered.

She shook her head, picking at some cheese on the wax paper. "Some cats need a scratching post, or they'll rip your upholstery to shreds. It's all about placating the unwanted behavior by transferring it to the proper spot."

Burk froze the cup halfway to the tailgate as if deciphering her meaning. "You're fixin' to eliminate the need for toe-stomping retaliation, aren't you?"

She allowed her pleasure to radiate in her gaze. "I hope he remembers to find out the hugging post's name."

"He will if he's interested…and something tells me he

might be."

A few minutes later, Cub walked back over with the lemonade cup in one hand and a tray of fries in the other. They appeared to be spattered with parsley. "Here you are, Lyndie. Burk, help me taste test these truffle fries. Brooke claims they were a hit at the state fair last fall."

Lyndie gave her date a fawning look. "Oh? Brooke is it?"

"Yeah, she's from Salina where her family runs a fleet of these food trucks. She agreed to come west and help with the relief effort. Her dad's worked with the Red Cross before, so they tag team off their initial effort and show up to ease the pullout."

Burk took a peppered french fry and hoisted it into his mouth. Within seconds, he was humming from the flavor. He soon reached for more.

"I hope you welcomed her to Ashland, Cub." She drew a truffle fry and sniffed it.

"I sketched my number on a napkin and told her to call if she needed anything. I mentioned going to Pratt tomorrow, in case she needs to restock her supplies. That seemed like enough." He took two truffle fries and downed them.

Lyndie ate her sample and experienced the musky-good flavor of the truffle oil. Those things might get popular fast. She swallowed and took a long sip of lemonade. On the tart side, at least it wasn't watery. "I think you did a fine job. Now, you know where she parks. Anytime you're hungry and in town, you could pop by."

"It's kind of convenient that I live in town right now," he replied, lifting his brow.

Burk doffed him with his hat. "Cut it out, will you. Enough fix-up talk. I really can't stand the plotting. Just be natural."

Cub emptied the sample tray with a nod. He crumpled up the sandwich paper, winked, and headed back to the food truck to dispose of trash. Burk moaned his disappointment at such a ready dismissal of his advice.

Lyndie slid off the tailgate. "I'm heading inside to go over some material with Tara. She took two interviews from ranchers who battled the blaze over near Protection. I might use the quiet time afterwards to write down my personal reflections on the voucher distribution. It helps me have flow while I'm live on the air."

"Remember, her afterschool program will ransack the place between now and your broadcast. Don't leave any paperwork in there." He stood, cleared the trash off the tailgate, and then slammed it shut. "Guess I'll go to the bank and possibly the lumberyard. Text me when you're done, and we'll head back out to God's country."

"When you meet Mr. Nichols at five, I'll come back to Ashland for tonight's broadcast. And don't forget, I want to ride by that apple orchard before we leave town."

"Planning on it," he replied with a smirk as he slid into the cab.

Lyndie checked the nonexistent traffic and tossed Cub a wave as she crossed the street. Maybe she'd press Tara for the name of a local real estate agent. If they were available on Saturday, she planned to set something up. She had an itch to become a property owner in tiny Ashland, Kansas, and it was high time to scratch it. Not worried in the least about putting space between her and a certain rancher with cedar-green eyes, she stepped into the library's atrium to get on her thinking cap for tonight's show.

~

Burk strode into the bank like he had every right to be there. With his account flush with the voucher money, he considered his assets beyond solvent. The fencing contractor might dent that sum a serious bit, but he'd keep expenses down over the first part of summer until the harvested wheat sold. He'd follow up by selling the cattle in August and reassess how things looked like by then. In total, he needed a little more donated hay, some grass to grow enough to sustain the herd, and a solid perimeter fence. If God blessed those, he could cover the rest.

He spotted the head banker standing to the side, speaking with Ken Ray. It looked like Ken had used his day off to tackle some banking, too. A glance toward the donation mural revealed that some funding had already collected at the base of the diagram. What a relief to know that incoming flow hadn't been staunched yet. They sure needed funds to accrue.

Ken saw him approaching and stepped out to greet him. "Hey, Burk. I had just mentioned your name to Neil. Do you have a minute?"

Burk shook his hand while the banker gestured to his office. He shot Ken a questioning look and received a wink in return. A bit relieved, he stuffed his hands in his pockets and followed the sizeable community leader into the inner sanctum of discrete money handling.

Mr. Goering stood behind his desk and motioned for them to sit. "Gentlemen, I've just received word that Kansas Farm Bureau intends to pay out an impressive amount to the wildfire victims in Clark County. Mr. Crosby, your name popped up for consideration under a special provision of their involvement, Farm Bureau's Young Ranchers program. Of the affected ranchers in Kansas and Oklahoma, those under the age of thirty will qualify for receipt of specially allocated funds. They have generous donors who are concerned about how this economic hardship might set back the younger ranchers of the county."

Ken leaned forward in his chair. "We want every rancher fitting the age restriction to fill out the paperwork. The Ashland Foundation will handle the applications to insure deadlines are made and the information is complete—like an agent of sorts. One thing we've learned, this money transfer business has to be gone about systematically."

Dazed by the offer, Burk sat back and tried to collect his thoughts. "Do you have this Young Ranchers' application? I don't know that I'm a member qualified to receive this money."

The banker sat with a dramatic plop. "No membership required, Mr. Crosby. The donation total will depend on the amount of money raised before the filing deadline. At that time, qualified recipients will be allocated their share of the sum, depending on livestock losses and the size of their operations."

"You have a full section down south, don't you?" Ken asked.

"Yes, sir. That's right." Burk divided his attention between the two men. "My livestock losses were next to nothing—only one steer. However, my fence replacement costs will be significant. I'm set to get a quote on that this afternoon."

"That's why you came in, I'm guessing," the banker said. "It's commendable to be certain you can cover your expenses, young man. That makes you the ideal candidate to receive this Farm Bureau allocation."

"I don't want anyone left out," Ken added. "Agriculture has a generous support system and a network of caring business connections. In fact, Cal just heard at the grain elevator that the Kansas Livestock Association plans to throw some of its heft at the burn-out area through their nonprofit foundation. That fund could rise into millions of dollars."

"I believe that's reported in this week's issue of the High Plains Journal," Goering said.

A lump formed in Burk's throat. "Garrett Guard should be at the front of that KLA receiving line. He had more livestock losses than the rest of us combined."

Ken nodded. "We'll keep an ear to the ground on that KLA dispersal. For now, I'd like to ask you to go ahead and fill out the paperwork for the Farm Bureau's Young Ranchers project."

Burk took a calming breath. The Lord had seen his need and made provision for it beyond his wildest imagination.

For some reason, Cub popped to mind. "Mr. Goering, do you have two forms? I just had lunch with Cub Haines. He's trying to finance a new modular home this weekend, as their entire ranch burned to the ground, house and all. I don't feel like I can blaze the Young Ranchers' trail and leave Cub behind. We're the same age—twenty-eight."

"We can certainly apply on Mr. Haines' behalf, though most of those assets are still in his father's name," the banker replied.

The truth hurt like a thorn lodged under a fingernail. Burk shifted in his seat. "His father is…incompetent, sir."

"Maybe Cub should see Sadie at the title office to gain some legal advice. If he held power of attorney over the estate, maybe that would be enough," Goering suggested.

Burk brought out his phone. "I'll ask Cub to join me in filling out the paperwork. We'll apply to Farm Bureau, and if they're seriously searching for needy candidates among the wildfire victims, Cub will qualify." He sent the meet-up text, adding *pronto* to the end.

Ken stood and regarded both men. "If this is the future of agriculture, then I'm greatly encouraged. Now, I need to check by the fairgrounds in case I have a truck waiting to unload. I sense the parade of donations may be slowing down, but I refuse to turn pessimistic over the lag. Burk, if I don't see you sooner, I'll see you after church on Sunday."

"Yes, sir. I'll be there. Don't forget that Lyndie plans to share some distribution stories tonight on her show." When he glanced at the banker, he already had the blank application form in his hand. Conscious that precious time ticked off the clock, he broke into a light sweat thinking he couldn't afford all this special attention.

Ken started to leave the room and paused. "Did you notice our display out front? Donations are already pouring back in to replenish the Ashland Foundation's fund."

"Thank the Good Lord," he replied. Though the banker chortled, he knew the source of all good gifts. A storehouse somewhere in heaven sat with its door ajar, right over Ashland.

154

Chapter 15

Lyndie cleared a wayward lock of hair from under her headphones. "That's how the distribution of funds went yesterday, ladies and gentlemen. No one got blessed more than the humble rodeo entertainer speaking to you tonight, I assure you. Now, it's my distinct pleasure to invite a local rancher to the show, Clint Hooper. Folks, I had the pleasure of meeting Clint that first night in the evacuation shelter at Coldwater. What I'd seen coming up from Oklahoma City ended up being mighty interesting to a group of ranchers that evening. Clint, let me thank you for being here with us tonight to share some of your recovery stories."

"You're welcome, Lyndie. I mostly agreed to speak tonight so folks could understand what we've been beset by out here on the open prairie. With the wind whipped up so furious that night of the wildfire, most of us had to shelter without knowing one way or the other if anything would be standing by the dawn's early light."

Lyndie keyed on the gravely quality of his voice that spoke authenticity over the air waves. No wonder Tara wanted to line up Mr. Hooper to speak. His voice carried the drama without any strains of pretense—only pure cowboy grit.

"My story is one of escape. The large operation across

the road caught the direct fury of the fire across their acreage, where they lost two homes, several outbuildings, and five hundred head of genetically-bred Angus cattle. Because the volunteer fire department arrived and fought with all their determination, my spread a mere stone's throw across the highway was spared. Now, two weeks later, we're all about replacing fire-damaged fences, so the surviving cattle can be contained and hay-fed until the grass greens up."

"The grass finally resprouted this week, thank you God," Lyndie interjected. "I had a little cheek-to-the-ground celebration in a pasture out south of town near Sitka. What a relief to be shed of that bare-dirt landscape."

"Relief? Yep, and then some. Everywhere you could turn, the damage loomed beyond belief. For ranchers, our stress level soared off the radar. We needed help. We asked for help. And we got an outpouring of support from all around Kansas." He paused to work through a catch in his throat. "It's been downright revitalizing to find out so many people care."

"Yet, there's still so much more to be done," Lyndie added. "The Red Cross pulled out of Ashland today, leaving the town standing on shaky legs. We've received word that Kansas Farm Bureau and Kansas Livestock Association have launched donation drives to continue collecting support for our ranches. Clint, would you like to say a word of encouragement to any possible donors out there?"

"Well, no one rightly knows when it's going to be their turn to be trapped beneath catastrophe. A rancher without grass is about as helpless a human as you'll ever want to meet. We're beholden to anyone who has a spare hay bale or an extra dollar bill to contribute. Growing season sits at our doorstep, yet we've got a long way to go until harvest. We've been down, shell-shocked, sleep-deprived, homeless, and other states of destitution—but we've never been without hope. Please help keep us going, as you're able." He rubbed his pointed chin as though he'd fully rendered his piece.

"I understand from the town librarian, you also wanted to promote a local project the library has undertaken."

"Yes, Lyndie. While the images still have sharp edges in our mind's-eye, Tara Daniels is asking for victims of the wildfire to schedule an appointment to have their account of that night recorded in what she's calling 'The Fire Book.' Each one of us had a different perspective of how the devastation rolled over Clark County that night. I've given mine. In fact, I even went to the hospital in Greensburg and interviewed Gene Shawboro as he recovers from his stroke. Part of Gene's memory has been blotted out, but he remembers that particular event crystal clear. Anyone who glimpsed the wildfire's fury should come in and give their account. It's our story."

"Thank you, Clint. If you go see Gene again, please give him Western Star's best wishes for a full recovery. I won't ever forget his bravery as he drove that plow-line around the town's perimeter while the rest of us had to flee under the evacuation."

"He's a hometown hero, that's for sure, a stricken one now, but still a hero." Clint stood and left his guest microphone on the table.

Tara waited by the door and escorted him out.

"Another story developing in the wake of the fire has to do with a remarkable testimony to enduring faith. Volunteer workers on the Miller ranch east toward Protection have fashioned and erected an oversized barbed wire cross from the discarded wire. That's similar to an Old Testament act where the faithful stacked stones to mark the landscape. Named 'Ebenezer' by the Israelites, it meant 'thus far hath the Lord brought us.' I think we can all sense the remarkable parallels spoken by this barbed wire gesture to those historic stacked stones."

A timing light blinked on her broadcasting panel. "I see we need to take a break here for a word from a loyal Western Star sponsor. Stay tuned for a story that has a real howl to it." She switched on the commercial, tilting her head back to refocus.

"Thank you for The Fire Book pitch," Tara said. "We have to take a box of tissues into those interviews with us. The hurt's too fresh yet, but we're getting there."

"Good luck with that project. Maybe it will be part of the healing process around here. I forgot to ask earlier, but could you write down the number for a local real estate agent? I saw a sign on the apple orchard west of town and wanted to inquire."

A slow smile crept across the librarian's face. "Let me get that for you, Lyndie. Right now, you have another walk-in guest. It wouldn't hurt your listeners to connect with him again, as he might be building a fan base of his own." With a wink, she disappeared into the dark recesses of the room into the central atrium.

Lyndie glanced at the panel and found she had less than fifteen seconds to segue into an intro for her next guest. When she looked up, Burk stood in front of the table wearing a hundred-watt grin. Her pulse rocketed on impact.

"I have some new donation links your listeners might be interested in," he said. Mischief painted his eyes a lighter shade of green tonight, which clashed with a red stripe in his plaid shirt. He sat down in the guest chair and fixed the lapel microphone onto his shirt placard.

"Allow me a few lines to reintroduce you, and then I want you to lead in with the behind-the-scenes dog story. Nothing says recovery like a rancher who wants a dog on his hearth once again. That's gonna tug on some heartstrings. Save the donation plea for last."

He nodded and slapped the papers face down on the table.

The idea came from left field, but she like it so much, she had to do it. She took a sip of water as the timer clicked down to zero. "Next, we have a walk-in guest you're sure to enjoy, but allow me to adequately set the stage for him with what

I'll call a prelude to an American landscape." She hummed a few low notes, dropping the song a full-throated octave. "Shenandoah, I long to hear you, look away, you rolling river." When she sang the river's name again, her gaze flitted up to Burk's face. Handsome in the shadows, her low alto began to tremble under his magnetic influence. "We're bound away, across the wide Missouri." When the river's name came out as a broken whisper, she realized she was in trouble. A radio broadcaster needed a voice, and a current of fluid emotion had sucked hers right out.

He leaned in with a twinkle in his eyes. "Why, thank you Miss Lyndie Leigh. On behalf of all us bachelors who have to spend the weekend alone, we sure appreciate you crossing the river for us tonight with that song. It was mighty special."

Lyndie fought to recover. "Folks, I hope you remember the rancher from down Sitka way, Burk Crosby. Last week, he gave us his story about being trampled as the fire headed in his direction. Tonight, he's got another doggone good story for us. Here he is, at six feet two-plus inches, handsome in a red plaid shirt that turns his eyes into a shelterbelt of cedar, planted to protect a gal from the late winter wind out here on the shortgrass prairie."

He leveled his gaze at her, settling like granite against her personalized introduction. "This is a story about a man who thought he'd lost everything, only to find he had what really counted." The timbre of his voice held an audible sincerity.

Moved, Lyndie reached across the panel for him and slid her hand into his. A new realm of challenge, she had to maintain professional distance for the sake of the broadcast, while courting him on the sly. In the shadows, Tara backed away from the atrium as if to contribute to their privacy. Even the orange panels lining the room seemed to fade to a dusky shade of tolerable peach. Maybe the world looked like this when love's influence fell, all shadows and shades of velvet. She sure had a bad case, amazing in every aspect.

~

Burk skipped up the makeshift steps behind Cub, knowing he had no right to be here. For once, his opinion meter had run dry. Each prefab modular unit looked unremarkably like the last one, except the kitchens. The sink kept switching places with either the stove or refrigerator. Otherwise, they all held the same combination of appliances and workspace. He blew out a breath and entered the next living room. Trimmed in brown tones, it resembled a bachelor's pad.

"Don't let this one fool you," the slender salesman said. "It's understated, but functional. Just have a walk-through and find out for yourselves."

Cub cut a swath through the kitchen, around the angled island, and headed down the hall to check the bedroom area. "It's got a walk-in shower," he yelled. "I like the looks of that."

Burk faced the salesman. "He has an aging father to consider."

The man nodded. "Are you also in the market?"

"No, sir. The fire spared my ranch house, so I have a roof over my head. Tell me, do you have your own contractors come out to prep the foundation?"

"Yes, we do the setup prior to the shipping of the unit. There might be a few tricky curves between our sales lot and Ashland, but nothing we couldn't handle." He clicked his heels together like a huckster.

"Since Cub lives west of town up north by Clark County Lake, you could stay on the highway through Bucklin to approach the ranch that way. Don't knock the Bucklin grain elevator down as you come through with your wide load."

"Yeah, the road narrows through there, all right." He polished something off the kitchen counter with his sleeve.

Cub reentered the room, his arms floating out in midair. "I'm getting a good vibe on this one. I like the layout—a lot."

"Brown's handy for hiding dirt," Burk offered.

"You're right on that. Let me look at the kitchen again." He drifted over and pulled out a couple of drawers by the stove. "Everything works like a charm. How about that?" Cub chuckled and opened a cabinet over the microwave. It held a thick booklet, possibly the operator's manual.

"I wonder if this one's big enough," Burk added, sensing Cub might be serious.

"Three bedrooms at sixteen hundred square feet," the salesman replied.

"Plenty big." Cub tossed a dismissive gesture over his head. "Let me snap a few pictures around the bar, and then I'd like to look at your financial paperwork. I brought a personal check for my deposit today."

The salesman's face animated. "By all means, let's go talk numbers."

Burk chewed his cheek as Cub took his photos. He'd never had to replace his home before, but it seemed like a major commitment to hang on a mere five-minute inspection. Ill at ease for the rush-through, he turned and faced his best buddy. "Maybe tour through a second time, Cub—just for the sake of saying you did your homework. Think about Bear and whether he could access the rooms, that kind of thing."

He seemed momentarily struck at the prospect. "I'm not sure I can talk him into coming back. He didn't appreciate that power-of-attorney conversation yesterday, not one bit."

"That doesn't change matters. You need the ranch in *your* name."

The salesman scratched his head. "You can join me back in the office when you're ready. I'll get the paperwork situated while I wait." With a nod, he left the model.

"Listen, Burk. I've got the money set aside for this and need to get the ball rolling. I'm no gourmet cook, so this kitchen will do. My new TV will fit in the front corner there. Add a sofa plus maybe a chair and, boom—you have a ready-made ranch house."

"Okay, if you like this one the best, then go with it. I need to step out and make a call."

Cub made a dismissive noise and headed for the door. "You can't leave that woman alone for five minutes. What's gotten into you?"

"I'm not going to honor that sore comment with an answer," he replied, kicking the door further open. For late March, the weather was almost pleasant. He reached for his phone and checked for messages. Nothing popped up. After deciding to run by the fairgrounds the second he returned to Ashland, he strolled along the back of the sales lot, staring into a row of scraggly elms as though they held some mystic secret. *What a total waste of a morning.*

~

Despite the neglect, Lyndie counted eight apple trees in the orchard. Each one held the promise of spring blossoms on its branches. If March would relent to April, then the new season could gain traction. She'd move right along with the advance and revel in every apple blossom.

"Follow me through this tree line, and you'll see the old home site I referred to earlier," the real estate agent said. The squatty woman dodged a low branch and maneuvered south, away from the highway.

"Miss Bert, does the property include that house on the corner?" She pointed to the cluster of outbuildings spattered around a small home with shingle siding.

"No, that's an outparcel. Good thing, too. That house blocks the gas station across the street. You wouldn't want to look at that all the live-long day and night."

"I'm thinking this portion might make a nice park, so people could stroll down from the hospital and sit a spell under the shade of the old apple tree. It's scenic enough." She stepped around what looked like the rim of a discarded wagon wheel.

"That's a nice sentiment—almost like a song, isn't it?

That also tells me you're really evaluating the place for its best use. That's quite discerning of you. Here it is—the old homesite. See how the rose of Sharon shrubbery still outlines the former foundation?"

"So I see." Unfortunately, most of it lay in ruins, and was no longer fit for use—at least not immediately. Even to get the camper functional, she'd have to upgrade the driveway and have the electric lines restrung. Though a stretch for immediate occupancy, the orchard sure tugged at her heart. Too bad the whole thing sat right on the main highway into town.

"It gets cozier back here off Fifth Avenue," Bert said. "You can barely hear the traffic from Fourth Avenue when you're inside. Plus, the pony corral on Beech Street would be gone after the sale. Anything you built here would have great rental potential, with the hospital being so close by."

"Good point. I hadn't thought about possible rental potential as times goes by. If my situation changes, that could be my fall-back plan." She crossed her arms and began to turn in a full circle. "How much are they asking for the two acres?"

The agent took two steps to stand in the shade. "They're asking eighteen thousand, but I think that is way too high. You might offer fifteen, just to see if they want to sell or not."

Lyndie tried to imagine the tree canopies leafed out and blocking the neighbor on the west corner. With the corral cleared out to the east, she'd have practically the entire block for her home. The possibilities began to grow on her. "Okay, Bert. Make the seller an offer of fifteen thousand, and not a penny more. I'm interested, but in no mood to haggle. There are plenty of derelict houses in town. I could level one of those and build, so there's no shortage of options."

She clapped her hands. "I'll make the offer before I go to lunch. Let me call you Monday with their response."

"Fine. I need to get back to the distribution site anyway.

Thanks for working me into your schedule. Hey, if you haven't stopped at the new food truck in town, their wrapped sandwiches are fabulous." She began to retrace their path through the trees.

"Thanks for the tip. I need to return an overdue book across the street, so maybe I will."

Lyndie glanced fondly at the apple trees as she passed. "There's my new hobby—applesauce and cider-making." When the agent chuckled, she had to join her. With only fifteen thousand reasons why she couldn't, she decided right there on the spot that she would.

~

Burk cleared the clutter out of his throat and determined to make the best of the stop, despite the circumstances. "We're all doing what we can. I helped Rodney, and then he came down and helped Garrett. We had two crews working that day, and the Methodists gave Garrett a check for five grand standing right there on the old fence line. It's exhausting work that fencing, but every time I ride by town and see our little community intact, I know it's all worthwhile."

His audience shifted in the hospital bed, one side of his face frozen and the arm dangling useless by his side. The floor nurse assured Burk that the patient could hear every word and needed that kind of stimulation. Still, the man didn't look like a hero by the world's standards.

"There's not a one of us that's not beholden to you for what you did, Gene. Ashland stands today, and we've got you and the Almighty to thank for that. Old Milt Enoch had been pretty devastated, and Clint Hooper's been low, too. I can't imagine having to face the ranch losses if we'd have lost the town, too. It would have been too much, so thank you. Get your rest and work hard at that therapy, so you can come back home soon. We're looking forward to it."

"Are you 'bout ready?" Cub called from the hallway.

Burk stood, his nerves frayed. The wildfire wouldn't

defeat them. No, it would not.

~

Down to a depressing two bundles of fence posts and a diminishing mound of square hay bales, Lyndie sure could have done without this particular visit. The sheriff paced down the picked-over distribution line, determined for the encounter. The wind skipped across the fairgrounds headed for a more festive locale. Even a cattle-heavy stockyard would have merited that distinction today. They should have closed up earlier and gone about their lives.

The sheriff planted his boots in the dust. "Wish I didn't have to keep coming out here with bad news, but we've received another report of rogue fencing sales down in Ralston, Oklahoma. Same thing, fence posts, wire, and this time, it included fence clips. The tipster didn't buy, but he found out later a neighboring rancher did. Since their support is coming in slower down there, the market couldn't be riper."

Ken kicked at a misaligned stack of mineral tubs. "Riper for rip-off, you mean."

The truth burned like an electric fence, searing an unquestionable recognition in her mind. "With the inclusion of fence clips, it sure looks like we're the origin of the load."

The sheriff harrumphed. "It's your siphon, all right. You can count on him being back by Monday, restocking to make more profit off your freebies. I think it's high time you sober up to the fact that your lack of registration only serves to enable the greedy hiding among us. That gives you two days to figure out what you're going to do to counter the abuse. I want a list of suspect names by midweek."

Ken nodded and walked off, his expression pinched.

Lyndie held a staring contest with the lawman a brief second as heartburn churned. For the life of her, she couldn't figure out why their help had to come with such a stinger of hurt. She had the voucher checklist she could use if necessary, but it would incriminate those most in need. As the sheriff retreated, she prayed for a solution that wouldn't needlessly blame the victim.

Chapter 16

Burk couldn't escape the somberness of the conversation over the lunch table at Ken's house. He hadn't asked for more, but when Leslie plunked down another slice of meatloaf, he attacked it as a dodge. Church had been a stalwart attempt to shore up the faltering faithful, but with Old Man Enoch sobbing hopelessly from the back pew, it fell short of full success by a country mile.

"I can try to be nonchalant about recording." Lyndie toyed with the peas on her plate, until they stuck to a ridge of uneaten mashed potatoes. "Since the ranchers already experienced the voucher list, something similar probably wouldn't alarm anyone."

Ken grimaced and shook his head. "What a crummy mess this siphon has caused. With the sheriff clamping down on us for a list of suspects, I'm at a loss as to what else to do."

Burk took a sip of tea, trying not to let his reaction show. He hadn't realized the situation had escalated. Maybe Lyndie could update him after lunch. He cleared his throat. "I'm coming by again on Monday, as my cost estimate from Mr. Nichols drops if I can continue to provide the fencing supplies. Guess that places me as the number one suspect on your list."

Ken gave a dismissive whistle and threw his napkin across his plate. "No, you're not. Plus, I've got my spy planted right in your backyard, so I'd already know if it was you, Burk."

Lyndie pressed her napkin to her lips and turned three shades of red. She shifted her shoulders, causing her hair to fall across her face. Her last bite of lunch caught in her throat. To rectify matters, she reached for her water glass.

The blare of a semi's horn cut through the open windows along the enclosed front porch. Burk's gaze caught Ken's as his pulse hitched. When the horn went staccato, he rose from his chair. Only a block off of Main Street, it sounded like they had company of the big rig kind.

"Special delivery," Ken said, "the kind we desperately need."

Burk rose. "Let me drop you off on Main Street, Ken, and you can guide the trucker back to the fairgrounds."

"I'm in with you guys," Lyndie replied.

Ken kissed his wife's cheek and headed for the front door. "Thank goodness for incoming traffic."

"Yes, thank the Good Lord," Lyndie echoed.

Burk held the door open and bumped shoulders with her all the way to the truck. When she finally graced him with a glance, he fed her a wink for dessert. In no time, they sat by the Bingo sign straddling Main Street as a big rig rumbled toward them. The first truck had a close shadow, and the next truck bore a string of shadows.

"A convoy," Lyndie said, her tone airy.

Once it appeared that the full length of Main Street would fill with laden semis, Burk let the wonderment run rampant through his frame. Goosebumps tightened the skin up his left arm. He reached for his light switch and flashed the headlights a few times. The lead truck signaled back and rolled to a stop. To his utter amazement, the driver was a woman.

Ken exploded out of the cab and trotted to meet her. "Welcome to Ashland! We're mighty glad to see you today."

The driver's face animated. "I've driven all the way from Michigan. The rest are from various parts of the upper Midwest. Let's get to unloading so we can have a look around and see what the wildfire left standing."

Lyndie clapped in support. "We'll meet you down at the fairgrounds, Ken."

"Call Tara and get some unloading help lined up," he replied. "Ma'am, I'll ride your running board and show you the way. Main Street hasn't seen this much traffic since the last cattle drive went through. Yee-hi!"

Burk let the distribution coordinator's jubilation crank up his enthusiasm a notch or two. Once Lyndie had gotten back into the cab, he shot her a loaded look. "Looks like our give-away committee just got a magnanimous boost."

"Yes indeed." She fastened her seatbelt and shifted the console down between them.

Sensing the need to break formation, he pumped the gas and took a side street past downtown. At the first stop sign, he caught her arm and locked gazes. "We hereby dedicate today to generosity—and forget the distrust fueled by the unidentified siphon." Prompted by the need to catch up, he let her go and whipped the steering wheel to head south.

Lyndie twisted her hair into a ponytail. She snapped a band around it and busied her hands tying a knot in the hem of her long skirt. "Will there ever be another day like this? I mean, one with so many gifts waiting to be opened."

He looked at her and let a smile warm his expression. Only one other day might come close. On that day, the bells would ring from the church tower to celebrate two hearts becoming one. He didn't know how to arrive at that commendable spot. Right now, he had a fence post thief and a sidecar of half-tended apples to outmaneuver.

~

Lyndie had to shake off the heebie-jeebies when the first

semi opened its trailer to reveal a load of replacement ammunition. Memories of the herd devastation came flooding back like a tidal wave. A warm hand steadied the small of her back and she glimpsed Burk crossing behind to get a foot up on the rear loading platform.

"Ammo—it seemed crazy to me at first mention," the woman driver said. "But the donors heard about the ranchers and wildlife officers running out of bullets when so many cows had to be mercy-killed. I think some hunting club sent these."

"I'm Lyndie Leigh Sessoms, a volunteer. We need whatever you've hauled in, because some folks are starting over from bare ground."

"I'm Barb King out of Grand Rapids. The other half of my trailer is filled with hay bales, so we'll need a loader of some sort."

"Sure, we keep a tractor over by the bale stack. Let me ask Ken, but he'll likely want you to pull over there once we get the ammo boxes cleared." Lyndie looked up to see Burk pass the top crate to Cody Collier who had answered their call for help. She'd have to thank Mandy later for sparing her hubby for the massive unloading task. Two other broad-backed men joined the crew. The sound of air brakes filled the fairgrounds as the big rigs crept up the distribution line.

"Oh, wow. What's in these wooden crates?" Cub's inquisitive expression made him look about twelve years old.

"Bullets, shotgun shells, and whatnot," Barb replied, "sent from Michigan straight to Kansas. We've been on the road for fifteen hours just to get here."

Cub tipped the brim of his baseball cap at her and elbowed the man with him to climb onto the rig. "Lyndie and Barb, meet my cousin Heath. He's taken me in, for the time being."

"This is Cub Haines," Lyndie explained, "one of those ranchers in the north county who lost everything when the wildfire boomeranged back on us."

"Oh, how horrible, Cub. I'm sorry to hear about your loss." Barb's graying brow knit again. "Will you rebuild?"

Cub hesitated to respond while catching the first crate from Heath. He grunted on impact and quickly looked for a place to set it down. "Yes, ma'am. I ordered a modular house yesterday, using the Clark County Proud voucher for my down payment." A whistle echoed from the trailer, calling him back to the task.

Lyndie seized the opportunity to guide Barb down the supply line so she could see how the distribution worked. "We can load two trucks at a time, if necessary. Some days are like that, and other days, business trickles in. Fortunately, the ranchers are beginning to hire outside contractors for the fence work, thanks to the first bank voucher distribution we held on Thursday."

"It's amazing to see what a pulse of cash flow can do for recovery work," Barb replied. "Guess I better get back in my rig and wait for my signal to pull up. Tell Burk to give a whistle when they've got the ammo cleared."

"There's plenty of parking here for the convoy after the trucks are unloaded. We hope you'll stick around. We can line up a tour of the county for anyone wanting to see what the fire left us." Lyndie nodded north, hoping they'd have some time to catch up.

"Believe me, the last thing we want to do is get back on that highway," Barb teased. "Now, if there was a restaurant nearby, that might be handy after a short while."

"We've got a new portable dinner store taking up residence in Ashland. Let me work some magic to see if it's available." She tossed a wave as the woman headed to the cab. Spying Cub working just below Burk, she stepped closer to the unloading team. "Hey, Cub. I need to ask you a personal question. Do you have Brooke's phone number, by any chance? The truckers might need a dinner delivery, and I wanted to check on her availability."

A grin flitted across his face. "Why, it just so happens I *do* have Brooke's phone number. Give me a few minutes to get these last crates stacked, and I'll bring it up for you."

"Perfect." Her tentative plan started falling into place.

Burk shook his head from inside the trailer. "Somebody's about to meddle where they don't belong."

"Nonsense. The truckers might need dinner later after the unloading, and I wanted to see if Wrappers on Wheels could come out here. That's all." She shrugged her shoulders with a prickle of indignation. "Hey, Barb asked for a whistle when you guys get done unloading the ammo. I'm going to wander down the line and see if Ken needs my help."

About the time she found Ken, Garrett Guard arrived with a posse of muscular men, all willing to help. She stood back and watched as a team of plaid-wearing laborers set about the task with a competent readiness. Hard work was no stranger here, a recognition that stitched the community a little tighter to her heart. With the distribution piles stacked high, she could hardly wait until Monday. What a difference a convoy of caring made. *God bless America.*

~

"Some day of rest," Burk confessed, leaning forward on the sofa so Lyndie could reach his lower back. Tighter than a drum, he should have eased off the fence posts earlier and helped align the hay. Two bales of that Indiana hay came home with him, a welcome addition. He'd helped Cub load his hay, too, which earned him a tasty square of carrot cake from Brooke's food truck. "Hey, turns out I was wrong about bringing Brooke into the fairgrounds. She had a strong day, and the truckers got fed. My humble apology goes out to my masseuse."

"Wait. You have to look me in the eye when you say something as meaningful as that." She flipped across the back of the sofa and tucked her knees up in her arms. "Now, tell me I was right again, so I can enjoy seeing your contrite expression."

He laughed and caught a tendril of hair between his fingers. "You're better than I am at all this networking stuff. I'm good at being a solitary rancher. Living out on the edge keeps me isolated from having to connect so much."

"I think that's part of what the wildfire is changing about Clark County ranchers. Your independence blew away with all that black ash, which left the bare ground of your heart to deal with the catastrophe. God's helping you sprout the new blades of grass that will keep the shortgrass prairie alive for the next decade. It's called the spirit of cooperation."

Her words sounded like a caress to him, so level and reassuring. He bent to better study the blue pools of her eyes. "Funny you should mention that, as it doesn't seem so lonesome out here anymore." He took more of her hair into his hand and enjoyed the silky sensation.

"Not to outright shock you, but I put an offer on the apple orchard along the west side of town. I'm supposed to hear back tomorrow if they accept. By the end of April, I could have power hooked up for my camper out there. Then I could tend my fruit trees."

He lowered until he could almost feel her eyelashes fanning his face. "Who's going to be tending me?" His inquiry brought a smile, magnetic at this close range.

"I honestly didn't know a young rancher like you needed such a high level of tending."

"This is a whole new rodeo you've got to learn, Miss Sessoms." He shook his head, mainly to brush his lips ever so subtly across hers.

"Aren't you sweet to play the teacher?" Her honeyed whisper begged a response.

Burk brought the day of rest to where it should have been, a place of togetherness.

~

Sad but true, none of this altruistic community involvement made his business any money. The banker paced behind the desk, staring at his diminutive guest. Her latest idea held the scant benefit of a feel-good gesture. He couldn't charge interest on that.

"Don't worry. I'll line up the speakers," Miss T said. "We'll give an ovation to the volunteer fire department members and invite the chief to say a few words."

"Where are you thinking to hold the service? An outdoor spot would be subject to the weather. You know how fickle spring can be." Tired of pacing, he sat down in his leather chair. By all signs, it would be a slow Monday.

"I think the high school cafeteria is the best we can do. We're inviting the entire community. I'm not too sure about the food, but whatever's brought will have to be enough. An ecumenical service will rally the residents and help us support the ranchers at the same time. We're all in this together. That convoy arriving yesterday has revitalized the foundation's efforts at the fairgrounds. We can ride that momentum to carry off the community-wide event."

He wiped across his face, trying to reframe the request. "Let's have a donation bin at the event. We should give community members every opportunity to contribute to the relief effort."

"Would this be an appropriate venue to thank the high-level supporters?"

"No, I have several who want to remain anonymous. Better to tout it as an every-man event and build rapport for Clark County Proud. Maybe Ken should speak for the Ashland Foundation."

"Right. I'll put Ken on the agenda. I heard that Gene Shawboro is coming home midweek. He can't talk yet, but he would be a sight for sore eyes if he could muster the strength to attend." She gave him an imploring look.

He wiped a hand over his desk to brush away the sentimental suggestion. They needed strong men who could handle speaking roles. A stroke victim hardly met the criteria. "Let me think about who we should add. Right now, I have a bank to run. I'd better get busy."

She stood and closed her notebook, clamping it against her ribs. "The Kansas Farm Bureau allocations should come in by the end of the month. That will help."

"Not today's ledger, it won't," he quipped. People had no sense about making the day profitable, he realized as he walked her to the door. No, that was his job, though the wildfire had dealt him a wicked blow. He waved goodbye without meaning it, numb for so early in the day.

~

Lyndie picked up the clipboard and made a checkmark by Cub's name. Ken helped Burk load his fence posts so he could get the contractor started this morning at the upper pasture. The week had a feeling of positive traction to it. Every rancher in the county knew about the convoy, thanks to Tara. If they gave away the new haul by midweek, what would be the harm? Fences were going up all over the county, making for a giant quilting party using metal thread. Large-scale patchwork had a beauty to it, plus it held the cattle in the right pasture.

She exhaled, thinking about the ranch tour later. Ken had two dual-cab pickups lined up to take the truckers around to see the sights. Her throat constricted when she remembered that Englewood would be included. The power poles had been replaced, but most of the recovery out there involved bulldozer work to bury all the charred remains. No one had plans to rebuild.

Someone approached so close that it startled her. She looked up to see Burk glancing at the checklist with disapproval. She rested a hand on her chest to still her heart.

"Well, I've got my load." His lips pulled thin as he looked out over the horizon. "Guess if you're putting Cub down, you might as well record me, too. Maybe I'm the siphon's sidekick."

She flattened the clipboard against her chest so he couldn't see the list. "Don't be ridiculous."

He shook his head. "Ranchers sure need these supplies,

but we don't need the suspicion that comes with it." He gave her a deflated look and headed back to his truck.

She should have replied with something upbeat, instead of letting him go dejected like that. Maybe they could have supper together and talk about it rationally. Her phone pinged with an incoming message, leaving her to fumble with the clipboard. When Burk pulled away, she didn't have a free hand to wave. She blew out her frustration and glanced at the screen.

Offer accepted! You now own an apple orchard.

She put the clipboard down to type in a reply to go ahead with the transaction. Maybe she needed some space. Burk could come court her the old-fashioned way where they could stroll arm-in-arm through her orchard. Somehow, the prospect didn't buoy her mood like it should have. Fifteen thousand dollars didn't purchase peace of mind, no matter how many bushel baskets you could fill with apples.

After typing the message, she took up the clipboard and studied the recordkeeping. In a willful act, she decided not to place a check by the name "Burkett N. Crosby." She realized that she didn't even know what his middle initial stood for. That began to bother her like a pebble in her shoe. What a mystery she could let something as trivial as that get to her. She never cared for intrigue and half-known situations, not the slightest bit.

Her phone rang, and she hastened to answer it in case it held an ounce of redemption. The gruff chuckle she heard next was unmistakable. Her hopes dropped into the pit of her stomach.

"Hey Lyndie. Bet you didn't think you'd hear from me this spring."

"Hey Ernie. What's up in the rodeo world?" She pinched the bridge of her nose. At best, she could make quick work of her manager's call and free up to help the driver of the burgundy truck pulling into the fairgrounds.

"Well, in short, we've got a calamity of major

proportions. The Strong City rodeo is coming up Thursday through Saturday and their headline entertainer, little Misty Mariposa, is down with that kissing sickness. I can't remember what it's called."

"Do you mean mono?"

"Yeah, I think that's it. Glad I'm not her manager, as that might not be so easy for the fans to forget. Anyway, the event manager sent out an SOS saying they'd pay top dollar to get a replacement filled in because of such short notice. I wasn't too sure how your community service might be going, but maybe you could take a break and come lend them a hand."

"I don't know about that, Ernie. My heart's about a million miles away from the circuit right now." She took a breath and put the clipboard back in the chair. The burgundy truck stopped on the far side of the distribution lane. When the driver exited, a three-legged dog hopped out. Her mouth fell open in disbelief, seeing the canine legend in real life.

"Seriously, Lyndie. This could earn you some big points. These event managers compare notes. If you bail this guy out of his tight spot, it's all gain, I can assure you."

One thing she knew, she couldn't accept the job at face value. No, there had to be some charitable component in there for the wildfire victims. The dog skirted around the post pile, sniffing for hidden morsels. Well, she had a nose for hidden tidbits, too. "Listen, Ernie. You tell Strong City that they have Lyndie Leigh Sessoms for a limited return performance, but I have a few extra conditions that must be met. We're going to hold an auction each night because I need to raise some money. And I'm not talking, 'Aw shucks, here's five dollars for your pity bucket.'"

"That's my spitfire Lyndie, getting back in the saddle again," he replied with a cackle. "We'll get 'em to do it your way, honey. I'll make that call right away."

Lyndie watched the dog wander down the loading lane, handicapped yet fully capable at the same time. Yes, there would be puppies bred this spring, and she would have the

farewell tour of the century, down to her flaming red boots—
which she'd sell without remorse to the lucky highest bidder.

Chapter 17

For a harmless Tuesday, everything felt rough as a cob. Burk had to leave the fencing contractor on his own to return to the distribution center for more supplies. He spat out the truck window when he saw the waiting line had backed up to the entrance. Noticing two semis were headed for the unloading area, he cut the engine and hopped out to expedite matters.

Several trucks ahead, he spotted a familiar burgundy club cab and headed for it. After assessing the rancher's under-aged passenger, he conceded it might not matter. "Hey Rodney. I'm going to help unload these big rigs, so we can keep the lines moving. Would your helper there be willing to move my truck up if the line advances? I'd be much obliged."

"Sure thing, Burk," Rodney replied. "Afterwards, if you're in any mood for company, maybe we could swap out the dog for a couple of days. I need him back by the weekend." A snout appeared over the man's shoulder that seemed to indicate willingness.

"I'd like that. Maybe I could pick up some dog food while in town." He wiped his face to refocus. "It's been a long time since I ventured down that aisle."

Rodney nodded as the teenage boy hopped out of the cab

to become his driver. "Maybe too long. Let's see if we can get on about this puppy-making business." The corner of his lips turned up, resembling a smile.

Burk thumped his hand on the rancher's hood in solidarity as he headed for the front of the line. He soon located Lyndie, shed of her denim jacket and working feverishly like the rest. He tapped her shoulder and stepped into the unloading sequencing, cutting her off without a word. The next item out of the trailer happened to be a water tank. By all rights, they needed a tractor, but there was little room to operate and no time to figure it out. Between the eight men, they slid it over to the outside of the loading lane and left it in a cloud of grit for the claiming.

Ken appeared from inside, kicking a wad of burlap sacks out of his way. "Let's get to the other truck, fellas. Hey, Burk. Thanks for joining in. That tank weighed a heifer and a half."

Burk reached with a helping hand to aid his descent. As he turned toward the other truck, he spotted Lyndie making her way down the waiting line, the clipboard in her hand. Gritting his teeth, he wouldn't consider any of those good men her culprit. Check marks weren't meant to be a seal of acceptable character. At the rate his contractor could burn through fencing supplies, the Crosby name would bear a check daily until the job ended. *So be it.* He remained the same God-fearing man, checked off or not.

Good fortune followed, as the second truck contained only thirty barbed wire spools, with the remainder of the load in hay bales. Ken tossed him a pair of leather gloves. They formed a snaky fire brigade and tossed the wire spools down the line until the wire could be stacked in the right location. Several of those would wind up at his place. In fact, he'd carry two back to his truck as he returned, one on each hip.

Breathing hard as he made his exodus, he soon caught up to Lyndie. "Hey, Rodney's loaning me Chip for a few days. I need to stop by the grocery store for dog food. Want anything else?"

She flattened the clipboard against her shoulder. "I'll be late. I have to take down the antenna at the library, since I'll be broadcasting on the road this Friday. You choose dinner."

He hesitated, breaking his gait. "What? You're going somewhere?" The wire spools started getting a touch heavy.

Lyndie puffed her hair out of her face. "Yes, the Strong City rodeo, starting Thursday. It's a three-day event. I'm stepping in at the last minute for a sick performer. Guess I'll have to do the radio broadcast from their media booth Friday night."

He tried to rein it in, but couldn't freeze the shock off his face in time. Forcing his eyebrows to lower, he improved his grip and grunted. "Guess you would have told me at some point before pulling out of my barnyard." Too proud to stand there with his ego bruised, he headed straight to the truck. He nodded to dismiss the teenage driver and managed to hoist a wire spool onto the tailgate before his wrist went completely numb. After two-handing the second spool, he shoved them both forward and retook the driver's seat.

Since he'd been fifteen years old, his world always fell into place as long as he sat behind the wheel of his truck. Today should be no different, except for the light-haired, blue-eyed woman up yonder forcing her clipboard ways on all the local ranchers. They all seemed immune, but somehow he fell susceptible to her feminine influence. Now that she'd announced her departure, where did that put him? *Left behind.* The line inched forward, and he eased up on the brakes, allowing the truck to creep right into her vicinity.

~

Definitely on her heels from his hurt-little-boy look, Lyndie's mind raced as to what to do about Burk. With so many onlookers, an exchange of affection seemed out of the question. Besides, she didn't need to resort to tactile placation when words would do the trick. After checking in Rodney Gillian, she continued down the waiting line to force the encounter.

Her next two stops became a perfunctory prelude to the direct encounter with Burk. She checked the second man's name off without a reply. Catching the omission in time, she nodded politely and tucked the pen into her back pocket. *A drink of water would sure hit the spot.*

She approached the next partially open window with guarded expectancy. "Burk N. Crosby?"

He turned slowly to face her, his expression too complex to read.

She needed to get him to open up some. Maybe chit-chat would ease the situation. "What does the 'N' stand for?" Dropping the clipboard out of sight, she hoisted a brow in expectation of an answer. Truck brakes hissed over by the hay bales, slicing the silence.

"Not…the…siphon," he replied with an elongated drawl.

She ran her tongue over the back of her teeth, a move her mother had taught her to quell any regrettable knee-jerk retort. "I was going to tell you about Strong City—"

"When? As you were pulling out of my gate?" His tone escalated with the second comment, full of hurt feelings and questioning motives.

Her knees began to quake, so she widened her stance. "I have some business to finish."

"Like what?" He rubbed across his brow, breaking his gaze.

"I need to sell my horse, for one. There are other open-ended matters I need to bring to a close. It's my farewell tour." When a sharp horn blared behind them, she noticed the line had moved up. She stood away from his truck to set him free of her hindrance.

"Sure feels like a farewell tour," he repeated, his tone bone-dry. Without a final glance in her direction, he pulled up a truck length and didn't look back.

Though she'd wanted to ask about dinner—or at least

offer a time she'd be home—the sting in her eyes wouldn't allow her to close the insufferable distance between them. *Good Lord above, what just happened?*

She stepped toward the road and soon discovered Cub leaning on his horn for the fun of it. She checked Jacobi Haines off her list, wanting to add a hangman's noose to the upturned mark. In two days, she'd be gone from western Kansas. The siphon could run wild and free in her absence. *What do I care?* Maybe she should take the long road back.

~

This time, the banker distrusted the visit. Donors never gave twice, not to his recollection. In an attempt not to make the rancher more ill at ease, he perched on the corner of his desk. "This time surely you've come about moving forward with the real estate deal."

"No, not here for a loan." The tall man hunched forward and feigned a cough. "The truth is…accepting the allotment didn't sit right with me. You know the wildfire spared my place. I only had to replace one fence line. Compared to the others, that cost proved trifling."

"So what? You don't want to use your voucher right now? Fine, then reinvest it. Many have chosen to save it for a rainy day, as we say in the banking business."

The man scooted to the edge of the seat as if not to be dismissed. "I'm donating the voucher amount back to the foundation, at least this first round. Should I find myself getting behind later, I might be more open to the second allocation."

He grimaced at the idea. "You're an outright fool. There might not be a second disbursement. Don't be so shortsighted. There's no trophy in life for just barely getting by."

The man stood and pulled the voucher out of his breast pocket. "I've signed the back, so you can deposit it to the Ashland Foundation. The mural out front shows red in the collection column which means the total's climbing toward the ceiling again, just like it should. I'll stick to my convictions today and ask for your help to make the deposit." He placed the voucher slip on the desk blotter and tipped the brim of his hat back in a farewell gesture.

Noncompliance trickled a bead of sweat down his neck. Somehow, his control of the situation appeared to be slipping. His subversive scheme planned out the windfall with utmost care, if everyone else would just cooperate.

The man hesitated at the door. "By the way, I'll not be doing any more of your runs."

"Don't even speak of it, as I don't claim to know what you're talking about." His sharp tone alienated the uncooperative man from his presence. Glad to be shed of him, he slunk into the chair with a clenched gut, thinking three moves ahead. He'd have to bring the drunk man back on, a desperate option—but one for which he held considerable leverage.

The abandoned voucher stared back at him, a noble talisman. Alas, he had no patience for nobility, not in this business. With big funds headed their way from the Farm Bureau and the livestock association, the bank would bog down with the paperwork for the transfer to ranchers while he invested millions in the market. He would skim off the cream to pocket it—a fitting analogy for personal gain if it weren't for the region's solid reputation for beef cattle, not dairy.

~

Burk could have written the familiar script. After all, he'd recently fallen for it himself. The male heeler took right to the female at first introduction. Together, they guarded the fence crew as it progressed toward the cemetery. After half an hour of cooperative existence, Chip walked close enough to Babe that her sturdy haunches helped keep his three-legged gait more balanced. Everything became a shared explore—two dogs in motion together instead of one.

On a water break, he kicked at the mud flap thinking

back to Lyndie's celebration of the grass sprouting on a morning not too long ago. She'd been content to roll under the fence with him and touch the miracle right by his side. An updated assessment reflected a lovesick rancher left behind for the lure of something more glitzy—a world with which he couldn't compete. He quenched his thirst with a long drink, but water couldn't remedy everything.

"Burk—bring up more posts," Conroy called between cupped hands.

He gestured back and slid off the tailgate. Work would make him feel rooted again in a world tipped over by the charm of a beautiful woman, one he couldn't get off his mind.

~

Lyndie wrung her hands as she sat at the library table. No longer compelled to rush out to Burk's ranch, she took a breath and decided to lay matters out for the honest librarian. A quiet confidante made sense. Maybe talking about the fallout would help. "A situation has arisen out at the distribution site. A dark cloud now hangs over the generosity that once prevailed, something I'm not terribly fond of having to handle."

"You can tell me as much as you want," Tara replied. Her eyes held an indescribable kindness. The empty public building shrank to their table.

"Since we're tasked with giving away the donated materials, we've been doing so without restraint. If we have supplies in stock, we can give some to anyone who drives up. Ken knows practically everyone, so we operated liberally, spreading the generosity of others."

Her crown of graying hair nodded. "And you did it kindheartedly, like the Bible says."

Lyndie stretched in the stiff chair, curving her neck back as she contemplated the comment. "I experienced so much joy from the distribution. To connect with the hurting like that, and be part of the solution—helped me find my true calling. I came in search of a deeper life…and I found it at the fairgrounds in little Ashland, Kansas."

Tara hummed. "I suppose that's when you began to fall in love with Burk Crosby, when altruistic deeds set your heart free."

She snapped forward as if being caught in a trap. "In love with Burk?"

"I sat several rows above you at the basketball game. That's when I first took notice. A woman under a mere infatuation doesn't react like that. Plus, a flighty woman hunts around for more sweet affection on the cheap, which you didn't."

Lyndie flattened her palms on the table. "From Day One—there was Burk and the burned-up prairie. I couldn't separate the two as they both began to mean something special to me, the man and the land. That part didn't seem like trouble. Quite the opposite, in fact."

"Take me back to the fairgrounds. You've had plenty of donations to distribute, yet there's still so much need."

"The need creates the never-ending demand for supplies, and that's what birthed the demon. An unknown party takes truckloads of fencing supplies and sells them for personal profit at locations around the fringe of the fire damage. Sheriff Waller shared that he'd been getting hints of illegal activity over the tip line, so he cranked down on Ken, demanding a registration. I understood he needed a list of suspects to narrow down the suspects, so when we had the sign-off list for the vouchers, we began to check off recipients as they came through the line."

"That must be agony for Ken. He's generous to a fault. That's why he insisted on starting up the Ashland Foundation in the first place." She rubbed her thumb across her eyebrow, as if the hurt threatened to spread.

"The heaviness of suspicion snuffs out the buoyant spirit of generosity—"

"So one bad apple spoils it for the whole bunch. I've seen

it happen time and again here at the library. One talkative child will ruin it for the rest, but after the hushing correction, I try to loosen the restraint to return the atmosphere to something more positive."

"Sheriff Waller calls the perpetrator a siphon. In his opinion, we enable the siphon by not structuring the distribution with more rigid parameters. He wants limits per day and demands a registration. Unable to see any way out once the siphon's activity increased, I caved and agreed to check off participants from the voucher list. Resolute, Ken would have nothing to do with it."

The librarian broke off her gaze, fingering a scratch on the table. "That doesn't make you a traitor, Lyndie. I hope your leaving has nothing to do with the sheriff's pressure to comply."

"No. I would call it a happenstance, but still, God is using it to test me. The performance will be my farewell appearance on the rodeo circuit. I took advantage of the manager's precarious position to leverage a few community service favors, if you will. Since the three-day commitment spans Friday, I'll need to make my Western Star broadcast from there."

"What am I missing? I see the sadness in your eyes that a nameless siphon doesn't explain. Is there another unsettled matter?"

Lyndie grabbed her forehead, wanting to hide. "Burk got...touchy regarding the registration. He said that the suspect list faulted the ranchers who needed help the most. His best friend Cub Haines usually comes through twice a day. When I brought that up, Burk reacted in a huff and demanded to be checked off just like Cub, so they'd both make the suspect list." Her throat constricted as she recalled the confrontation.

Tara leaned forward. "He's not picking his best friend over you, Lyndie. Because there's been some instability out at the Haines ranch, Burk plays big brother to Jacobi rather than best friend sometimes."

"Nothing makes me feel more like an outsider than being treated like a Johnny-come-lately that doesn't have any real stake in the matter. I'm the newest citizen of Ashland, as I just purchased the old apple orchard on the west side of town."

"I trust that means you're coming back," she replied, her tone calming. "I have an opening on my Friends of the Library board. It would benefit us to have someone in the broadcast industry serve in that capacity. We need a vision for our future. I'd like you to consider the offer and let me know. We meet again in two weeks."

"Let me get past this weekend, Tara. When the dust settles after this change of direction, maybe all of this community involvement will make more sense."

"Sure thing. I'll come hold the ladder while you get that antenna down." She rose and headed for the door.

Once she stood, Lyndie felt somewhat lighter. She'd shared her burden and received some encouragement in exchange. She doubted that scenario would be repeated back at the Crosby ranch, her next destination.

Tara bumped shoulders with her as they walked outside. "Don't let a lawless man dampen your spirits, honey."

"No, an upright man has managed to do that, though right now he's leaning out of kilter more than this ladder will be." She sighed and stooped to pick up the aluminum frame.

"I'll pray he leans toward you, then, when everything is said and done." She gripped the ladder and helped position the rungs beneath the antenna.

"Please pray for me at the Strong City rodeo. Like basketball players are fond of saying, I plan to leave it all on the court. Plus, I'm auctioning the very shirt off my back." They exchanged glances as she hoisted up the ladder to put herself out on a limb.

Truth occurred to her as she climbed. When stepping too far out for anyone else to help, the long arms of God provide the only safety net. *Help me, Lord. Precariously yours, Lyndie Leigh.* The antenna detached at first tug, its weight almost knocking her off the upper rung.

Chapter 18

Burk knew it wouldn't be an ordinary evening at home, not with the way he'd spoken to Lyndie at the fairgrounds. He stirred the frying pan contents and looked at the combination he'd tossed together in mild disgust. Even though her truck had pulled in over an hour ago, she hadn't graced him with her presence yet.

The dog grumbled from a nearby rug.

"I'm not saying I don't deserve the cold shoulder. My problem is that I've let some vague evil intent overshadow the good in my life. The Lord said there would be trouble in this world, but I guess I don't have to explain that to a three-legged dog."

His canine companion made a noisy yawn in return.

"That used to be my life, before she came along. A boring man on the fringe of nowhere—and I laughably thought I was happy." When the food stuck to the pan, he cut off the burner. A plastic tub in the dish drain seemed to offer a solution. "Okay, one carry-out order on tap. If she won't come to me, then I'll go to her." He split the pan's contents into two portions and shoveled one serving into the container.

The dog bounded to its feet as he left the kitchen. Its tail thumped the bar, begging the invitation. Trained to heel, it stood motionless.

"Come, Chip," he called from the rear hall. He popped open the back door and held it for his acquired companion. "Maybe you'll earn me some attaboy points. Turn up that canine charm." Instead of traipsing along beside him, the dog ventured off and soon watered a pole.

Burk studied the light shining from the camper window and thought he saw a figure cross in a hurry. He cleared his throat trying to be ready to meet the tempest inside the tin can, with the hope he could match momentum with an angry woman. He brought food and a dog—about all he could offer her right now. He blew out a tense breath and knocked on the door.

Lyndie appeared in the open doorway looking a touch startled. Chip rushed up the steps to make himself at home. She blocked the dog's entry with her knee, bending to pet its head.

He lifted the container for her inspection. "I brought you dinner."

"Oh, guess I got a little busy in here and lost track of the time." She reached for the container with both hands. Unblocked, the dog nudged the door open and went right in.

One glimpse at the scene inside became his undoing. Glittery costumes and fancy accessories sat in piles on every available surface, evidencing her serious pack-up mode. The reality landed on his chest like a round hay bale, heavy and awkward.

After some pleasant cajoling, Lyndie returned with her fingers wrapped around Chip's collar. "Here's your mascot, Burk. Sorry, I don't have an inch of space left for entertaining him right now."

His gaze skittered back to her face. "I, uh, can see why. Okay, it's a dinner drop-off without a tip tonight. So be it." He grabbed for the dog and drew it down the steps to depart. He'd couch his damaged ego by keeping farewells short and sweet. "Have a good one." Once he'd stepped outside of the camper's glaring light, his blood pressure began to drop a bit.

"Say," Lyndie called, leaning from the doorway. "Would you happen to have any boxes? You know, gift boxes about so big?" She gestured a width a little less than her shoulders.

He nodded. "Probably. There's some heaped up in the rear bedroom closet. Help yourself." He continued back to the ranch house, but let the dog's wandering slow him down. Maybe she would take that as a courtesy, like he had waited for her. The image of how the two dogs had walked alongside each other popped to mind. Such strength-lending-strength shouldn't be avoided, if the opportunity availed itself. Guilt nudged his ribs.

Lyndie jogged up beside him. "Thanks for waiting up. I'm running out of minutes in this day. What a pistol."

He reached for the knob on the back door. "Bang, bang."

"Did you notice? I got the antenna back on the camper. I'm all set to roll."

With her gypsy sentiment knifing him in the back, he pushed the door open and led the way inside instead of being the gentleman. Afraid he'd speak his blunt mind, he headed up the hall in silence. He turned for the spare bedroom and flicked on the lights. *What a mess!*

Lyndie followed him inside and made a tiny gasp.

"Ignore all that, I'll get around to straightening up. The Christmas stuff stays over here." Kicking a pile of magazines under the bed frame, he cleared a walking path. He shoved open the sliding closet door and revealed a similar mess, only this one stacked in vertical disarray.

"There, I see several boxes," Lyndie said. "Can you hold up that storage bin on top and let me get to them?"

He answered with a grunt, shuffling his feet closer so he could attempt the lift. "Come over here and get ready to take them."

Lyndie shifted under his arm and put her hands on the stack of boxes. "Okay, go for it."

"Let the record show, I'm aiding and abetting your pack-up, although that doesn't seem to be in my best interest." He heaved the storage bin and held it up for a five-count.

Lyndie snatched the flattened boxes out and began to count. Slipping them onto the bed, she returned and patted his arm. "One more time, please."

Without removing his grip from the container, he wiped his face across his sleeve and looked at her. All the feminine attributes that brought him pleasure began to swarm him at close range. "I…I'm not sure I can." He dropped his arms and rotated his shoulders to pull out of the lightheaded spell.

"You've probably overdone it working today." She patted his back like she'd petted the dog earlier. "Go put your feet up after I leave."

He took hold of the container again and drew a deep breath to fuel the exertion. In the quiet of the moment, his muddled thoughts focused on a profound truth. He'd be a lesser man if he didn't express it. "After you leave, the world goes flat lonesome for me again. You'll be the sweetheart at center stage, but I'll be bankrupt behind the scenes." He rubbed his chin on his flannel sleeve, wishing the heartache would ease up a notch.

Lyndie hummed a sympathetic note for a brief second. Inching inside the closet, she ducked his arm. "I'll only be gone three days. Just think about me, Burk. My heart to yours, we'll still be connected." She looked up through her lashes.

"Better remind me how that goes, because I'm drawing an honest-to-God blank here." He searched her face for any sign of willingness and must have flat-out missed her gradual approach in his sorry state. Only when her lips skimmed his chin did he snap out of it.

He scraped his stubble across her cheek. Dropping his arms around her back, he transferred affection's fire to her lips and held it there for prolonged burn. With arms clasped around each other, only her pending departure marred the moment. By the second kiss, his heartache surrendered to an abridgement that came dampened by her tears, a pain-against-pleasure mix he'd have to cope with for survival while separated. *Three days feels like thirty.*

~

The banker gave a stern look at the early-bird guests sitting across from him. They hadn't even given him time to read the newspaper online this morning, let alone have his coffee. Some succinct treatment would be in order, to regain the regularity of his day. "How may I help you both this morning?"

The old man straightened his stooped frame. "We were having a cherry cola at the drug store soda fountain yesterday when we heard tell that the foundation fund is rebuilding. A cowboy mentioned that Milt Enoch can't get any water to his herd out west by the Krier pasture because his windmill burned to the ground. My grandson researched the cost of a new one from an outfit in Meade, so here's a check for that amount to the foundation."

"I can only put this in the general fund for the foundation. Ken hasn't set up a means to designate recipients within that collection." He held up his hands to be shed of the complication.

The old man stood and helped his fragile wife join him. With a thumb through his suspenders, he turned toward the desk. "For a man who built his reputation by putting money where the best gain is, you sure seem mighty impotent all of a sudden when it comes to the foundation. I'll speak to Ken, and he'll make sure it happens the way I requested it."

Dressed down by the crinkled waif of a man, he stood to defend himself. "I'll have you know—"

"No, you listen up. Not every man's the same, though every dollar appears to be. Hardship brings out the hidden flaws, all right. Rest assured that Milt Enoch will get his windmill this week. You deposit my donation, Neil. I'll have Ken handle the rest." He pressed his lips so hard the tip of his nose nearly touched his chin, toothless and no doubt swallowing residual fire as he shuffled out.

The banker held up the transfer slip, noting the sizable amount. Exhaling his immediate regret, he stood to make the deposit and grab his much-needed coffee. Money, money everywhere, and not a drop to link.

~

Burk didn't even know how to hold the thing. A fleshy pea-green wrapper folded around a fluff of bean sprouts and avocado. He sure hoped some meat came with today's lunch offering, labeled the Californian.

Cub sauntered up to sit beside him. His rolled sandwich came flanked by two pickle spears. "My, oh, my. Brooke really fixed me up today. She suggests something new every time. I like it all. Say, thanks for agreeing to meet me here today."

Several more customers wandered up to the ordering window, making him grateful he'd parked down the way. A catalpa tree by the sidewalk showed signs of greening up. With the last days of March unfolding, it seemed high time. "I needed to come in for more wire anyway. Conroy thinks he'll finish up today. His two boys need to take off for the weekend."

"How about you? Any weekend plans?" Cub flounced his eyebrows for intrigue.

"Nope. Lyndie's gone back to the rodeo for a three-day show. I plan to go to the community-wide service on Sunday, but that's the sole event on my agenda."

Cub started to bite the rolled sandwich, but lowered it instead. "I'm thinking to ask Brooke out to a movie Saturday after her lunch session. Maybe we could go into Pratt instead of Dodge City."

Burk elbowed his arm. "There you go. That sounds like a good first move. Plus, you could wander by the housing sales lot and point out the model you ordered."

Cub bit his sandwich and glanced over at the purple

panel truck. After a sip of his drink, he turned to him. "You don't reckon that's too much too soon, do you, Burk?

"Look, you're the only man in Clark County getting a new house put up. I think you could make her a small part of that remarkable feat. Consider the contrary if you didn't show her. That's like avoiding the obvious. The fact that you're asking her out on a date means you want to bring her into your inner circle of friends, right?"

"Dude, you make too much sense." He flounced the pickle spear at him and then bit off half its length. After some exaggerated chewing, he hung his head. "Something's not right with Dad. Can't tell whether it's a health issue, or a mental glitch. That's why I wanted to meet up."

The turn in conversation leaked ice water down his back. He cleared the sandwich out of his throat. "Tell me you went to Sadie's title office to gain power of attorney on the ranch."

"Oh, I took Dad in all right. He signed the papers giving me authority, kicking and screaming that it was cruel and unfair treatment. Welcome to my world, the retaliation of a thankless son." He slapped his thigh to accent the comment and returned to devouring his lunch.

Burk hardly knew what to say. This particular conundrum had been brewing for some period of time. The recent disaster might have been too much for the old man. Shoot, he had a hard time coping with the added pressure. When the fencing contractor flitted to mind, he became aware of the time. "I need to down this and get rolling to the fairgrounds. If I have any fencing supplies left over, I'll bring them by Heath's for you."

"Thanks, as my pile seems to be evaporating. Wish I could hire out like you did, but my voucher money went to the house. Poof!" He mimicked an explosion with his free hand and gave an animated wink.

"Good luck with Brooke. Remember to be a gentleman cowboy." He slid from the tailgate and motioned for Cub to do the same. In his peripheral vision, a car crept down Main

Street and passed with a weak toot of its horn. Through the passenger window, the silhouette of Gene Shawboro shot his pulse into orbit. "Hey there!" He jogged toward the middle of the road.

The car halted to a stop abreast of the library. Several patrons emerged with books tucked under their arms. A woman made an exclamation and headed for the vehicle's far side.

Burk stooped, smiling into the window. When the passenger struggled to turn toward him, he angled toward the front of the car. "Welcome home, Gene. What a great day for Ashland to have you back in town." He patted the man's shoulder and caught the twinkle in his eyes.

His aging wife leaned over the gearshift. "Gene hasn't spoken yet, but he can hear you plain as day. We've got a ways to go still, but I can't wait to put him in his favorite chair. You may come by for a visit anytime." She turned to greet the woman who offered to bring a meal.

Burk hesitated to remove his hand from the man, sensing a connection of the spiritual kind. Maybe the power of touch held healing. *Which one of us needs it the most?* He swallowed the lump trying to form in his throat as he cleared a smudge on the mirror with his thumb. "Say, if I'm in town tomorrow, I'll drop by so we can catch up. Hope you can find enough strength to attend the community service Sunday at the high school. That's a strong goal for you to work towards, Gene." He patted the man's arm for good measure and stepped away.

The car eased down the street, soon turning left to take the town hero home. When the idea struck to spread the word of Gene's return at the fairgrounds, Burk hurried to his truck. Cub flashed a thumbs-up from the food truck window in passing, and somehow the world shifted a degree back in order. Now, he needed three spools of barbed wire to finish a costly four-strand fence. He launched a prayer down Main Street, eyeing the grain elevator up ahead. Both pointed skyward, where his ultimate help resided.

~

Lyndie stomped her boot in ladylike objection. Determined to bring her auction plan to fruition, she wouldn't let the lanky site manager stonewall her intentions. "You let the concession stand run the entire time of the event. My shop is similar, only a sidecar."

"We have a strict vendor exclusion clause, so the rodeo doesn't become a fairway for every carnival act that wants to ply its wares. I think you're rubbing against that restriction mighty hard." He tugged at his graying mustache that dripped below his jaw.

"But I'm under contract, so I hold exception to the clause already. Look at it this way, my farewell tour starts and ends right here in Strong City. Only these fans will have the opportunity to take a little souvenir of Lyndie Leigh Sessoms home with them. That's pretty exclusive, which I'll be sure to tout during my nation-wide Western Star broadcast on Friday night. That might bump up attendance on Saturday for the finals, so we all stand to gain."

He harrumphed, eyeing the men loading the roping calves in a pen. "Here's the deal. You set up the auction display like you want it. I'll come by and pass final inspection on the whole shop. If it doesn't sit well with me, I retain the right to shut you down."

She closed her eyes in a delayed blink. At least she had her toe in the door. "Thank you, Wes. I personally think the fans will respond to this gesture. People can be surprisingly generous when given the opportunity. Those Clark County ranchers deserve the effort."

He dropped his hands off his hips with a growl. A commotion in the pen drew his attention next. He stepped over to lend the men a hand at the gate.

Lyndie blew out a breath. Thanks to her extra stop along the way, the auction sheets were all color coordinated in print, not handwritten. She'd also succumbed to the print shop manager's suggestion for a farewell banner. Now with permission to set up shop, she strolled by the concession stand's perimeter, eager to choose her spot.

Once Ernie arrived, she could set out the boxes and be ready when the gates opened. Fortunately, her act led the evening's program. That allowed her to sing to the nation's flag and cast her plea for the burned-out ranchers. A tug at the heart would launch her farewell tour. She needed to keep it genuine with the audience, or why else had she come? Having stepped into a small recess guarded by two massive poles, she visualized her little auction shop right there. "Bless this effort, Lord," she muttered to the wooden pole. *This* is why she had come.

~

Burk loaded the fifth spool at Ken's insistence. The line had been mercifully short, so he'd be back to the ranch by one o'clock. "Oh, I just saw Gene Shawboro being delivered home. Praise God for that return. I guess it means he's recovering from the stroke."

"Yeah, talk about some good news," Ken replied. His back pocket beeped so he fished out his cell phone. In seconds, his expression soured. "No joy in this. Neil needs me at the bank. Without Lyndie here, I haven't even had a lunch break yet. Say, could you possibly stay an hour or so and run the distribution line, Burk?"

Aggravated at the bind, any other day he would stay without a second thought. "Sorry, Ken. My fencing contractor needs to wrap up today, and we're shy this wire. I've gotta get these spools right out to him, so we don't have any downtime." He glanced over the fairgrounds and spotted a stocky figure over by the hay bale stacks. "Who's that over yonder?"

"That's Barb King, the truck driver from Michigan. She's staying for the Sunday community service. I put her on the agenda to speak."

"Guess she couldn't run the loading line here?"

"No, that wouldn't do. Sheriff Waller has driven through twice already. We can't appear that lax, or he'll nail me with neglecting my civic duty again." Ken shot him a fake smile that melted into a grimace.

Burk looked toward the road and saw Cub's pickup heading into the entrance. Sensing a solution, he'd toss it out there to see what Ken thought. "Listen, here comes Cub Haines. How about we ask him to man the loading dock after he gets his supplies?"

Ken's glance shied from the approaching truck to the clipboard resting on a nearby chair. His mouth twitched to one side as shook his head. "No, I can't let him do that."

Burk stared at the man, a squint stretching his cheek. The gist surfaced plain enough. Ken saw him as trustworthy, but Cub, not so much. The siphon's threat reared its ugly head again.

Ken snapped his fingers. "How about this? Ask Cub to run your wire out to the ranch, so your fencing contractor has what he needs to stay busy. That way, you can plant yourself here and guard the fort until I can get back. Consider my position here, Burk. Waller's got me under his lawman's thumbscrews."

He refilled his lungs a time or two, working through the scenario. He reckoned if Cub would make the run, he'd have no major objection. "Okay, Ken. Let's see what Cub says. Maybe if the girl in the food truck accepted his date invitation, he'll pass the kindness on to us."

Ken's expression warmed. He finally chuckled and wiped his upper lip. "Life sure has a funny way of working out sometimes, doesn't it?"

Burk gave him a knowing look and leaned closer. "Yeah. You're not the only one missing a certain female sidekick today."

"Welcome to the spot where misery loves company." He threw his arms up right in time to welcome Cub to the loading area. When Milt Enoch pulled up behind him and almost rammed his rear bumper, they suddenly had a waiting line.

Burk slapped a hand on Cub's arm resting out the window. "Ken's being called out to the bank. I need to stay here and cover for him, but my barbed wire has got to be delivered pronto to my fencing contractor. Can you do me a huge favor and deliver this wire?"

Ken held his phone over his head as if to add leverage.

Cub glanced back and forth along the loading line. "Okay. I'll do it. Let's get me loaded first. I'll put your wire on top poised for special delivery."

Ken saluted the decision. "I'll have Milt pull around to the other lane. Heads up, fellas. Don't turn your back on Old Man Enoch's driving." His warning held a tease.

Burk winked at him. "See you in an hour, Ken. Enjoy your lunch break."

"Hey, that food truck on Main Street is worth the stop," Cub added, sliding out of the truck's cab.

Burk bent down to keep the message personal as Ken walked away. "Did she say yes?"

Cub's smile widened. "Yep, she most definitely did. I now have a date for Saturday."

Burk lowered his best friend's tailgate, wondering whether to congratulate him or warn him about women. Last night's tactile scene at the closet replayed in his mind. Even after the tender moment, he couldn't figure out Lyndie. He reached for the first post bundle, allowing the rigid metal to offset a softer sentiment seeping through his chest. "Here's my advice, Cub. Always do things for the right reason. Trust your heart. It'll help you sleep at night."

Cub's confused expression filtered back to regular geniality. "Double up my load," he whispered. "Lord knows I need these supplies."

Burk nodded, fully aware he would ignore the clipboard in Ken's absence. *Good riddance.* The slight translated into a sucker punch right when the siphon wasn't expecting one.

Sheriff Waller would stew over the lapse, but that recognition failed to motivate him. He picked up the post bundle and slid it onto the truck bed, determined to give Cub a generous stack.

Chapter 19

Lyndie chose her green satin western costume for Thursday's opening performance. Considering she'd be modeling it when she made the announcement for the silent auction, maybe the showy outfit would bring a high price. She had always loved the braided gold star on the back yoke that matched the detail stitching on the jacket cuffs. Some rising rodeo rider might need to own it next. She could only hope.

Her manager approached with the bid sheets in hand. "I figure these are the equivalent of real money, so I don't feel comfortable leaving them on the table when I'm not there."

She allowed his insight to ease her tightness a bit. "Good thinking, Ernie. If you can hold down the booth while my act is underway, I'll come right back and spell you afterwards. Keep that old playbill in the box until I return this green jacket."

"Got it. Hope you're not having any regrets, Lyndie Leigh. It sure seems like you're cutting your career in half to me." He shook his head, though his eyes held a gleam.

"There's more for me than the rodeo show circuit. You probably knew I would grow up enough to see that one day. I found both purpose and a place suited for me in Ashland. Those dear folks have been through so much."

"Losing to gain—that's one of life's little ironies, ain't it?" He grinned and glanced down the entrance corridor. "Looks like they've opened the gates. Are you about ready?"

"Guess I need to get Tracer out of the trailer." She scanned the approaching crowd, wondering how hard to pitch the items in the auction booth at the start.

"Here, take these," he replied, shoving the bid sheets at her. "I'll get your horse. You talk up the crowd some. What those wildfire pictures don't say, you can fill in better than I could."

She tilted her head, not anticipating the support. "Thanks, Ernie. Watch out, your tender heart might be showing tonight." She took the papers and headed for the booth, ready to rid her life of its sparkle and shine. A contemplation of whether the switch to plain would suffice caused Burk to pop to mind. *Cedar-green beats satin-green any old day.* She'd make sure to get her fix when she returned as they sat hand-in-hand at Sunday's community service. With a sigh, she slid behind the table as the first couple strolled past the concession stand headed her way.

~

The Crosby ranch would seem mighty lonesome once he gave the visiting canine back on Friday. With the fencing contractor pulling out, Burk couldn't justify the loan any longer. He'd swing through town tomorrow, check on Ken at the fairgrounds, and then make the haul out to Rodney Gillian's so he could have his three-legged champion back. From the close attention Chip had given Babe, he had no doubts there would be puppies this summer.

Dry from an afternoon fencing the upper pasture, he stepped to the sink for a glass of water. Gazing out the window, he heard the blue heeler plant its haunches on its favorite throw rug. He figured he had half an hour of daylight left, maybe forty minutes. Sadly, the hay wouldn't throw itself over the pipe gate to feed the herd. He gulped the water and smacked the plastic glass down on the counter. "Want to see some cattle, boy?"

The dog lifted its head from the braided oval, ever watchful.

"Come, Chip." He headed down the back hall to escape to the barnyard. As he passed the rear bedroom, the open door reminded him of his heaped-up accumulation. "You're next to rectify—even if it takes me all night." Thinking to haul off the discards on his way to the fairgrounds, his empty days began to take shape. If he stayed busy enough, he wouldn't miss Lyndie at all. The dog knocked against his shin, so he threw the door open to a worthy diversion— ranching.

~

Midmorning on Friday, Lyndie hiked the trail from the historic main house to the old schoolhouse at the National Tallgrass Preserve. Only four miles from the Strong City rodeo grounds, the preserve offered a passive escape during her free time. She could have sat in the camper and stewed about how few auction bids had come in last night, but this seemed like a healthier alternative. She'd even stopped by the grass-covered visitor's center and autographed the rodeo playbill for the gift shop manager. Her celebrity status would be fading fast.

Friday always seemed to bring the best out in the week, so tonight's performance would represent an upswing, for certain. Plus, she had her Western Star broadcast to fit in right before show time. She walked past a winding dry-stack limestone wall that held the main grounds off the prairie. Picturesque in its own right, the rolling hills and rocky outcrops in this area didn't strike her as inviting as the shortgrass prairie of western Kansas. Maybe the humility of never having enough water made that landscape more appealing to her. Thirst could be interpreted as a sign of questing—a longing for something more. She could fully relate to such a sentiment.

Her boots parted the bunch grasses growing along the

trail as she made her way up a hill to a blocky limestone structure that appeared part schoolhouse and part chapel. She'd attempted the climb to speak to God from the hilltop, a great way to reduce the distance between heaven and earth. Before she returned to the distribution site in Ashland, she needed some major resolution on certain mounting issues. One day, the supply distribution would conclude. What would her life look like then?

Perhaps she'd missed her calling by not joining forces with the Red Cross. With a bit of training, she could obtain certification as a disaster team member. By summertime, the next natural disaster would likely happen somewhere on the continent, and she could mobilize to meet the immediate needs of that struggling population. Familiar faces began to flit to mind, starting with Ken Ray. A parade of ranchers came next, old to young, big operations to small. Cub and Burk trailed along behind the rest, making her cherish the various friendships she'd formed.

The truth seeped into her conscience as she approached the flagpole outside the hilltop limestone structure. Not merely a checklist of disenfranchised ranchers—it was a tight-knit community—and this particular one in Ashland had stolen her heart. To trade away such welcome-home contentment for a gypsy-rescuer lifestyle struck her as inconceivable. Her days in the camper were numbered, whether in the apple orchard's shade or not. *Here I am, Lord. Where could you send me?* The vastness of the grassland stretched westward for the answer, connected by a link of successive barbed wire fences and one ever-caring God.

~

From the time he'd rolled out of bed this morning, Burk felt off-balance and challenged for proper direction. This side stop represented that aimless inertia. Still, a promise remained a promise. He knocked on the bare wood door as the dog sat at his feet. The porch's planking needed a new coat of paint. If he looked hard enough, he could probably generate a list of chores. When the door squeaked open, he focused on the occupant. "Morning, Wanda. Is Gene awake?"

She pulled at her gray hair to loosen some curls. "Yes, he's up and already exercised this morning. Those physical therapists mean business, I declare. I have three different exercise lists he has to do twice daily." She pushed open the screen door to let him inside. Leading through the living room, she brought him into the eat-in kitchen.

The humble scene bathed him in purpose for the first time all morning. "Happy Friday, Gene. There's nothing like waking up to springtime in your own home, is there?"

The hero sat hunched in his wheelchair, barely able to make eye contact. In slow motion, the index finger on his right hand rose from the chair arm.

"One finger means *yes*, he's in agreement," Wanda said, wiping crumbs from the plastic tablecloth. "Two fingers means *no*. I've only had a few of those, as it takes him more effort. Can I get you a cup of coffee?"

"Yes, ma'am, that'd be nice of you." Burk pulled out a chair to face the old-timer. "Gene, I have Rodney Gillian's three-legged blue heeler sitting on your front porch. One of the goings-on I wanted to tell you about is my far-fetched scheme to gain a new puppy." He paused to let Wanda place the coffee mug on the table between them. When he looked back up, the man's eyes twinkled with the inference.

"Sugar and cream?"

"Yes, ma'am, I can hardly stand the best brew without some additives. Anyway, my fencing contractor came down from Hoxie with two sons and a nice female heeler bearing a fancy Hanging Tree bloodline. I made sure the two dogs met up while Conroy Nichols ran four wires around my upper pasture all week. He's willing to let me have the pick of the litter should anything come of it this summer. I've been too long without canine help, plus I about got trampled to death that day the wildfire came up. Sure makes a man wonder why he's held off for so long without a dog."

Gene closed his eyes and lifted one finger in slow agreement.

Burk leveled a spoonful of sugar into the mug and then splashed the coffee with milk until it lightened up. The first taste set him back on the level. *Praise God.* Maybe the morning had some redemptive value, after all. "Rodney's had a rough go of it. Most of the northern ranches burned to the ground when the wind switched around. Cub Haines' place went up in flames, too. He's pulling in a modular house next month, the first rancher to rebuild in the county." The mug beckoned to him and he took a long drink. The hot liquid held healing.

Gene opened his eyes and lifted one finger in support of rebuilding.

Wanda padded around the kitchen and soon began to rinse dishes in the sink.

"The Good Lord knows that Garrett and Barrett Guard have the longest journey back to normal. Honestly, you would not believe the level of help they're getting. I worked with them the first week and saw a regular stampede of volunteers making tracks out there. Lots of strong college boys came during spring break. The Methodist relief team brought its own equipment, including a skid steer that could pull posts faster than a cat can wink its eye. The day they handed Garrett a collection check for five thousand dollars marked a turning point for most of us. Guess we felt like, with so much of the state backing us, we'd somehow make it through this disaster."

"Tara mentioned you might have gained a lady friend out of all the influx of helpers," Wanda said as she dried a frying pan. "She said some celebrity rodeo singer has been running her Western Star radio show from the Ashland Library, of all places."

Burk laid the smooth ceramic mug against his cheek, wondering how much to admit. Before he could put together a reply, he saw the old man's finger float from the chair arm—a single finger. Maybe that was all the validation he needed. Either the coffee or the exposure caused a warm rush down his trunk. He finally gave Wanda a smile.

"Lyndie has gone to Strong City to say farewell to the rodeo circuit this weekend. Get this, she's buying the old apple orchard on the west side of town because Ken Ray told her she needed to be a citizen to have her voice heard. I didn't fight the purchase, because it sounded like a truckload of apple pies arriving in my future to me." He grinned and bent closer to his stricken friend. "If that dad-blame siphon doesn't come between us, we might just hit it off."

Gene blinked in a millisecond. Two fingers floated up a scant half-inch.

Burk took a sip of coffee and glanced at Wanda for input.

She hung a pot up on a rack over the stove and came closer, her expression reserved. "I reckon he doesn't know about that siphon you mentioned. We don't talk about the negative too much." With a wipe of her hands, she took off the apron and hung it around the back of a chair.

Burk braced his elbows on his knees to stay close to the wheelchair. "Sheriff Waller received several tips that a man had been spotted in the surrounding vicinity selling fencing supplies to those in need out of the back of his pickup. Naturally, he blamed Ken and Lyndie for abetting the thug's efforts, because they felt led to give away the donated materials without any recordkeeping. The more donations rolled in, the more pilfering-for-profit went on. Waller dubbed him the siphon and it stuck—a bad apple stinking up a beautiful heap of generosity."

Gene rocked back in his chair, seeming to stretch his neck. When he straightened, he began to cough with a dry hack. The second round, it sounded more like whooping cough.

Wanda knelt beside the chair, concern etching her features.

"Maybe Gene needs a drink of water," Burk suggested. He'd probably stayed longer than the stroke victim could handle. The realization landed like a load of rocks.

"Hoooop," Gene croaked. "Hooo…hoo."

"Lord, help us. Gene's trying to talk," Wanda said. "Quick, grab the notepad there."

Burk scanned the bric-a-brac on the table and saw a square notepad behind the salt shaker. He fished it free and grabbed for a pen. "Can he write, Wanda?"

"Not exactly. I write down what I think Gene's saying and let him move the pen around afterwards. It can be a real lesson in phonetics by the time it's all said and done." She took the pen and pad to print out the message. "Gene, look at this now. Is this what you're telling Burk?"

Gene angled toward the pad, stretching his neck as if ready to vocalize again. An indiscernible croak came out. He raised the two finger combination again, knocking against her writing hand. The pen scratched a mark on the paper. Gene looked up and grunted.

Wanda studied the pad and then passed it to him. "I can't make out a blame thing."

On heightened alert, Burk took the pad and stared at the characters. Beside Wanda's block letters spelling out "H-O-O-P" Gene had made a mark that resembled the letter V. Running several possibilities through his mind, if he closed the gap, it could pass for the letter R. The skin tightened up the back of his neck. "Gene, do you mean Hooper?"

Gene blinked, looking relieved. He lifted one finger and held it up.

Grit threatened to clog his throat, but he'd dig to get to the bottom of this, God as his witness. "Gene, are you telling me Clint Hooper can tell me who the troublemaking siphon is? Be real sure when you answer, as nobody's been able to pin any blame on the guilty party yet."

The man leaned back in the wheelchair, a messenger with a locked-up message. His hands clamped the padded arms of the chair and slowly released them. The index finger of his right hand rose, and then the hand joined it, followed by his entire arm.

"Oh, that's good movement, Gene," Wanda gushed. "Real good. Now, hold it for a five count, and we'll try another round." She placed her hand under his arm, braced for his falter.

Burk locked gazes with the crippled man, ready to alter his next stop along a route he hadn't seen before. "Ashland stands, Gene—like they said that first night in the evacuation shelter. We depended on your heroism that day…and now I'm depending on it again. Thank you for trusting me with your message. I'll update you at the community service on Sunday."

The man's trembling finger pointed at him, as though to level the responsibility squarely onto his broad shoulders. A single finger of affirmation, one he wouldn't take lightly.

~

Lyndie dropped the brush into the bucket and ran her hand under Tracer's dark mane. The buckskin horse flinched, muscular and lean. Though she had tried to make the mental transfer of this grand show animal to the cemetery pasture just west of Sitka, the two seemed ill-matched at best. "We've truly given them a good show, haven't we fella?" She kissed the horse's blaze as it pulled against the halter line.

"Look at all that affection," Ernie said in a bombastic voice.

She turned to find her manager had brought a visitor along. From the looks of his high-end cowboy boots and tooled leather belt, the trim man wasn't any stranger to affluence. She released the horse and dusted off her palms for the introduction.

"Lyndie Leigh Sessoms, please meet Will Banner," Ernie said. "He's the horse rancher interested in breeding Tracer here."

She leaned forward and offered her hand. "Mr. Banner."

"Ma'am, my pleasure." He took her hand and gave it a firm pump. "I appreciate Mr. Matthews letting me follow-up on my initial inquiry. If this spring would suffice—"

"I no longer have that kind of time," Lyndie said in a blunt tone. "I've just decided to sell Tracer after Saturday's finals." She paused strategically after the man failed to constrain the flicker of gain in his eyes. "You may not realize that this is my farewell tour. I'm clearing my assets, as showmanship doesn't match up well with the ranching life I plan to pursue."

"That's a horse of a different color," Banner replied with a hitch of his brow. "I'm highly interested, I assure you. When you're ready to talk numbers, let me know."

"Catch me Saturday before I pull out after the show. The silent auction for the western Kansas ranchers will draw to a close then, as well. I hope your proposition comes with a bonus donation for that charitable endeavor, or I might find the offer somewhat lacking." Confident she held the upper ground as the seller of a well-trained horse, she stood firm.

Banner's mustache twitched. "Let me do some ciphering on that and get back to you on Saturday. In the meantime, don't accept another offer ahead of mine."

She tilted her head, but her gaze held fast. "Are you *asking* me?" From what she heard, it sounded more like a demand. Not to turn down the man's money, but she had to drive this bus.

Standing on the sidelines like a puffed-up rodeo clown, Ernie made a child-like whimper. He had demonstrated many negotiation tactics in his day, but hard-lining didn't match his style.

"First offer or last, I'm most definitely asking for that exclusivity," Banner replied.

Lyndie nodded. "You can bid with or without the horse trailer included, whatever your preference. I'll pull it empty if I have to—or sell it separate."

"Good enough for me," he replied, stepping away with a tip of his hat.

Ernie filled the void with his bulk, stroking the horse's neck. "I can't believe you could part ways with this horse, Lyndie. You two have made each other great."

"Best I can tell from my prayers and clear thinking, this is what I need to do. Should I keep my trick pony, there's always the lure to go back to the show. What does that say to God, if he wants to take me from here and lead me to greener pastures?"

He shook his head. "Your faith is stronger than mine, young lady. I'm afraid I would hedge on those tough decisions."

"I'm coming around that third barrel, Ernie. What's left is an all-out dash for the finish line. I've got two shows to go and counting down." She winked and untied the horse to find some hay. After that, she had a radio show to outline, her not-so-usual Friday night endeavor.

Chapter 20

Burk slowed the truck for the driveway into Clint Hooper's ranch, putting the dog on high alert. A small house boasting a wraparound porch sat right off the highway, with a tiny yellow cabin next to it. Both were dwarfed by the massive outbuilding in back where a line of bare-branched trees formed a shelterbelt from the north wind.

With his pulse elevating at no signs of life, he allowed the truck to drift toward the shop. Maybe he'd knock on the back door and draw Clint out for the necessary conversation. He hated to namedrop Gene, as Clint might have shared something in confidence, thinking the disabled man represented a safe risk. Whistling out his tension, he killed the ignition and threw open the door. He hadn't come out to be combative.

Before he could get a boot planted, the heeler scrambled across his lap and hit the scent trail at a trot. He shut the truck door and tugged at his shirttail on the way to the back door. The dog circled around the bottom step, sniffed the corner of the cabin, and took off for the outbuilding. Not willing to run up a wayward canine, Burk started to call a command when the heeler let out a raucous series of barks. It nosed into the twin sliding doors with a fevered pitch.

He turned and headed for the commotion, several

possibilities swirling through his mind. At the entrance, he heard a low mechanical noise between the dog's protests. Once he'd gotten a strong grip on the tin door, he gave one panel a sideways shove. "Clint?"

From the row of antique cars, a motor hummed. The stench of trapped exhaust knocked him back into the opening. Then, behind the steering wheel of a pea-green Chevy, he spotted a hunched figure. "No, God—please no." He ran to the driver's door, heaved it open, and switched off the ignition. Once he got his arms around the unconscious resident, he hauled the rail-thin man out with care. Too far from town to wait for an ambulance, he made headway for his truck.

Frantic, Burk negotiated the passenger-side door open. Chip hopped in without a prompt, skittering into the floorboard. He pulled Clint's lifeless figure onto the seat and thought to check for a pulse. A weak response drummed his fingertips. "Thank you, Lord—now please keep him alive for me." The dog whined as he slammed the door. Racing to the driver's side, he scanned the property and noticed a stockpile of fencing supplies near the rear of the building. *What?* A truckload's worth seemed to be missing from the center of the pile.

In reverse, he floored the gas pedal and turned the truck around. Headed down the driveway, he checked for traffic and then pulled out onto the pavement at breakneck speed. The dog lowered its center of gravity, yet remained on high alert, its ears pinned back.

The speedometer peaked at eighty-five as several pastures of burnt ground blurred by the windshield. Panic clamped his chest. He soon drove up a rise and could see the outskirts of town. The hospital wouldn't be far off from here. Weighing the current tragedy against another potential one, he sacrificed speed and slowed for town. His composure held until he passed the apple orchard, bringing his absent girlfriend to mind. His hands began to tremble on the steering wheel. *Lord, help the poor state I'm in.* As he hooked the last corner, the man leaning on the console beside him groaned, a tepid sign of life that delivered a sliver of hope.

~

Lyndie finished writing the note with the phone cradled on her shoulder. "I can't believe the wildfire would climb up and over a pickup truck like that,"

"That poor rancher looked scared out of his wits when he told me his story," Tara replied. "I think the insinuation is they all got caught off guard by the wildfire's speed. Even that fire chief from Slapout, Oklahoma claimed he drove sixty miles an hour in his suppression vehicle, yet couldn't keep pace with the fire as it spread. Yes, it had all the makings of a first-rate calamity with wind speed up like that, and it headed right for vulnerable little Ashland."

"This is great material, Tara. Thank you so much for sharing these stories with me. I want the broadcast to relay the genuine human impact, so the listeners can relive the threat."

"I guess you won't have your typical guest speaker on tonight's show. Sorry about that. Burk has gotten pretty good at fleshing out his radio personality. I'm quite surprised, actually."

Lyndie laughed. "I doubt he'll miss having radio duty tonight. Well, I better scoot and sketch in this outline. Thanks for everything, Tara."

"Let me know if you need any further help, Lyndie. My reference section is only a phone call away." A soft chuckle played down the phone line until it went silent.

Her pen scratched the paper while details remained fresh in her mind. The radio show held top priority, but once Lyndie's rodeo days were history, would Western Star still want her? Finishing the script, she stood and exited the camper to check her equipment setup. Maybe the question should be whether she still wanted Western Star. *Will I?* The smell of fresh sawdust accompanied that consideration all the way to the media booth, her perch for the early evening.

~

Burk surveyed the tranquility of the fairgrounds. Maybe Sheriff Waller would find something incriminating beyond what he'd been able to see when he tore out to race Clint to the hospital. A minor miracle, he spotted Rodney's burgundy truck in the distribution line and made a beeline toward it. When he pulled up and stopped, he didn't have to waste a command on the dog, as it practically leapt from his lap. Rodney waved and let Chip inside his truck.

Burk searched for Ken to catch him up with the breaking news on the siphon. Given a little recovery time, Clint might be forthcoming with more truth on the matter. Never one to accuse, he'd hold off for more details before placing blame, especially on a familiar face. Finally, he picked up on Ken's spirited stride as the man returned from the hay bale stack.

"Hey, Burk. Are you here to pick up fencing supplies?" Ken asked, shrugging one shoulder toward the distribution line.

"Nope, my upper pasture's done. I dropped off what little I had left in Cub's truck bed before stopping in to see Gene Shawboro this morning."

"Oh? How's Gene getting along?" He waved Rodney off the far end of the line and picked the clipboard from a chair nearby. With a flick of his wrist, he had the man marked down.

To avoid the recordkeeping jab, Burk assessed the amount of supplies remaining. "Gene's trying to talk, but he mostly signals 'yes' or 'no' with his index finger. Interesting, when I brought up the siphon problem, he seemed to know something about it. He tipped me off to track down Clint Hooper, but when I got to Clint's ranch, I found him slumped in a running automobile, half asphyxiated inside his garage. That led to a speedy trip back to the hospital."

Ken's expression went blank. "Well—how's Clint?"

"He's on oxygen right now, but the emergency room staff thinks I found him in time."

"Thank God and Gene Shawboro, once again a dynamic duo." Ken shook his head. "I have a hard time swallowing that Clint played the culprit selling supplies for profit. That simply doesn't add up. I'm not saying Clint is oblivious to the underhanded goings-on, but that man doesn't have a plotting bone in his body."

"Okay then. Who's your top suspect?" Burk set his hands on his hips to force the inevitable showdown. He'd had about enough of this random speculation.

Ken twisted his head first one way and then the other. He turned the clipboard. "Here's what the record shows. You read between the lines." He shoved the registration into his hands.

Loathe to read the record, Burk glanced around the fairgrounds. In the distance, two ranchers helped one another load up with round hay bales. Nonpartisan, the grain elevator lofted its towers in the background. *If only evil intent could be more evident.*

He raised the clipboard and traced down the list of familiar names. Clearly, one rancher had more visits for loading supplies, almost twice as many. He fingered the line and double-checked the name. No doubt about it, the list incriminated Jacobi and Byron Haines. "Tell me you don't think that Cub is the siphon, Ken."

He shrugged and stared at the ground.

Burk started to defend Cub's exuberance to load up early, knowing his plans for the date over the weekend. Before he could verbalize any rationale, his phone vibrated. Seeing the name on the screen, he brought up the incoming call on speaker phone. "Go ahead, Sheriff Waller. I'm standing here with Ken Ray. Did you find out anything?"

"Enough to know that Clint Hooper isn't the siphon."

Burk blew out a breath. At least one friend was off the

hook. "What gave you that impression? I saw his heaping pile of fencing supplies with a divot taken out of the middle."

"You failed to notice the new fence line along the north pasture beyond the hedgerow, Mr. Crosby, hence the dent in his stockpile. But an even more prominent clue sat right under your nose. You missed the brick holding down the accelerator in the old Chevy. Somebody wanted Clint dead, which leads straight to my next question. Why?"

The sheriff could have struck his head with a two-by-four. Too numb to string any thoughts together, Burk nearly dropped the phone. He eased the clipboard under it for support.

"I'm headed back to the hospital to see if Clint's in any shape to talk yet."

Ken leaned forward to speak into the phone. "I'm shutting down the distribution site for the evening, sheriff. I'll be at home if you need to get in touch with me." He locked gazes momentarily and took possession of the clipboard.

"I'll be in town a while longer," Burk added. "Let me know if I need to file a report on what I found at Clint's place." Not waiting for a reply, he ended the call and pocketed the phone.

Ken zipped his jacket closed against the cooling air. "Where are you headed, Burk?"

"I'm going to the temporary address of one Jacobi Haines. He'd better have a convincing justification of his need for so many fencing supplies." He practically grumbled the last few words. Maybe Ken's suspicions swayed him somewhat. The six check marks popped back to mind, a record hard to refute. When he got back in the cab, he missed the dog right away. *Alone once again—and on a Friday night, to boot.* He turned up the radio to fill the void.

He exited the fairgrounds, set for town. A familiar voice echoed from the speaker, instantly adding to Burk's dilemma. Western Star had begun its Friday night broadcast, with Lyndie Leigh Sessoms singing to everyone in the country—but him. A slow song he hadn't heard before, some glock-amore-a bird was supposed to deliver a cheery word across the distant landscape. By all accounts, he truly needed a message like that.

Lyndie sang the next verse about a brook and a weeping willow tree noticed by a lad who might be sad and dreary, given the singer's absence. Hitting a bit too close to home, the doleful lyrics tore at an exposed part of his heart. In no time, moisture rimmed his eyes and his throat thickened. He centered the truck down the middle of Main Street to avoid sideswiping anyone.

Lyndie's tempo slowed as she asked a final question about the well-being of the town in remembrance. Her voice cracked on the last few words, causing her to shorten the final note. Next, a soft whimper sounded across the airwaves. "I miss you, Ashland, Kansas" she confessed in a sultry whisper. "Would you hold me in your heart till I come back?"

When the show cut away to a sponsor's spot, Burk knuckled the radio off. Too late for fortification, extensive damage had been done. Now, his heart possessed a hole big enough to drive a camper through—if only a certain someone would. Wiping across his eyes, he exhaled and tried to make the mental shift back to his troublesome best friend, wondering for a short second if their boyhood bond remained worth the hassle anymore.

~

Lyndie stomped out of the cowgirls' room and headed for the auction booth. What had she been thinking to sing that show tune from Finian's Rainbow on the broadcast? A resounding ovation had followed her theatrical performance back in eleventh grade, but these cowboys didn't seem to want Irish music tonight. A spirited call went out for the calf roping event as she maneuvered around a couple with small children. Both little boys wore chaps, boots, and hats, reflecting a fine western tradition. No, Glocca Morra didn't seem to fit in here.

She sighed, regretting the somber mood she'd set for announcing the charity fundraiser with the Ashland Foundation. Maybe the tallgrass prairie residents had no sympathy for their neighbors on the shortgrass end of the state. The possibility tweaked her mood toward sour. For now, she needed to see how Ernie had made out in her absence. If the bid sheets hadn't gained many signers, she just might migrate to the bitter end of sour—a spectrum she didn't cherish.

"Lyndie Leigh?" a man called behind her. "Hold up a second, will you?"

She turned to find Wes tracking her down in no uncertain terms. Hatless, his face held an expression she couldn't name. If he brought more censure, she wanted no part of it. "What gives? You're not going to make me fold up early, are you? I'm just getting back to the booth."

He gave a dismissive sweep with his hand. "No, you're a hundred miles off. Come on out to the arena with me. There's something you gotta see." He held out his bent elbow to insist.

She pulled her hair over one shoulder of her glittery blue jacket and tried to level off. Ernie could last a few more minutes, especially since his station sat right beside the concession stand. Manufacturing a crooked smile, she linked up with the site manager and let him lead. *Only one more show left on Saturday.* She could do this.

The lights blazed over the grandstand where they walked out beside the chutes for bull riding. If she squinted, they appeared to form a halo above the rodeo grounds. More sawdust than saintly, she wasn't about to hallow these grounds as holy. The opposite argument could be made.

"Up there in the seats—can you make it out?" Wes pointed to a lower row where a man passed a two-tone boot to his neighbor. "They started it up on their own—somebody on the far end yanked off a hat or boot and sent it down the way. It's a collection for your burned-out ranchers in western Kansas. I'm telling you, that old Irish song scarcely left a dry eye in the stadium during your radio broadcast. Then when you followed up with that heartfelt appeal at the end of your act, it seems like everybody positively itched to give."

Lyndie gazed out in wonderment as hats and boots passed from hand to hand. She hadn't wanted to trivialize the need by asking for pocket change, but such a spontaneous effort held much more honor. When her host reached up to smooth his hair, her intuition linked his absent hat with the donation solicitation. "Wes, would you like to admit how your hat went missing?"

"No, ma'am," he replied, his mustache twitching. "Sally from the concession stand is helping me collect all the money. Once she brings it to your booth, have her count it behind you to double check the total. Let me lock up that money with the gate proceeds tonight. I don't want to have to worry about someone breaking into your camper after it."

"That sounds great. I'd better get back to relieve Ernie. He dearly loves the calf roping event." She turned to leave, but couldn't get over the feeling that something more needed to transpire. With her charity burden lightened, she could have floated back to the booth.

"Heaven help those ranchers who have to rekindle from ashes," Wes said. When he glanced her way, his eyes had misted with the sentiment.

"Thank you for helping make my farewell an unforgettable one, Wes." She threw her arms around his neck, surprised when he hugged her back. "Heaven help those ranchers," she repeated, meaning every single word.

~

With one leg inside his luxury SUV, the banker had all but missed the waif of a woman standing amid the back alley's brick rubble. Since the bank had closed over two hours ago, what could she possibly want? Using the handhold, he hoisted into the seat. Uncomfortably cramped, he adjusted the seat back a couple of notches. "We're open Saturday until noon. Can't this wait until the morning?"

"Sorry, Neil. I might run up to Strong City to assist Lyndie Leigh Sessoms tomorrow. She texted that the crowd volunteered a strong collection at today's show. She closes midday Saturday, so I thought I'd lend a hand packing her up and transporting the money here."

Cheered at the aspect of incoming cash, he immediately began to make a savvy plan for Monday's sidecar investments. "Well, well. That is good news, isn't it? That girl is a real go-getter. Use the deposit drop box after one o'clock. I can't stay much later than that."

"Fine, we will. The Kansas Farm Bureau may be ready to send aid by this time next week, so financial help is coming our way in waves—but at least it's coming."

"Enjoy the rodeo, Miss T," he quipped, right before slamming his door closed. He keyed the ignition and backed away, leaving her standing in the alley's construction zone. That epitomized the entire county, didn't it? Left to rubble and ruin, their only way to climb out was a fence post at a time. He chuckled, wondering how much cash the rodeo singer had finagled.

~

"What do you mean you can't find your father?" Burk jammed his boot heel against the curb, determined not to linger. If his hunger could hold off, he'd stop at the hospital and visit Clint before heading home.

Cub scratched his ear. "My aunt from Bucklin called. Bear hasn't been there since Tuesday. She wondered if he was here at Heath's with me, so I told her no."

"Did you check up at the ranch? He could be sleeping in the new shed."

"I'm running fence supplies up there twice daily, but I really wasn't looking for signs of a squatter. It'd be hard to live up there, but I guess a man of simple means could do it."

Since the fencing stock-up had entered the conversation, Burk had to pursue it. "Ken Ray tells me you've been through the distribution line double the amount of trips anyone else has. Sheriff Waller's going to look at that number pretty hard. You want to tell me why?"

Cub held up two open palms. "That's no big secret. Let the sheriff read my bank statement over the last month. Every dollar I have is going into that modular house. My perimeter fence will have to be built from donated materials—and I mean, one hundred percent."

Burk looked for holes in his argument. "Yet, you're going on a date tomorrow."

"Right—a date I can't afford financially, but I have a few dollars in my pocket and deserve to have some female companionship. Not every guy has a woman pull her camper into his farmyard, after all. Some of us have to work through more inconvenience."

His comment raked over a touchy spot, but Burk didn't want to shift the conversation into personal territory. "I'm playing devil's advocate right now, so you can hear it from me instead of Waller. If he comes in with a search warrant, he'll be looking at more than your bank account."

"Great—let him," he replied, gesturing over his head. "My life's an open book with scorch marks around the edges. Except for my cuckoo father, I'm leading the regular ranching life—lots of endless work with hardheaded cattle."

Burk let that claim settle a few seconds. Maybe Bear's erratic behavior did shift the spotlight on Cub by mere association. Plus, some of the checks on Ken's list could belong to his father. Lyndie's story of Bear fuming at the voucher pickup sure served as a ready example of double-dipping between the two men. He recalled the old man's wanton helplessness that night in Dodge City and shook his head. "What's your dad driving around now anyway? Did he get that old truck fixed?"

Cub laughed. "There's no money for that. He asked, but

I turned him down flat.”

“Well then, someone else is financing his wheels.” As soon as he’d said it, he wished he’d only thought the accusation instead.

Cub recoiled, backing from the curb. “All I ask is that you keep an eye out for Bear. I’ll be out of town tomorrow most of the day. He’s liable to stumble up and need a place to lay his head. I’ll have Heath keep a lookout, too.”

Burk nodded and slipped back in the truck cab. He rolled down the window with a steady crank. “Try to forget about all of this hardship and enjoy your date tomorrow.”

“I appreciate that, Burk. I’m still undecided as to whether to show Brooke the model home or not, but I’ll figure it out at some point.”

“That’s probably the kind of thing you need to hold in reserve—to make sure the date’s going like you want it to.” He winked, trying to end the visit on a friendly note.

Cub chuckled. “I’m just hoping to get a word in edgewise. Brooke’s a talkative thing, but her cute factor offsets the chatty tendency at any given moment.”

“That’s the spirit. Just keep looking at her lips.” He pulled off with a reserved wave, headed for the hospital two blocks away. His phone pinged, so he slid it off the console. The sheriff’s name came up on the text.

Two tips over the hotline late this afternoon. Oklahoma again.

The night began to hold a deep uncertainty. With Clint in the hospital and Cub here in town, that eliminated two top suspects. Dread took up residence in the cab, nameless and lacking any welcome.

~

Lyndie folded the blue jacket into the auction box as a departing guest made a farewell comment. She smiled and tossed the family a wave, exhausted but buoyed by the collection response. A quick check on the bidding sheets revealed activity had increased in that department as well.

Her phone pinged and she whipped it out, hopeful to hear from Burk at long last.

Am planning to attend Saturday's performance. How can I find you?

She tried to quell her disappointment. After all, she needed girlfriends, too. *Great, Tara. Can't miss me beside the concession stand. Starts at ten. My show's at ten-thirty. Don't be late!* After sending the reply, she pocketed the phone and reached for the tarp to cover the display. Only one more show to perform. What a blessed relief. Maybe she would finally sleep like a baby tonight.

~

The second box Burk hauled out to the truck weighed more than the first one. Why had he saved every issue of Kansas Farmer and High Plains Journal for the past two years? He groaned, shoving the box up to save space for more junk. Well past midnight, he might need to eat a bowl of cereal to keep up his stamina. By the time Lyndie returned tomorrow afternoon, this spare bedroom had to be impressive.

On his way back, he stopped at the kitchen sink to get a drink of water. He missed her company more than he would readily admit. *Who am I fooling?* He felt the lonesomeness in every square inch of his frame. He should have called her after the show just to touch base, another tactical debacle. With little good news, maybe that call could wait. Cool from the tap, the water slaked his thirst as he took a long drink. Next, he had to get right back to the cleanup.

When he stepped into the rear bedroom, he felt compelled to plop down at the makeshift desk he'd set up for conducting his paperwork. There, an unruly stack of bank statements occupied an entire quarter of the desktop. Thinking he should have given those more notice upon arrival, he reflected back to his conversation with Cub. At least his records remained on hand, where Cub's paperwork had gone up in smoke. The bank had its records, too.

A worrisome thought pestered him, so he picked up the statement that arrived in yesterday's mail and looked for the Clark County Proud voucher deposit. When he couldn't locate the seventy-five hundred dollars recorded as a line item, he studied the upper edge of the statement to verify the closing date. The mismatch sent a quivering sting down his spine. *What am I not seeing?* By all rights, the deposit should have posted three days before the banking period ended. So where was his voucher money?

The disparity needled him into action despite the hour. He pulled the cell phone out of his chest pocket and brought up the number to text. *Voucher money missing from my bank account. Could this be related to the siphon?* He needed help figuring this out while the walls of trust ever crumbled around him. With the press of a button, the message disappeared into a silent vacuum.

Chapter 21

The early hour contributed to the eclectic mix of men shoved into the tight space. The convenience store proprietor added a folding table onto the snack table and dragged in some crates for additional seating. The headcount stood at eighteen ranchers and one gruff sheriff. At this point, if he was wrong, Burk would be making a colossal—and highly public—mistake.

When the sheriff made rumblings that he needed to start, Burk guided Milt Enoch into his seat and stepped out to cap the far end of the second table. Several men shot skittish glances beyond him. He turned sideways and quickly allowed Garrett Guard to join the huddle. The proprietor slid two more crates over, and they all took seats.

"Gentlemen, I cannot let this suspicion continue another day," Sheriff Waller said.

Rodney Gillian gestured at the papers on the table. "Is this about the siphon?"

"Maybe," the sheriff replied. After shooting a look at Burk, he cleared his throat. "Most likely. That's part of what we're trying to figure out this morning. For those of you who haven't heard, someone tried to kill Clint Hooper by asphyxiation yesterday morning."

Milt slumped over the table and had to take a wheezy

inhalation. The papers in his hands shook with a palsied grip. The old man's severe reaction cast pallor over the proceedings.

"That likely was a desperation act to hush up Clint," Waller added. "Now, it's up to us to figure out what Clint was going to tell us. I'll let Burk Crosby take it from here, as he stumbled onto something odd last night. He might be onto a connection. We simply don't know yet."

Burk looked down the table and saw men he had labored beside fighting fires and fixing fences for nearly a month now. Before that, they had ranched next to one another every day. He trusted these men. "The siphon never made sense to me from day one and here's why. The fencing supplies that poured into Ashland represented gold to all of us ranchers, so who would go to all the trouble to trade gold in for cash? The whole notion's illogical from the get-go."

"Maybe not—if you don't need fencing supplies," Garrett Guard offered.

Burk snapped his fingers and pointed at the renowned Angus breeder. "What seemed like wealth to us—food and clothing from the Red Cross, hay from the Anderson Creek fire ranchers, and fencing supplies donated from Meade to Michigan—represented out-of-reach opportunity to someone else in the community."

"We called him the siphon," Waller said. "Even though I sensed he had crossed the line of legality, we were only talking hundred-dollar loads of posts and wire. Looking back on the bounty of what's come through here, that occasional selling off could be dismissed as petty pilfering. I fault myself for magnifying those acts out of proportion. If I had treated it more like the tip of a dirty iceberg, Clint wouldn't be laying in the hospital struggling to breathe this morning."

Burk felt compelled to offer the lawman a slight rescue. "We need to stand together in this, or we continue to give the siphon the upper hand. Lyndie Sessoms was the first to recognize how all that suspicion tainted the distribution process. It sucked every last breath of generosity out of what should have been a joyous allocation."

"I don't intend to sit here and wonder who else will fall victim like Clint," Garrett said. "If there's corruption at a higher level, it could only be accomplished by a few people."

"You're welcome to throw out some names before I continue," Burk replied. "The last thing I want to do would be to overlook the obvious suspects."

"Ken Ray runs the Ashland Foundation," Rodney stated with a shrug of his shoulders.

"All the online funding comes through Tara Daniels at the library," Red McMinimy added. "That includes the Clark County Proud funds—a right sizable contribution."

Burk conceded the point, though the meek librarian had never been a blip on his radar.

"Still, all the money flow ends up at the bank," Milt Enoch said in a gravelly voice. "That throws Neil Goering into the suspect pot—for me anyway."

"Let's get into the banking aspect." Waller folded his hands together in forced restraint.

"Mr. Enoch may have spoken the truth that I stumbled onto late last night," Burk admitted. "Collections are being made. Large sums of money are being transferred locally, and then get distributed to us. Odd though, when I looked on my latest bank statement to find my Clark County Proud voucher, paid out and promptly deposited on the same day, March twenty-third, it was nowhere to be found. By all rights, that money should have landed within the latest reporting period, as designated by the closing date."

Garrett Guard stood up, kicking the crate in his haste. "What are you saying, Crosby? Our hometown bank is against us? I'm about to float a hefty loan to rebuild two houses, so now's the time to tell us anything you know."

"I only suspect," he replied, shaking his head. "Look at your March bank statements and try to find the amount of seven thousand five hundred dollars on or around the twenty-third of the month. The Ashland Foundation had received the money, the bank distributed the money, and—for those of us who trustingly deposited the voucher back into our accounts, it appears not to have been credited to us. My voucher money disappeared off the record."

Papers rustled around the table as ranchers began to scrutinize their accounts.

"It's not recorded in my account," Rodney Gillian said, his face blanched white.

"Mine's not there, either," Milt Enoch growled.

"Hold up," Waller insisted. "Let me record these claims one at a time. State your name and whether the voucher money appears on a line item in your statement."

Burk had to suppress his sky-rocketing blood pressure as the response remained the same around the table. Not one rancher had the voucher in his individual account. His turn came, and he was not about to be left out. "Burkett Crosby—no voucher money recorded in my account."

"Jacobi Haines," a frail voice said from behind him. "I've got no money showing in my account—which means the down-payment check will surely bounce for a modular house I've already ordered. To make matters worse, my father has gone missing."

Pandemonium broke out after that remark, as another local rancher seemed imperiled by the siphon's scheme. Several men started shouting at the sheriff, demanding their money. For his part, Waller maintained a modicum of self-control, carefully recording Cub's last comment.

Now that they had corroborated the missing funds, Burk sensed that time would be of the essence. Too many wagging tongues could easily slip and tip off the guilty party, given they were even on the right trail. Several ranchers began to murmur threats. Behind him, a deafening metal crash sounded. He turned to find the store's proprietor looking mildly sheepish with two trashcan lids reverberating in his hands. At least quiet had been restored.

The sheriff stood up. "I'll have to call in Kansas Bureau of Investigation for backup since this has the appearance of bank misconduct. I need advice on how to proceed."

"With Bear Haines missing, I don't think we have the luxury of time," Burk replied, forcing the lawman's hand. "We need to set a trap—a money trap. By regular hours, Goering's still at the bank until noon today. If he's involved, maybe we can get him to tip his hand."

"For one thing," Waller replied, "I'm not sure I can get KBI down here that fast. For another thing, who's got any money to bait such a trap?"

Silence fell over the entire group. Garrett clenched his teeth and buried his fist in his palm. Milt Enoch started to cough. Rich in fencing supplies, no one had ready cash.

"Lyndie Leigh Sessoms has the money for the trap," Burk said with resolve. "She's bringing back a large cash collection from the Strong City rodeo. Tara left me a text late last night. I wanted to leave her out of this, but I don't know if we can manage that, given the critical timing." His stomach started to churn with the added tension of involving Lyndie.

"Let me get with KBI," Waller said. "It may come down to stalling Goering after the bank closes. We can't afford to give him the rest of the weekend off, in case he bolts on us."

Rodney stood, showing more conviction than he had all month. "I think we bring Ken Ray in on our side. Even though I posed his name earlier, every one of us here knows Ken isn't the siphon." Several grumbled in agreement around the table.

"Tara Daniels is with Lyndie in Strong City, to help her bring the cash back safely," Burk added. "That leaves us focused on Neil Goering for the trap."

Waller nodded, clutching his notes. "Let's meet back here at high noon. We'll position for the trap from there. Until then, no one speaks a word of this to anyone else. Clear?"

"The ranchers of Clark County will stand together," Garrett said, offering a hand in the middle of the table. Other hands stacked readily on his, a real team effort. The stack gave every appearance of strength renewed.

Burk added his fist, kicking the crates back so the others could exit. He saw Cub disappear out the door without a word exchanged between them. Maybe his buddy would opt to keep that first date in Pratt and leave the mayhem on Main Street to the sheriff. That would become a matter of prayer, right after he begged God to keep Lyndie safe. When Garrett Guard offered his hand, he shook it as if hanging onto the veteran cattleman for dear life.

~

Lyndie spotted Tara's profile hiding under a palomino-tan hat and motioned her over to the auction table. From the moment the gates had opened, folks had flocked in to Saturday's rodeo. Word must have gotten around, as more individuals seemed aware of the fundraiser. Sally had given her an empty pickle jar from the concession stand for cash donations. Early yet, it already stood three-quarters full. "Good morning, Tara. Thanks a million for coming out today."

The off-duty librarian gave her daypack a push aside and leaned over to give her a quick hug. "The more I thought about this, the more I simply couldn't miss the show. Goodness, your auction display looks great. I love the farewell tour banner."

"Thanks. Bids for the auction items have picked up, too. Somehow, I think the Western Star broadcast elevated the cause this weekend."

"Or maybe the combination of on-air appeal and on-the-ground presence brought the success. We'll have plenty of time to analyze that later. Remember the gambler's sage advice—never count your cards while still sitting at the table."

"Oh gosh, wouldn't that song be a hoot in my final

show?" She laughed as she sat out the last auction box, stroking her green satin jacket with fondness.

"Red is definitely the color to wear today. You'll look like an asteroid blazing through the darkness of space as you go out." Tara's eyes twinkled as her tone carried a tease. "If I were you, I'd sing Dolly Parton's 'Nine to Five' on my way out, not the gambler's song."

Lyndie laughed so hard at the suggestion, she had to hold her side. Having a friend along made all the difference in the world. A couple stopped by the pickle jar and let a handful of cash tumble in. "The Clark County ranchers sure thank you for that donation." The man tipped his hat and continued toward the grandstands while the woman did a double take over her shoulder. She seemed to like the red jacket. Lyndie hoped she had the money to back up her fine taste.

"I don't know why this green set hasn't had much bidding," Tara said. "I've been contemplating bringing some memorabilia back for the Friends of the Library annual book sale. Since you're going to be our newest resident, it only follows that we would want to add a token of your fame from the rodeo circuit."

She sensed a blush burning her cheeks. "Come on, Tara. I'd rather be plain old Lyndie to the folks in Ashland. There, I can pull a dog out of the dumpster and be a local heroine for the day. That's really about all the notoriety I want to claim from here on out." Two more patrons stuffed the pickle jar with cash on their way into the arena.

Tara leaned across the table. "I had an idea come to me for your final song today—to keep the farewell from seeming too solitary. It's an old librarian's trick, I'm afraid."

The toes of her red boots inched forward toward the collusion. "Please, tell me. I sure don't want to go through a meltdown out there after the last note."

"Simply this—invite all the children out on the arena floor with you. Somehow, when you close the distance between you and your audience, they become a part of you—

and you belong to them."

"That's a most excellent idea. Plus, it definitely works for the song I've chosen to end the performance. Let me work on the invitation some, as I want to word it just right. Oh, goodness. Here comes my manager. It must be time for my act."

Tara patted her arm. "I'll go find my seat. This is exciting. Give it your absolute best."

"I plan to. Hey, can you drop by from time to time and help Ernie count the pickle jar?"

She gave her an authentic librarian's shush, complete with a finger to her lips. In a swift gesture, she lifted a bank deposit bag from her daypack and gave a little wink. "Here to help."

Lyndie's palms began to sweat. She sensed a compelling need to retrieve Tracer. When Ernie approached, she dashed through the side gate to her trailer. Showtime—for one last time.

~

Burk rolled the hay from the pickup's bed, eyeing the gate to the upper pasture. He planned to move the herd up on Monday to ease the pressure on the sprouting grass here. The cemetery gate would allow him plenty of access to drop more hay. By this time next month, they wouldn't need the hay supplement any longer. That lent him a distant hope that things would improve, though he could scarcely project beyond the noontime showdown.

Milt Enoch's comment about all money flows leading to the bank came to mind. He fought off the anger that rose from such a domestic betrayal. Despicable greed likely drove the entire scam. No matter how generous people around the state and entire country had been, someone who knew their individual names had placed his own financial gain over their collective well-being. If he mulled it over for too long, he'd lose his ability to stay in control. His phone pinged, grating his patience further. Seeing the text was from

Waller, he had to look.

KBI agreeable to trap. Need to leak money amount to dangle bait. Contact Tara for rough figure to lure Goering. Also get ETA in Ashland. Share no information.

Relief flooded Burk's senses. Waller might be his favorite person right now, but only until Lyndie could return. He'd shift allegiances in a heartbeat. Right now, he needed to bait a trap with the smell of money. He knew the rat would reach for it—a fatal affinity.

Thinking about his message, he decided to keep it simple. *Negotiating to keep bank open today for your cash deposit. Can you send me a general $ figure and estimate what time you ladies will roll in? Your welcome committee host.* He slammed the tailgate and left the cattle to be contented herbivores. The land tenders had a battle to wage in town.

~

Lyndie waved at the attendant leading Tracer away, creating a pause to set some distance between her previous song and her final number. She removed her red-banded black hat and set it on a speaker while the applause thinned around the arena. "Bless you, everybody. Thank you so much. Oh, me. It's come time to say goodbye to the rodeo circuit so God can grow me into the next phase of my life. I'll be hiding out in tiny Ashland Kansas, helping the burned-out ranchers rebuild and watching my apples grow. If you ever get out that far west, feel free to drop by and see Lyndie Leigh, will you please?"

The crowd roared in response, its message indiscernible.

She took a moment to scan the full breadth of the grandstands as her audience quieted. From now on, she'd be up there looking down. The new perspective held loads of appeal. After checking her microphone, she cleared the emotion from her throat and swirled around. "I don't think I can do this last part without some help. Could you loan me your children from the stands? I sure could use their help breaking free. What about it, kids? Can you come stand with me?"

As planned, Wes opened a railing midfield and created an access on one side of the arena. His helper soon cleared the other side. A vivacious wave of little ones ran onto the well-groomed grounds, adding levity to the moment. Many wore western attire, making it a real posse of miniature cowboys and cowgirls. *Thanks, Tara, for steering me in the right direction.*

She motioned the children closer and several little girls readily responded. Seeing an adorable cowgirl with her hair in braids, Lyndie stooped and offered her hand. Once the girl took it, she had everything she needed. She delivered the song's challenging first line clear and crisp, suggesting that the listener remember to feel small when they stood beside the ocean.

As soon as she got to the chorus about choosing to dance no matter the circumstance, the children instinctively picked up the message and began to act it out. Several locked arms to square dance, while others two-stepped. A line dance formed on the far left and began to parade around the perimeter. Hoots and calls rained down from the stands. The audience seemed to love the spontaneous cahoots.

With a happy heart, she launched into the second stanza where doors had to open and close on life's journey. Nothing could hold more truth about her life that that analogy. She grew a bit teary-eyed when she posed to the audience once again the choice to dance. When the little girl holding her hand wanted to promenade around, she followed with a rhythmic shuffle.

A musical bridge offered her a vocal break, which she used to soak in the moment. The audience clapped to the beat while the children cavorted around the grounds in unrestricted fun.

Drawing deep breaths to replenish her air supply, Lyndie felt drawn to the line dance, so she led the little girl over and linked up to lead the rest. On cue, she sang out the chorus one more time, flinging gestures from her heart toward the crowd. After the last note ended, she bowed from the waist, her long hair cascading down like a final curtain. She straightened and gestured to the children to include them in the tribute. From the back of the line, a lanky teen strode up, took her hand, and kissed it while sweeping off his white hat.

Sobs joined her tears at that point. While she tried to collect herself and retrieve her hat, a rodeo clown appeared with an oversized broom and swept the children back toward the gates. Laughter rippled from the stands, helping lift her mood. She located her hat, clipped the microphone onto its stand, and walked toward the exit. Her final gig had ended. Once under the building's overhang, applause circling the arena grew muffled. The haunting question now remained— would she miss it?

Chapter 22

Burk approached Sheriff Waller's vehicle. He had everything he needed, but a clear way out of this mess. He caught sight of Ken Ray in the front passenger seat, looking like a flattened armadillo on the side of the road. Wishing he could have spared Ken this pretend role, he opened the rear door and slid inside. The trap had to maintain the appearance of standard operating procedure, so they desperately needed Ken's involvement.

"Sheriff, here's the information you wanted from the Strong City contingency." He handed his phone to the lawman to let him read the text directly.

Waller stared at the screen. "Lyndie raised forty-five thousand dollars at the rodeo?"

Burk stifled a tense laugh. "Yeah, that includes the auctioned off wardrobe items and the last-minute selling of her horse. She wants to donate all proceeds, so she lumped her personal items in with the charitable collection." Respect for her selflessness swelled at the admission.

Ken turned and gave him a knowing look without saying a word. His face appeared wax-like, stiff and pale. From all signs, he'd taken this forced play to ferret out the siphon pretty hard.

"Thank you for being here, Ken," he offered. "The other

ranchers asked for you by name. Know that they're standing right behind you on this thing. I hope that helps some."

The man nodded once, staring out the windshield.

"At any rate, we have what we need," Waller said. "Their two-thirty estimated arrival gives KBI more time. We formulated an op plan. I remain the arresting authority. KBI provides backup muscle for the operation. There shouldn't be a hitch unless Neil flat-out refuses to stay."

Burk chewed the inside of his cheek considering that possibility. "Once he hears how much money is coming in, won't he want to line up where he's sending it for immediate investment? Isn't that his usual trick—using the donation money to generate interest that he steals while stalling to make the sum available locally?"

"I'm guessing that's how it goes," Waller replied. "Underhanded banking."

A muffled retching noise echoed from the front. In seconds, Ken threw open the car door and emptied the contents of his stomach onto the ground behind the convenience store.

As Waller passed him a sharp look in the rearview mirror, Burk sucked in a breath and reassessed the risks. Their amateurish approach to setting the trap began to feel like a sieve, chock full of holes. He reviewed the plan of action and realized he fell within the inner loop by virtue of his friendship with Lyndie. *So include me.* Fortified, he leaned forward to relate the decision. "I'm going in with Ken to set this trap. Goering won't question it when I play the role of the bragging boyfriend. I'll emphasize how excited Lyndie is about the fundraiser's success."

"Yeah," Waller replied. "I like that a lot. Then Ken would have some help. Let's do it."

Ken closed the door and wiped his mouth on his sleeve. He made a faint groan as the clock ticked ever toward the forced encounter. His countenance took a demotion from wax replica of a living man to all-out corpse.

"I want both of you to know that I'm a praying man," Burk said, his tone anything but light. "For this particular caper, I'm about to hit overdrive on that aspect. Ken, let me drive us to the bank. We'll come up from the south, like we're heading in from the fairgrounds."

"Which is where I'd rather be," he replied dryly.

"Good luck, gentlemen," Waller said, "and remember the part about pressing for voucher distribution early in the week. We want to get his excuses recorded to use against him in court."

Burk needed to patch another hole in the sieve. "Is Ken wired and ready to go?"

"He's wired, all right," Waller replied.

"One out of two ain't bad," Ken added in a meek tone.

When the reluctant player leveraged his door open, Burk followed his lead. He doubted that would last long, but he'd be there to shore up the situation if Ken faltered. They had too much at stake not to fully commit. His thoughts drifted to Lyndie as he walked to his truck. Funny that he'd taken up showmanship right when she'd relinquished it. He'd call that laughing all the way to the bank—yet one more thing he'd have to pretend.

~

Still numb from selling Tracer, Lyndie increased her cruise control speed a notch to keep pace with Tara's aggressive lead. A last-minute decision she felt good about, they'd stuffed all the cash bags into Tara's locked trunk. Checking her rearview mirror as second nature, she momentarily forgot that the horse trailer was no longer her concern. From now on, she only had the camper. She sighed, spying a more immediate mess. The jumble in the backseat could be dealt with later. Maybe Burk would enjoy seeing her farewell tour banner after-the-fact.

Her phone pinged from the console. She saw Cub's name come up. Too unexpected to ignore, she grabbed the phone and gave the text a quick glance.

Do NOT trust anyone in Ashland today.

Uncertainty pulsed through her veins. Could Cub possibly know about their sizable deposit? Still, if something was up in town, surely Burk would have let on. Instead, his earlier text had read like a sweet welcome home message. She blew out a breath. The tension would lessen once the money sat safely in the bank's vault, of that she could be sure.

Up the highway, Tara's white car had become a mere dot on the horizon. She mashed the accelerator with her socked foot, having sold the red boots along with the jacket and hat—all to the lady with fine taste. In a momentary lapse, she wondered if Tara fell within Cub's trust-no-one warning. "Forty-five thousand dollars—come back to momma." Suspicion ruled yet again.

~

The last thing the banker wanted at eleven forty-five Saturday was more traffic through the door. Once he recognized Ken Ray headed towards him, he gave an exhale of relief. Ken had a knack for brevity, a quality he admired. They were both businessmen, after all, and understood the value of time. He led the young rancher who lived out by Sitka, possibly Ken's helper for the day. He stepped toward them, his hand out to shake Ken's. "Gentlemen, how are you today?"

Ken made quick work of the handshake. "We're here with some big news for the Ashland Foundation. Do you have a minute to give us private audience in your office?"

"One solid gold minute, coming right up," he replied, gesturing to his door.

Burk Crosby entered first with long strides. He plunked down in the second guest chair. Ken followed in mincing steps and slipped into the closer chair.

Thinking to pace behind the desk to feign impatience, he reconsidered and parked his heft on its corner instead. "I love big news, especially if it has a dollar sign leading it."

Ken nodded. "How about forty-five thousand dollars, to be precise?"

"That's what Lyndie Leigh Sessoms is bringing back from the Strong City Rodeo," Crosby added, a catty grin splitting his face.

He modulated his pleasure with a faint smile to placate his audience. "Well, well. It must have been quite a show then. I instructed Tara to place the proceeds directly in the deposit box when they got back into town this afternoon."

Ken slid to the edge of his chair. "About that, Neil. For such a big lump of money, I'd feel a whole lot better if you could stay open and take in the deposit personally. The Ashland Foundation needs that money right bad. If anything was to happen—"

Crosby held up his phone. "Lyndie texted me she'd be here by two-thirty, coming straight to the bank."

"If you stayed open to log in the deposit today," Ken posed, "we could make a quick distribution to the ranchers by midweek—or possibly sooner."

That suggestion crimped his operating room. He'd have to flash some caution. "Hold on, Ken. You're too worked up about this. Money-handling is a slow procedure, all things considered. I have to go through protocol to make sure the sum is well-documented and makes its way through the proper channels. There's always a day or two delay to using your money following the deposit. You know that." He dusted off his palms to be done with the deal.

The young rancher's expression dropped like someone had stolen his candy. "Lyndie practically begged to have you wait. She won't feel safe until the money's in your hands. Folks like us aren't used to such big amounts of money. After she and Tara counted it, they had upwards of nine or ten bags."

Have mercy. He'd forgotten to take into account the bulk of such a sizable collection. "Oh, really? That actually may pose a problem then. The deposit drawer is designed for five bags at most. No wonder she wants me here. She really does have a big load to drop off."

The rancher laughed. "Now you're seeing it our way." He stood as if the candy was back in his hand. "So what can I tell Lyndie to expect?"

He studied Ken for a protracted second. "Okay, I'll keep the bank open until two-thirty. Tell her to come inside. Ken, can you drop back by on Monday to work out a schedule for the pending distribution? Maybe by then, you won't be in such a frantic rush."

Ken stood and wiped his sweaty face. "I reckon I can do that. Thanks for hearing us out, Neil. I sure appreciate it." He led the way out of the office, looking a little worse for wear.

Once the taller man had darkened his doorway, he slid into his chair and brought the computer back up. *Where can I place forty-five grand for forty-eight hours?* The singular enjoyment of clandestine money management brought the sensation of leisure back to his weekend. What an entrancing hobby, a hidden gem of indulgence.

~

Though the banked curves south of Bucklin had been quite the challenge at their speed, Lyndie felt a flutter of joy crossing the bridge into Ashland. She reflected on that first day when their access had been denied. So much had changed since she met Burk that day. Seeing Tara's indication for turning onto Main Street, she slowed and pulled on her turn signal.

Main Street appeared as broad as ever. When she got to the corner of Fifth Street, she spotted Mandy strolling the baby with little Abby trailing behind on a tricycle. She gave an enthusiastic wave as she passed, thrilled to see a familiar face. The library seemed quiet, having already closed for the day. Each nuance became more endeared to her, block by block. Passing two cars parked at the grocery store, she slowed at the corner and pulled across from the bank.

Tara wasted no time in releasing her trunk latch to fetch the money. She soon appeared outside the vehicle, searching for her helper. Her gesture to hurry could not be misinterpreted.

Lyndie took her keys, hopped out, and trotted across in socked feet to Tara's hybrid vehicle. "Here, load me up with as many bags as you can. We may have to make two trips."

"Not if I can help it," Tara replied, heaving two bulky bags into her arms. Two more followed, leaving room for a fifth bag right under her chin. "Hold up and let's walk in together. I don't see anything suspicious, but we don't want to let down our guard at this late juncture."

"I can't thank you enough for coming to help. This might have been too much for me."

"Nonsense. Still, it was my treat to help out." Once the last bag cleared, Tara slammed the trunk. They walked to the bank entrance, and she tugged at the door.

A wave of relief washed over Lyndie with the final hurdle out of the way. When they walked into the bank's lobby, the head banker stood there to greet them.

"Hey, Neil," Tara said. "Thanks so much for waiting for us. Glad you can take this cash off our hands."

"Anything to help," he replied, his arms outstretched. "Let's take this cache up front and I'll note the deposit. Guess you had quite the final show, young lady."

Lyndie rushed through the last three steps just to get the weight of the money onto the counter. The tile floor made her feet cold. "Yes, sir. It proved highly memorable in every way."

"She went out in a blaze of singing glory," Tara added, slipping her bags with the others. "I'll take the receipt on Ken's behalf, just to document the deposit for the Ashland Foundation."

The banker looked up at her a split second and kept logging into the cashier's station. "Sure, that's fine. I'm afraid the paperwork might have Monday's date preprinted on it, since the bank day officially ended at noon. Everything's pre-programmed nowadays."

"Highly understandable," Tara replied.

Lyndie unzipped the first bag. "Should we start placing the bills in piles?"

The banker stuck out two stiff arms. "No, I'll trust your total until my clerks can verify it on Monday. Where's your tabulation, Tara?"

The woman searched for the requested slip in the recesses of her daypack. "Oh, here it is. Forgot I tucked it into the side pocket."

"We both counted the money, so I'm fairly confident of the amount," Lyndie added. She blew out a breath and sent Tara a supportive smile.

The banker soon held out his handwritten receipt. "This will do until the printers are up on Monday. Please come back by, and we'll finalize your transaction."

As her grateful reply sat on the tip of her tongue, several stern-faced men wearing blue polo shirts rushed into the bank lobby. "Everyone down on the floor," the lead man shouted. He held his position about ten feet from the counter.

When Sheriff Waller strode past, Lyndie knelt in stunned disbelief. The money still sat on the counter, exposed and extremely vulnerable. Someone's hand shoved her shoulder, forcing her to the floor.

Waller nodded at the lead man and approached the counter. "Neil Goering, you're under arrest for embezzlement of funds from your customers, as well as from the Ashland Foundation. We're taking you in, plus we're confiscating your computer and your transaction records as evidence of your patterned offenses. Once we get Clint Hooper's full testimony, I stand ready to add attempted murder to those charges against you."

Her cheek crushed against the tile floor, Lyndie managed to make eye contact with Tara. The woman looked wounded beyond belief. "Dear God above," she whispered.

The man standing over her produced a pair of handcuffs from his cargo pocket. His muscular jaw tensed as the confrontation intensified. Emblazoned on his polo shirt in gold thread were the letters KBI.

Tara locked her hands behind her head as a hapless victim. When her forehead pressed the dirty floor, her anguish became unmistakable. What a helpless pair they made.

Sheriff Waller spoke over his shoulder. "You ladies can get off the floor now. I believe the atmosphere may be much more to your liking outside." With a curt nod toward the door, he closed the distance between lawman and violator.

Dazed, Lyndie squatted, stood and walked to the rear of the bank where another KBI agent guarded the door. Without so much as taking a breath, she pushed through the heavy glass door and found a contingent of her rancher friends standing in an arc around the bank's entrance. A line of sleek muscle cars had parked along Main Street, as if to seal off access. Several matching SUVs lurked behind them. None of the spectators moved.

Sheriff Waller shouldered through the door, his grip clenching the shackled hands of the heavy-set banker. Several KBI men followed, carrying laptops and stacks of bank records. As if on cue, someone standing in the rear started clapping at their sudden appearance. The applause picked up with regularity.

Burk stepped onto the sidewalk and approached her with a timid smile. "You just helped catch the head siphon, Ms. Lyndie Leigh. Sorry we couldn't let you in on the trap, but now we can say what we really mean. On behalf of the ranchers of Clark County, welcome home."

A rowdy cheer went up as many others repeated the sentiment. Lyndie pressed her temples to hold back her over-the-top shock. Tara clamped a hug around her middle and gave her a validating look. Beyond her, a parade of confiscation headed for the sleek cars.

She scanned the faces in the crowd, all area ranchers she had the pleasure of serving from the distribution line. She tried to blink back pent-up tears, knowing they would come anyway. Cub's warning evaporated like the final sinister suspicion. At last, she beheld only good guys.

Hearing the sheriff's gruff voice behind her, she turned to see him help escort a protesting Neil Goering across a break in the sidewalk. With hands cuffed behind his back, his indulged profile jutted out even more. He resembled a bloated cow carcass, not a sinister siphon. Still, he had extracted something from everyone with all the suspicion he'd planted, something of utmost value—trust.

Two men opened the rear doors of the SUVs. A computer soon topped the confiscation pile. When Goering refused to step off the sidewalk toward the sheriff's vehicle, Waller leaned in to add a bit of muscular persuasion.

Lyndie felt the caress of Burk's touch when he reached for her arm. Out of nowhere, the sound of screeching tires pealed up Main Street. From the far side of the sidewalk, a little girl screamed. An old truck careened into view. Before she could draw a breath, it inexplicably veered straight toward the bank building.

At Sheriff Waller's shouted warning, Burk lunged to knock him out of harm's way. The KBI agents scrambled to take cover behind the last SUV. The runaway vehicle rammed into the bank with a horrendous crash. Dislodged bricks tumbled onto the truck's hood.

Shackled and lacking any assistance to dodge the truck, Neil Goering had been mercilessly pinned against the building by the truck's protruding bumper. His lifeless torso now lay across the truck's crumpled front fender. The whole scene spoke of surrender.

Lyndie held her hands over her face, reluctant to view the gruesome outcome.

Burk maneuvered through the onlookers to check on the errant vehicle's driver. The man's head rested on the steering wheel, his face covered with blood. Burk touched his neck and turned to face the crowd. "Somebody call in the ambulance. It's Milt Enoch. He's bleeding from the impact. It looks like he's having a spell."

"Yeah—a spell of justice," Tara said under her breath, all the while dialing her phone. In mere seconds, a distant siren pierced the air.

Waller returned with a noticeable limp. He hobbled over to aid Burk with the jammed truck door. After a couple of tries, their combined strength overrode the buckled metal.

From where she stood, inertia had ruled for too long. Lyndie closed the distance between her and the accident victim. She placed a caring hand on Burk's back as he tried to ease the driver's discomfort. Several of the KBI agents pressed by to assess Goering's status. She had no sympathy in that particular direction. "Hang in there, Mr. Enoch. We're going to buy that new windmill for your Krier pasture, don't you worry. I bet she'll sing like an angel in the Kansas wind. Once we get her running, there'll be water aplenty for your cattle."

The old man held a bloody hand out to her, so she took it with a squeeze. Burk placed a kiss on her temple as Tara appeared with a tissue, trying to mop the smeared blood from the crash victim's fingers. Somehow, despite the betrayal and ensuing upheaval, the whole scene settled to feel more like a homecoming. Their community stood undivided once again.

A siren rounded the corner. Garrett Guard stepped down and motioned toward the victim. "The ambulance crew is here, Burk. Let's yield Milt to their expert care now. We've all done what we could do."

Burk stepped back onto the sidewalk and beckoned to Lyndie. In no time, he held her in his arms. Their embrace became a nucleus of sorts, as the ranchers surrounded them in a packed huddle. Feminine voices soon revealed the inclusion of Tara, Mandy, and little Abby. In the midst, Burk began a prayer that many soon echoed. His lips pressed her forehead as his petition took wing, flying beyond the grain elevator towers toward a kingdom in the sky.

"Milt's going to be just fine," one EMT called out. "Just his diabetes flaring up."

She felt Burk's lips lower in search of hers, so she rose on tiptoe to close the gap. *Home at last.* What a magnificent feeling it brought, from head to toe.

Little Abby snaked an arm around her neck. "Can I have some of your apples, Lyndie?"

She ended the kiss to hug the girl back. "Yes, honey. Since I'll be staying right here in Ashland, let's pick them together." That earned her one wink and a few laughs around the huddle. She'd remember that particular cedar-green wink. Yes, she would cherish the source of that wink for quite some time to come.

Chapter 23

Sunday's ecumenical service had proven quite the magnet, as everyone in the county seemed to be in attendance. Even their oldest members, the Fellows, attended. When Lyndie spotted Clint Hooper and Gene Shawboro sitting side by side in matching wheelchairs, it made her reflect on the night of the evacuation. Despite all appearances of what the wildfire had taken from them in its vicious raid, the residents still had assembled to give thanks to God and celebrate their fledgling recovery. That intangible resilience made her want to stay—that and a few other persuasions.

Burk laughed heartily from a loose collaboration of ranchers at two adjoining tables. The Guard family had shown up in full force, a major contingency that embodied the comeback spirit. Garrett fired another good-natured volley and everyone chuckled at Burk's expense.

Tara grabbed her arm and pulled her toward a quieter corner. "Here's the scoop. Ken has a major announcement to make. He's absolutely giddy about it. I'm not positive about the contents, but I sure hope it has some money attached."

"Me, too," Lyndie replied. "Do you know if the KBI confiscated my cash donation with their evidence yesterday?"

Tara shook her head, making her graying bob sway. "Nobody's saying a word about the details. Did you hear? Sheriff Waller doesn't want this service sullied by any mention of Neil Goering or his tragic demise. I can't say as I blame him for that censorship."

"Burk promised to tell me more, but he did allude to how gut-wrenching every decision seemed when they planned out the trap. He mentioned Ken's struggle, in particular."

Tara rallied with a smile. "Well, let's honor the sheriff's wishes, shall we? Today, we celebrate the rebuilding of a resilient ranching community. That should be our main focus."

When Lyndie glanced up, Burk approached with a determined look on his face. "Okay, I need to go take a seat. See you in the food line after the speeches."

Burk leaned between them, ready for her company. "With so much food over there—I hope the talking runs short." He took her elbow and guided her past several tables to his spot.

Cub stood momentarily while she took her seat. He leaned over the table as if he had a secret. "Hey, guys. I heard from Bear last night. Get this—he's in Branson, Missouri playing banjo in a regular nightly show. He always wanted to do something flashy like that, so I guess this proved as good a time as any."

Burk laughed and shook his head. "We didn't exactly have him all figured out, did we?"

Lyndie patted Cub's hand. "I'm so relieved for you. Don't you want to sneak down there and see the performance for yourself?"

His expression grew comical until the red-haired woman on his right side leaned in and hugged his arm. "I think we'll plan that in the next week or two. Everything gets arranged around the delivery of that new house. My, oh, my—that arrival is larger than life."

Lyndie smiled at Brooke and adjusted her chair to better

view the stage. Soon, a warm breath tickled her ear. She leaned back to get a close-up of Burk and inhaled a hint of his aftershave.

"Just to look at you heals my smoke-weary eyes," he whispered through her hair.

"You don't say? Do you need more ointment applied, Mr. Crosby?" She gave him an evaluative look over her shoulder, but couldn't spot any visible wounds.

"Ladies and gentlemen," Ken Ray said. "If I may have your attention this morning, we'd like to begin and end with a word to the Lord, given it's his holy day of rest. With this morning's invocation, we have the pastor of Community Church."

Validated to have familiar faces at the podium, Lyndie tucked her arms around her waist and prepared to bow for the prayer. When Burk's arm wrapped hers, she welcomed it into the fold. The prayer came as a simple expression of gratitude for provision and guidance, sentiments which she fully shared. Upon speaking the benediction, she sensed a cleansing wind that must have dropped straight from heaven onto the high school's occupants. What a blessing.

A commotion began by the double doors leading out front. The sound of heavy wood scraping the floor soon repeated. Ken retook the platform with a grin spreading across his face. "We knew we couldn't hide this particular donation from you—so here it is. Members of the Kansas chapters of Future Farmers of America hereby donate fifty hand-crafted picnic tables to Ashland with this message. 'To the ranchers of Clark County, we believe in the future of agriculture, and we believe in you.' Let's give these FFA students some thanks."

A round of applause filled the building. Several young men wearing blue corduroy coats stopped hauling tables long enough to take a bow. Brooke held up a finger to Cub, putting in a claim for her table. Lyndie thought his responding smile was adorable. They made a cute couple.

"Okay, on with the program," Ken said into the microphone. "Ten days ago, we celebrated the first voucher-driven payout from our online donation site, Clark County Proud. I'd like to publically thank Tara Daniels for making that tremendous transfer of funds possible."

Lyndie searched for her confidante and found Tara at a table predominantly occupied by women. Her associates prompted her to stand. Tara capitulated as the applause rose, but she soon flashed them her trademark shushing gesture and then sank back into her chair. The little smile that snuck out from beneath the librarian's finger made the day seem all the more precious.

"We also want to thank the nameless donors who contributed to this and all the other funds being received by the Ashland Foundation," Ken said. "You make our recovery possible, so we thank each one of you from the bottom of our hearts."

When the humble man touched his chest, Lyndie felt a wince of emotion deep inside. With all that Ken had received and distributed, he still acted in earnest on behalf of the townspeople. It had been her version of Clark County Proud to serve beside him daily.

"I think we need to show Ken some appreciation," a voice boomed from the corner. A familiar figure in uniform stepped out of the shadows, gesturing to the podium. The audience applauded in ready agreement.

Ken wrenched away from the microphone as if trying to dodge Sheriff Waller's accolades. His discomfort with the public recognition caused a giggle to bubble up Lyndie's throat. How many times had those two been on opposite ends of the topic at hand? This time, the friendly rub didn't worry her in the least. One of them finally had their civic responsibilities in proper order—or perhaps, they both did. Burk's warm hand slipped around to trap hers.

Ken motioned for the return of quiet. "How am I supposed to tell you about this next miracle if nobody can hear me?" The room soon settled into a lull. "Okay, this news just came in from Kansas Farm Bureau. 'Dear Clark County ranchers, you cannot imagine how much you've been on our collective minds in the wake of the wildfire disaster. Please know that we've gone to bat to support your recovery, so that every operator of an agricultural endeavor that wants to carry on will have adequate resources to do so. With this in mind, we have two distinct funds being collected right now for your benefit. We hope you'll bear with us as we approach the closing dates for collection, with distribution to follow immediately thereafter.'"

Lyndie leaned back in her chair and soon felt Burk's breath on her neck. When his chin came to rest on her shoulder, she laced her fingers between his. Instead of quelling his slight tremble, she became an extension of it. Electricity seemed to run through their connection.

"So," Ken continued, "we don't know how much money will be divided, only that it will come our way. However, I do have the results of the Farm Bureau's Young Ranchers selection process, for which the Ashland Foundation provided oversight during the application process. It's my honor to announce that Burkett Crosby and Jacobi Haines of Clark County both qualified to receive extra funding through this supplemental program. Congratulations, gentlemen."

Applause swamped the building in hardy affirmation. At Garrett Guard's insistence, Burk started to rise from his seat. He clamped an arm around Cub's shoulders and brought him up alongside as a slightly shorter sidekick. Cub's expression twisted with emotion as he swiped at the corner of one eye.

Lyndie could hardly contain her joy. Applauding didn't seem like enough, so she started praising God's name right out loud. Several around her picked up and spread the sentiment, giving God the glory. When Burk slid back into his chair, his chin returned to her shoulder. Unable to resist his proximity, she planted a kiss on his cheek.

"What in the world am I going to do with all that

money?" His whisper carried an extra nibble at her earlobe.

"Well, you can replace your burned-up ATV for one," she replied, lifting an eyebrow.

"I've given some thought to building a horse stall with a lean-to for foul weather out back. Does that seem forward-thinking?" His voice held a mystified gravelly texture, like he'd spoken something out of reverence.

Lyndie pressed her lips together, charmed at his inclusion of her in such future plans. "You do have a lot of riding room out there. What about adding a dog run in the backyard?"

Burk moved closer, so that only inches separated them. "The whole ranch is a dog run. There's room for all of it—every part of the dream."

He held her in such a mesmerizing gaze, she could scarcely pay attention to Ken's introduction of the lady truck driver from Michigan. "We probably should go some place quiet to talk after this," she whispered against his cheek. She caught his wink as he pulled back into his seat, making her wonder what he might have planned. One trap had already played out in her immediate vicinity, but she didn't sense another. No, if today proved anything, suspicion had no place in Ashland, Kansas. Only trust and truth prevailed, proof of their lasting virtue.

Burk leaned forward and nosed into her hair. "Don't get too neighborly afterwards and lose track of me. I have something else in mind for us this afternoon."

She turned to search out his sincerity and found a blaze instead, not unlike a wildfire in its intensity. Those cedar-green eyes had turned incendiary, ever heightening their appeal. *Good Lord above.* Nothing else seemed to matter beyond the greening of that immediate landscape, a most pleasurable horizon that held a hidden promise of something more.

Epilogue

Burk drove west, knowing they had to revisit this spot. With Lyndie pressed against his right shoulder, he considered overshooting the entry drive to preserve their closeness, but Dodge City seemed much less romantic as a date destination by comparison. He turned the truck and let it amble up the approach to the parking lot. Relief washed over him. They had the place to themselves again. Once the truck tires tapped the telephone pole outlining the lot, he turned off the ignition and planted a kiss in her hair. "Okay, little Sweetheart of Naptime—we're here."

Lyndie straightened and stretched. She soon spied the sign for the Living Water Monument and sprang for the far door. "Oh, yes. I so want to be here. And this time, I'm wearing my trusty cowgirl boots." The door popped open, and she gave a feisty kick as if to show her readiness for the challenging climb.

Burk slid his hand into the front pocket of his jeans, making sure he had adequately prepared for the terrain up ahead. Once confident he could approach the water's edge, he quickly caught up to his eager passenger. "Hey, remember how you called this the most honest place on earth when we visited the first time?"

She tucked her loose hair up and glanced at him over her

shoulder before descending. "I'm totally for honesty Mr. Crosby. In fact, now would be a fine time to tell me what the 'N' stands for in your name." Impish, she took off down the stone steps as if wanting to be chased.

Burk laughed, tickled by her infectious spirit. In a burst of energy, he caught up to her and halted her progress on that same bottom step that caused her hitch-up the first visit. After taking a brief inventory of her fine facial features, he felt the time for truth had arrived. "The 'N' stands for Nelson—and yes, I'm afraid to admit it's borrowed from Willie Nelson, my father's favorite country music singer."

She giggled, her gaze caressing his. "Well, who could have guessed it would come back around to country music? I kind of like that."

"No," he insisted, planting a finger across her lips. "Not like—there's no room for *like* in that offer." With that overdramatized delivery, he plopped down the stone step and extended his arms. "Come on, you're going down riding piggyback, cowgirl."

"Wahoo!" In seconds, she'd made the jump to climb aboard. "Take me to my fish friends and let the nibbling begin." She stole his hat and put it on her head.

Happiness exploded inside his chest, a depth of happiness like he'd never experienced before. In half a minute of jaunty progress, they had arrived at the water's edge, as tranquil a spot as the local landscape held. He eased his grip and let her slide down to stand near the pond.

"Imagine what a permanent water source meant to the thirsty," she said in a whispery voice, her tone almost musical. "The shortgrass prairie seems to be questing in a similar way, which is why I truly love western Kansas." She placed his hat on a nearby rock.

He couldn't wait—not with her speaking from the heart like that. When she started to squat by the water's edge, he pulled against the motion. "Hold up for a second. Let me say something before you get too distracted by the residents here—something to do with truth."

Her brow flinched as if to assess his earnestness. She straightened and looked deeper into his eyes. "I want to hear everything you have to say, Burkett Nelson Crosby."

Unable to do this without some kind of bridge between them, he reached out and took her left hand. Reinforced when she clamped her grip on his, he drew a breath. The pond mirrored the sky, and not a single creature moved. The time had come—to be honest with her and with his feelings. "Lyndie, when you went away, somebody stole the sunshine right out of my sky. There I stood, in the same old house the wildfire had spared by the grace of God—but it wasn't the same at all. Everything changed when you came into my life, and that change happened for the better. Your love turned every day into a feast, but when you left town, I only had crumbs."

She moved closer and gave his hand a squeeze. "I had a few things I needed to give up. Believe me, it didn't feel like a feast to me either when we were apart—especially at night when you weren't there to share a comforting perspective on the day's events."

Fighting the urge to wrap her in his arms, he gave in to his trembling knees and sank into the pond's sandy shore. "Give me the feast then, and don't let us be apart ever again. I'm asking you to marry me, Lyndie Leigh. Let me live the love every day—the love I see in your eyes. Would you marry me and be my happy wife?"

"Happy?" she questioned, leaning into him as if to search out his sincerity. "No—there's no room for *happy* in this offer. Ecstatic, yes…a devoted wife, yes. Sharing in the feast of a life together, yes. I hope that's the answer you wanted, Burk, because it's the only answer I have to give." She tilted her head ever so slightly, inviting his response.

He tugged her down to kneel in front of him, knowing her affinity for the pond's surface. "Yes, it's the answer I wanted all right, and here's a little something to prove it."

He produced the diamond ring and slid it in place, right before he stole her next breath with a kiss. When she molded to perfection in his grasp, he took that as another truth the landscape held as certain.

After the embrace, Lyndie sat back on her ankles, her blue eyes a banquet. She leaned toward the pond and slid her ring-bearing hand underwater. Within seconds, the fish began to validate their claim of promised togetherness with a few harmless nibbles.

From a place of trust and truth, they would build a lifetime of happiness. Peace encircled the sheltering willow tree. All wariness and suspicion had been cast aside. Burk reached for Lyndie, taking his place at the watering hole as a man blessed through and through.

Author Bio:

Cindy M. Amos writes about ranching life with "man on the land" fiction from the heartland of America. Dedicated to the family's ranchland in both the tallgrass and shortgrass prairies of Kansas, she enjoys mixing honest sweat equity and nature appreciation as she accomplishes her ranching chores. In March 2017, a devastating wildfire evacuated her in-laws from their western ranch in Clark County for a sleepless night in her Wichita home. The story-line of "Rekindled from Ashes" emerged from the real-life recovery experience of local ranchers and the author's hands-on involvement in rolling up damaged fencing across miles of scorched land. Factual testimonies of Clark County residents surviving the Starbuck wildfire have been compiled into "The Fire Book" which is available for purchase at the Ashland Public Library.

A work of fiction, "Rekindled from Ashes" represents the author's 38th book with Winged Publications and owner/editor Cynthia Hickey, in the Forget Me Not Romances imprint.

Member: American Christian Fiction Writers and Heart of America Christian Writers Network.

The author's entire booklist with Winged Publications can be found on her website:
http://cindymamos.wixsite.com/natureink

Her author page on Amazon is found at:
https://www.amazon.com/Cindy-M.-Amos

~Writing romance onto nature's landscape~

OTHER BOOKS BY CINDY M. AMOS
Landscapes of Mercy Series
Redeeming River Rancher
Saving Bicycle Man
Justifying Sound Strider
Sanctifying Ace Aerialist
Lifting Lock Runner
Salvaging Doctor Junk

National Parks 100th Anniversary Romance Collection
Everglades Entanglement
Mesa Verde Meltdown

Holiday 3-in-1 Collection
Running Out of Christmastime

Taming the Cowboy's Heart Collection
Warming Stone Cold Lodge

50 States Collection
Secondhand Flower Stand (Kansas)
Red Cloud Retreat (Nebraska)
Tidewater Lowlands (North Carolina)
Canyon Country Courtship (Utah)

John Denver 20th Anniversary Collection

<u>Calypso Reimagined</u>

Loving the Town Hero Collection
<u>Cascading Waterworks</u>

Cowboy Brides Collection
<u>Renegade Restoration</u>

America's Fabulous Fifties Series
<u>Oil Field Maven</u>
<u>Airfield Aptitude</u>
<u>Camp Field Capable</u>

Small Town Christmas Collection 2018
<u>Gift Tag Tree</u>

Romancing the Rancher's Daughter Collection
<u>Waylaying the Hauler</u>

Romancing the Farmer Collection
<u>Furrowed Hearts</u>

Adventure Brides Collection
<u>Ocean's Edge</u>

Romancing the Bachelor Collection
<u>Impasse to Springtime</u>

Romancing the Boy Next Door Collection
<u>Forty Acres on Loan</u>

Romancing the Doctor Collection
X-Raying the Doctor

Vote for Love Collection
Ballot Box Rumors

A Secret Santa Romance Collection
Sweet Regrets from Sourwood

Christmas Cookie Brides Collection
Pizzelles for Elves

Romancing the Drifter Collection
Derailing the Drifter

A Family to Love Collection
Skinny Ranch Romance

Nonfiction Little Lift Gift Books
Signs of the Seasons: Hints from Nature

The Men of Mustang Pass Series
Silver Lining at Mustang Pass
Copper Halo at Mustang Pass
Sapphire Skies at Mustang Pass
Holiday Hitches at Mustang Pass